Midnight Spells

The Witches of Hollow Cove
Book Two

Kim Richardson

FablePrint

This book is a work of fiction. Any references to historical events, real people, or real locales are used fictitiously. Other names, characters, places, and incidents are the product of the author's imagination, and any resemblance to actual events or locales or persons, living or dead, is entirely coincidental.
FablePrint

Midnight Spells, The Witches of Hollow Cove, Book Two
Copyright © 2020 by Kim Richardson
All rights reserved, including the right of reproduction
in whole or in any form.
Cover by Kim Richardson
Printed in the United States of America

ISBN-13: 9798688442892
[1. Supernatural—Fiction. 2. Demonology—Fiction. 3. Magic—Fiction].

BOOKS BY KIM RICHARDSON

THE WITCHES OF HOLLOW COVE
Shadow Witch
Midnight Spells
Charmed Nights

THE DARK FILES
Spells & Ashes
Charms & Demons
Hexes & Flames
Curses & Blood

SHADOW AND LIGHT
Dark Hunt
Dark Bound
Dark Rise
Dark Gift
Dark Curse
Dark Angel
Dark Strike

TEEN AND YOUNG ADULT

SOUL GUARDIANS
Marked
Elemental
Horizon
Netherworld
Seirs
Mortal

Reapers
Seals

THE HORIZON CHRONICLES
The Soul Thief
The Helm of Darkness
The City of Flame and Shadow
The Lord of Darkness

MYSTICS SERIES
The Seventh Sense
The Alpha Nation
The Nexus

DIVIDED REALMS
Steel Maiden
Witch Queen
Blood Magic

Midnight Spells

The Witches of Hollow Cove
Book Two

Kim Richardson

Chapter 1

I stood before the basement door, my heart thumping with excitement. My aunts had slipped away early this morning, leaving me alone in Davenport House. The six-thousand-square-foot farmhouse boasted enough bedrooms to be considered an inn and enough secret passageways, hidden places, and mysterious closed doors to keep me busy for months. What I *should* have been doing right now was the dishes, or even weeding the herb garden that looked more like a patch of grass ready for the cows. But my curiosity had a mind of its own, and before I knew it, I was standing in front of the basement door, my toes wiggling in anticipation.

My aunts kept avoiding my questions about this male-lobotomizing basement. The fact was, I had no freaking clue what had happened to those three men down there. They'd gone in, and they'd come out a few days later—alive, but with a few screws missing in their heads. Cheaters, indecent exposure to minors... I guessed Davenport House had done something to them. It had taken away some of their life force, their own mojo, the inner energy all mortals possess. I wouldn't know anything for sure until I went down there and looked for myself.

Clearly, my aunts didn't want me to know what happened down in the basement, which only cemented the fact that it was either bad or dangerous. As a witch, dangerous and bad were in my DNA, qualities I was proud of, thank you very much.

A wicked smile spread over my face. *I'm going through that door and I will discover House's secret.* So what if I lost a finger? It would be worth it.

I had no idea when my aunts would be back, but I couldn't think about that right now. I only needed a few minutes, enough time to allow me to snoop around the basement to finally unearth what the hell was down there.

With my mind made up, I reached out, grabbed the doorknob, and turned.

"It's locked," I announced to the universe, tugging on the doorknob hard, but the door wouldn't budge. "You've got to be kidding." Apparently, my aunts *didn't* want me wandering in the basement. Either that, or they didn't trust me to know its secrets. How bad could it be? What the hell was down there anyway?

That's it. Now I *really* had to know.

"It's just you and me, door. And you're going down," I told it.

Angling my copy of *The Witch's Handbook* against my hip, I flipped through the pages until I found what I needed.

"How to open a lock," I read. "This is too easy."

After reading the instructions—which were again, way too easy—I grabbed a spare piece of chalk from my bag and drew a key-shaped symbol on the door. Focusing, I tapped into the power of the elements around me and said the incantation, "Reserare secreta."

An influx of power washed through me, and the key-shaped symbol on the door glowed a bright gold, looking unreal like a brilliant jewel. I held back the surge of energy that wanted to slip my control, allowing only the barest amount to spill forth. The symbol flashed one last time and then returned to its dull, chalk-like state.

Smiling, I reached out and pulled on the doorknob. But it was like trying to pry open a cement block.

"What the hell?" I twisted the handle again and even yanked it hard for good measure. But still, the basement door wouldn't open.

Crap. I was sure it would work. I glanced at the incantation, wondering if I'd said the words incorrectly though I'd felt the magic spread through me. Hell, the key-shaped symbol had glowed and reacted to the magic. No. I had done it right. Which could only mean... another force was at work here and wasn't allowing me to unlock the door.

"House?" I called out, knowing it was the only explanation. "Are you doing this? You better not be." I put a hand on my hip and looked around the kitchen, the hallway, not sure what to expect.

The pipes in the wall gave a sudden groan and pop that sounded a lot like laughter.

There was my answer.

Frowning, I snapped my book shut, disappointment and anger fluttering inside. "Why? Why won't you let me through? What's down there, anyway? I'm a Davenport witch, damn it. I should be allowed in."

I waited for House to answer, which in itself was a little foolish. House didn't utter words. It was more like an invisible and mute butler. But hey, you never knew. Weirder things had come to pass in this town.

After another minute of silence, I watched as my chalk-drawn key symbol vanished in three strokes, like someone had taken a cloth to it and wiped it off the door.

"Nice. Real nice."

"What's nice, darling?"

A slender figure came through the kitchen's back door. The petite witch wore beige linen pants with a white linen blouse, which accentuated her tan skin and shoulder-length blonde hair. Her kitten heels clicked on the floor as she dropped four large shopping bags onto the kitchen island.

"You look pale, Tessa," said my Aunt Beverly, her green eyes pinched. "I have a new bronzer that'll fix that problem. And you could use some lip gloss."

"Mmm-hmm." I stood there, my heart pounding against my chest and feeling like I'd been caught going through my aunt's closet. Maybe House had erased all evidence of my break-in attempt to save me from further humiliation.

But I wasn't giving up yet. *One day, I will get through that damn door. You just watch me.*

"What's all this?" I asked, moving to the kitchen island. I set my book on the counter and peered inside one of the bags. "Definitely not groceries." I spied a light blue box with a metallic sheen. "You went on a shopping spree? Looks fancy." I smiled, knowing my Aunt Beverly was the only one of us Davenport witches who cared about following the latest fashions. I just wore whatever looked clean and didn't smell.

"... that's exactly what I told him," said my Aunt Dolores as she pushed through the kitchen back door with a shopping bag similar to the ones Beverly came in with hanging in her hand. "You can't mix Avena Sativa and Damiana and sprinkle it on your penis in the hopes that it will grow. The herbs are to *maintain* an erection. Only a fool would do something so reckless."

At five-ten, Dolores was the tallest of the Davenport witches. Lean, with a knife-edge wit, her long gray hair was pulled back neatly into a braid. Her dark brown eyes were bright and intelligent as she stood with the posture of a professor, prompting a stumbling student.

"I wish I could be there to see the look on his wife's face when she sees him naked." Ruth giggled as she pushed in behind her sister. Nearly a head shorter, all smiles and bouncy on her tiny feet, her white hair was piled into a bun and held in place with two pencils. "Unless she's into green penises... then, she might like it," she added, as she made her way toward the kitchen.

Now, *that* was interesting. "Whose unfortunate penis are we talking about?"

"Jim Forrester's." Dolores hung her purse on the wooden peg rack on the wall next to the back door. "The idiot wanted to lengthen his penis. But these herbs are for maintaining sexual arousal. A more natural version of Viagra, if you will."

Men. "So, now he's stuck with a stiff green one, huh?"

Dolores snorted. "Yes. He's in a bit of a panic. But there's nothing we can do. He'll be fine. He just has to… wait it out."

I laughed. "Until little green Jim goes limp again."

Ruth burst out laughing, her smiling face beaming at the sight of me. She swung her shopping bag up next to Beverly's on the island. "Are you hungry, Tessa? I can whip up something for you. Pancakes? Or would you prefer an omelet?"

"I'm fine, thanks," I said, slightly embarrassed that at twenty-nine, I was still a disaster in the kitchen and cereal was my go-to food. Wasn't everyone's comfort food cereal?

My gaze darted over the three sisters, a smile creasing my face. "Are you gals all going on hot dates tonight?" Beverly had a date with a different man nearly every week, so that was no surprise. But I hadn't even known Ruth or Dolores were dating. The three sisters were all widows, at least a good decade since their husbands died. They should be dating. No one should live their life alone. Strange thought, coming from someone who'd sworn off dating after my ex—John the douche—had dumped me four weeks ago after five years. I shook the thought of him out of my mind. This was not the time to wallow.

A pair of mesmerizing gray eyes, framed by thick, black lashes and accompanied by a pleasant musky scent, strong muscular arms, and a wide chest flashed in my mind's eye instead.

Marcus. The chief here in Hollow Cove.

Heat rushed from my neck to my face. Damn hormones. We didn't get off to a good start—totally his fault—as he'd called my mother a "waste of space" in front of the entire town. But after what Martha had confessed about my mother's terrible decision-making by leaving her post, which resulted in the death of Marcus's best friend, I could understand his hostility and open hatred for me.

Still, he'd helped me take down Samara and her followers. He'd even protected me and carried me home after the battle in the woods with the sorceress. I wasn't sure where we stood now. Friends? No, we weren't friends. So, what did that make us?

"You don't know?" asked Ruth, leaning forward on the island, her eyes wide with disbelief.

I looked at her, my eyebrows meeting in the middle. "Know what?"

Dolores put a hand on her cocked hip. "Didn't your mother tell you anything about our town and its festivities?"

"Yes. She said you were all crazy."

"Sounds like her," muttered Beverly as she tucked a strand of her blonde hair behind her ear.

I shrugged. "I give up. What festivities?"

"Here." Beverly handed me one of her bags, a trace of a smile on her mouth. "This is for you."

My mouth hung open for a moment. "You got me something?" I took the bag from her and peered inside. It was the one with the metallic blue box.

"Open it," encouraged Beverly, her eyes flashing. "Oh—and this one too," she added and handed me a smaller bag with a white box decorated with purple stars.

Doing as I was told, I pulled the blue box out of the bag and settled it on the island's counter. The label Boutique Marie France was stenciled elegantly on the top in black letters. Fingers shaking slightly with excitement, I lifted the top of the box and moved the white tissue paper to the side. A sheen of black material peeked up a me, smooth and elegant with thin spaghetti straps, begging for me to pick it up. So, of course, I obliged.

I lifted the article of clothing and gave a tiny gasp as it fell, swiping against my ankles. "You got me a dress?" I stared at the most beautiful dress I'd ever held in my life. Hell, I didn't even own anything this expensive or elegant. The only dress I owned was a cotton one I got at the Gap a few years back. I'd never felt the material on this one before, smooth and silky under my fingers like liquid metal. It must have cost a fortune. I spied that the price tag was conveniently missing.

"You like it?" asked Ruth, a touch of worry in her voice, as though I'd be crazy enough not to like it.

"Of course she likes it," said Beverly. "Just look at her. I can always tell when a woman knows that *this* is the dress. It's perfect. Fancy and ritzy."

Dolores snorted. "Like the cracker."

Beverly was right. "It's beautiful," I answered, having a hard time looking away from the silky, uber-sexy dress. "And it looks *really* expensive. Can we afford this?" Guilt threatened to stop my heart. I was swimming in debt. I could never afford something this exquisite and expensive. My aunts shouldn't be spending the little money they had on me or this dress. It didn't feel right.

"We have to look our best tonight, ladies," announced Dolores, like that was answer enough. She grinned at what she saw on my face.

"Why is that? And why do I need a dress?" I pressed the beautiful black dress against my chest. I couldn't help it. It was spectacular.

"Because, my darling niece," said Beverly, a hand on her curvy hip, looking like a classic movie star from the fifties. "Tonight is the Night Festival."

Chapter 2

According to my aunts, the Night Festival was an annual get-together, a paranormal festival extravaganza that featured a multitude of famous faces, both influential and powerful in paranormal circles, with a few mingling humans sprinkled in.

I'd never heard of such a thing. The only festivals I knew about were the common Winter and Summer Solstice festivals, Spring and Autumn Equinoxes, and let's not forget Samhain—my fav. So, this was news to me. The festival was a five-night event, and it sounded strange and mysterious. Coming from a witch who'd missed out on most of all the paranormal stuff growing up, I was as giddy as a little kid who had fallen into a box full of puppies. Of course, I *had* to check it out.

It was a chance for me to see how the rest of us paranormals lived. I could get a glimpse of our world without having to take a plane or a bus, which I couldn't afford at the moment. Let's not forget I was deep in the debt crapper. Every single dime I made went toward paying down my enormous debt. I'd managed to bring it down to forty-nine thousand four hundred and fifty. But at the rate that I was going, I'd be eighty-two by the time it was fully paid.

The thought of my ginormous debt plunged me into a deep depression. I quickly shook out of those morbid thoughts, opting for something that would lift my mood. And I knew just the thing.

Light on my feet, I hit Shifter Lane and made my way to the downtown core of Hollow Cove, which was basically the main road and the town square. I tried to walk as normally as I could without looking like I was jogging. Who was I kidding? That's *exactly* what I was doing.

By the time I made it to the town square, I was panting and my armpits and back were wet. I probably smelled too, but it was worth it.

I tried hard not to gawk at the cluster of paranormals. I'd never seen so many gathered in one place before outside of the town meetings, and definitely not if you took out all the townspeople from Hollow Cove.

Voices flowed around me from half-breeds and even a few humans crowded onto the town square in a blur of color and motion, talk and costume, like some kind of paranormal circus. The humans were easily spotted with their plastic vampire teeth and stick-on rubber pointy ears. They appeared to be geared up for a Trekkie convention.

And it was fantastic.

I moved along the throng of half-breeds, trying to see everything at once while attempting not to look like a tourist—which I was, in a way. The tallest female I'd ever seen, measuring at least nine feet tall, walked by me. Her skin was rough like leather and was the color of leaves in the spring.

"...that's not yours. That's mine," a short, old female was saying to another older female, as she tugged on a purse. That would have been totally normal here in Hollow Cove, except for the fact that the two old ladies were covered in gray fur, and a puff of tail peeked from below each long skirt.

A pack of half-breeds in silver robes embellished with purple runes and sigils clustered on the gazebo, moving their hands in gestures, while green drapes floated up and secured themselves magically along the gazebo's ceiling. Witches.

In the park around the town square, set up out in the streets, was a line of vendor booths and stands like you would see at a local fair. They proffered bottles, boxes of potions, charms, wands and amulets, pottery, clothes, and more jewelry than I'd ever seen.

A young witch with bright pink hair stood next to a cart that proclaimed GET YOUR OWN PERSONALIZED VOODOO DOLL! A doll about twelve inches high stood on a tripod next to the witch, its dull blue eyes darting around from the bleak, impassive face. It was an exact replica of the witch, except that its head was abnormally large. It even had matching wisps of bright pink hair and wore the same clothes. The doll's eyes fixed on me and wouldn't look away. Creepy.

More paranormals in various forms of dress meandered by—some sporting modern fashions like me and some dressed in vintage mortal fashions with layers of skirts and lace.

I spotted six portable pavilions and an enormous water tank the size of a minivan. When I moved closer for a better look, a man swam up to the glass and flashed me his pointy, fish-like teeth.

I jumped back. Okay, *not* a man—a merman. And a hot one at that.

Long navy hair lifted around him. His skin was a metallic blue, almost painted over his large muscled chest and arms, with black shark-like eyes and a tail. His upper body was all man, but his lower half was all fish. So weird. I loved it.

"Well, hello there," I said not sure if he could hear me, or even if he spoke English. My whale song was a bit rusty.

His lips moved as he said something, his handsome face smiling. He waved. I waved back.

Moving along, moving along...

Echoes of rich voices and the distant sound of a mocking laugh reached me. A group of beautiful half-breeds stood next to a booth. They were all tall, slim, perfect, and looked like a bunch of models getting ready for the runway. Vampires? But I caught sight of some pointy ears and smiling mouths filled with pointed teeth—faeries.

Though just as beautiful and mystical as vampires, faeries were equipped with their magic mojo. And with that magic, they could spell you into believing just about anything, just so they could slowly drink your soul away, making you their slave for as long as they wanted.

Yeah. Faeries creeped me out.

They all stopped and stared as I walked by, their cold, beautiful faces screwed up in disdain. From their group came several distinctive hisses.

Trudging along, trudging along...

A group of vampires walked past me, stoic, beautiful, and merciless. The strong scent of old blood and the shivers that rolled up my spine as they moved past me cemented my thinking that these were full-fledged vamps and not the half-human variety like Ronin.

Speaking of the half-vampire, I spotted the tall guy across from me with a beautiful young woman hanging from his arm as he strutted his stuff like a proud peacock.

"Vampires," I muttered with a half-laugh as I made my way deeper into the throng of paranormals.

"No, no, no!" shouted Gilbert, holding a clipboard in his hand while he stomped his foot. "I told you before, and I'll tell you again, because apparently you're a simpleton, Adrian." He glared at a young guy who looked ready to punch Gilbert in the face if he wasn't on a fifteen-foot ladder holding up a sign that read 86TH ANNUAL NIGHT FESTIVAL. I recognized him. Adrian was a twenty-something witch who helped my aunts with some of the landscaping chores around Davenport House. He was a really nice guy too.

"It needs to be higher. H-i-g-h-e-r!" commanded Gilbert. "Everyone knows... signs are supposed to be ten feet *above* our heads. Not at eye level."

"Then I'll need a taller ladder," growled Adrian, eyes narrowing.

Gilbert's face reddened. "It's the same ladder we use every year. If Marty could do it last year, you should be able to do it too."

The rest of Adrian's comeback was lost as I moved away, laughing. Seven black limousines were parked at the curb along with a dozen two-story motor homes painted with stars and moons and suns.

I felt eyes on me. A man standing next to a group of important-looking people was watching me. The sun reflected off his sun-kissed skin, and his tall frame was dressed in a simple black T-shirt and jeans, which showed off his fantastic fit physique. His short blond hair was just long enough to make me want to run my fingers in it—not that I would. In the light, his beauty was startling, like an ageless elven prince, elegant and dangerous and merciless. His ears were rounded, so not an elf or faerie. With handsome good looks like that, he could be a vampire. But he could still be fae with a strong glamour.

His handsome face creased into a smile as he caught me staring back at him.

Instant flush-o-meter skyrocketed to my face like molten lava.

I spun around to keep him from seeing the flush on my cheeks—and crashed into a hard body.

"Oops, sorry, my fault," I said as I stepped back and looked up. "I wasn't paying attention—Marcus?"

Damn. Of all the people I would crash into today, it had to be Marcus.

The uber-sexy chief of Hollow Cove gazed at me with those stupid mesmerizing gray eyes. "You should look where you're going." A tiny smile crept along his full lips. "You could sprain an ankle on the curb if you're not careful."

I hadn't yet prepared myself mentally for how I was supposed to behave with him now. Friends? Acquaintances? I could do acquaintances. His tone was cordial, not at all like the rough tone he'd used on me before. Did that make us friends?

I wasn't sure how to handle myself, now that I knew the reason behind his hostility toward me. Still, we'd have to get used to each other since I had taken up permanent residence in Hollow Cove.

My eyes drifted down to his chest, which was covered in a low V-neck white shirt, causing the heat on my face to increase. What the hell was wrong with me? I was acting like a schoolgirl with a crush, not a soon-to-be-thirty grown woman.

Control yourself, witch!

I pulled my eyes away from Marcus's chest and found the handsome stranger staring at me, the smile on his face still there, open and inviting.

Now my face felt like I'd stuck it inside an oven. I was in hell.

Marcus looked over to what I was staring at before, and his jaw tightened when he spotted the sexy blond guy still watching me. Interesting.

"Will this be your first Night Festival?" asked the chief, his eyes still on the stranger.

Was he trying to make conversation with me? "My what? Oh, right. Yes. The Night Festival. I can't wait. Looks exciting."

Marcus turned his eyes on me and smiled. It transformed his face from dark-sexy-chief to it's-time-to-go-pantie-shopping. I didn't think he'd ever smiled at me before. Hell, I didn't even know his face could do that. Wow.

Even though my body and hormones were reacting to this stupidly handsome male, my brain wasn't. I had just come out of a bad relationship, so now wasn't the time to get involved with anyone. The last time I'd listened to my stupid hormones, I'd ended up wasting five years of my life. I needed to take care of me first.

Still, it didn't mean I couldn't look. And there was so much to see…

"You look nice," said Marcus. Something in his soft tone made me want to purr and snuggle against his neck.

I was losing it.

"Thanks. Same here." *Same here?* What kind of blabbering fool was I?

I swallowed and straightened, reluctant to let him see how much his words or voice affected me.

"Gilbert always throws a few tantrums this time of year," continued the chief. "He takes the festival thing a little too seriously. Drives everyone crazy."

"Uh… mmm…" Apparently, I was suffering from another mental fart. I shifted from foot to foot. I did that sometimes when I was nervous or when I tried to jumpstart my brain to function again.

"You can use the bathroom at Brooms & Brew," added Marcus with a knowing half-smile.

Oh. My. God. He thinks I need to pee.

"What? No? I just… too much caffeine this morning. You know what I mean?" I was mortified. But it *was* kind of funny. "Are you going to the festival tonight?" Of course, he would, but it was the only thing that popped out of my mouth. It was weird and exciting that we were having a conversation, and I found myself not wanting it to end.

"Yes," answered Marcus casually, his gray eyes rolling over my face. Gone was the tough exterior, replaced by a gentle and kind one. I liked it. "I need to make sure things run smoothly for everyone tonight. But mostly, I need to keep an eye on Gilbert before someone kills him."

I laughed, spotting Gilbert waving a tape measure at Adrian. "Looks like Adrian might be suffering from some murderous thoughts right about now. Poor guy."

Marcus laughed. It was a very pleasant, deep kind of laugh that made me want to make stupid jokes just to hear it again. "I think you're right. See you tonight," said the chief as he turned and went to rescue poor Adrian from Gilbert.

I watched him walk away. "Yeah," I whispered. "See you tonight."

Chapter 3

Sleep wouldn't come. Under Dolores's instructions, I was supposed to take a nap before the Night Festival, seeing as it opened at midnight tonight. But I was so excited I lay on top of my bed in my T-shirt and undies, listening to my heartbeat and waiting for my phone alarm to go off a half-hour before midnight.

Beep. Beep. Beep.

I vaulted off my bed, turned my alarm off, and jumped into the shower. Thirty minutes was way more time than I needed to get ready. Hell, I only needed fifteen, but I needed to look my best—according to my aunts. I had a feeling they were about to parade me around to some important people tonight.

After a record five-minute shower—I made the mental note to ask Martha for a hair-removing spell because I did *not* want to shave my legs, pits, and bikini area for the rest of my life—I towel-dried myself and blasted my wet hair with a hairdryer. I stood before the mirror on the dresser naked, contemplating how much makeup I was going to use. I didn't want to be too done up. I always thought it looked fake. With that in mind, I added a bit of concealer under my eyes to hide the dark circles, some light taupe eyeshadow on my top and bottom lids that made my brown eyes pop, a touch of mascara, and a dab of lip-gloss.

I blinked at the mirror. "You clean up well, Tessa," I told myself and then let out a sigh. "Now. What are we going to do with your hair? Up or down?"

I decided to go with a messy low bun. It would look more sophisticated but also would take less time. I was all about being practical.

Next, I slipped into a black thong—trust me, you don't want panty lines showing in a dress like that—and wrapped a strapless black bra around the girls (courtesy of my Aunt Beverly) which was surprisingly comfortable.

Excitement had my pulse thumping as I pulled my new black dress off the hanger in my closet and slipped it on. I ran my fingers over the sweeping, soft material from my waist and hips. I practically moaned at how soft it was. Light tingles rolled over my skin as I admired the shining black material. And of course, the dress fit like it was made for me, snug in all the right places but leaving material in the places that needed more, like my ass and thighs. How did Beverly know my size? When I felt another tingle, I knew.

Magic. The gown was magical or spelled to fit the wearer exactly right, as though it had been molded to me.

Grinning like an idiot, I slipped into a pair of black pumps, feeling like Cinderella before the ball, and stood. Thank god Beverly got me low kitten heels. Otherwise, I would have been a giant. Though these were comfortable enough, heels weren't my thing, and the last thing I needed was to fall over on my face in front of Marcus. I wasn't sure why I even cared? Maybe it was because I couldn't stop replaying our earlier conversation.

No. Tonight was for my aunts. They didn't go to all this trouble to get me ready for something they deemed unimportant. I was a Merlin. I needed to act like one.

"Tessa! Get your butt down here. We're leaving!" came Dolores's voice from downstairs. Grabbing my phone and dropping it into a black leather clutch (thank you,

Beverly), I slipped off my shoes, hooked them over two fingers, and ran down the stairs.

"Where are your shoes?" Beverly's pretty face was mortified at the sight of my toes, which I'd totally forgotten to paint. Whoops. But the pumps would hide the fact that I had the toes of an ogre, judging from my aunt's expression.

I hit the bottom step and lifted my shoes. "Here. Don't worry. I promise I won't go barefoot." Though the idea was tempting. It would be so much easier.

"Thank the cauldron," commented Beverly in her exquisite silver gown that oozed sensuality. "You can't catch a man with goblin toes, dearest."

"I wasn't planning on catching anything," I told her.

Ruth snorted. "She's funny." Her lithe form was wrapped in a snug red dress that made her pale skin and white hair pop.

"Let's go. I don't want to be late," ordered Dolores. Her long black dress swayed at her heels as she hurried to the door, her matching flat shoes scuffing the floor.

We all followed her out to the Volvo station wagon.

"We're driving there?" I asked, surprised. I'd figured we were going to walk.

"Did you think I would ruin my hair walking down to the festival?" Beverly didn't wait for my reply as she opened the front passenger door and sat while Dolores positioned herself behind the wheel.

I followed Ruth into the back and then we were off. It was a two-minute drive to the town square, but it took another five minutes to find parking that was arguably neither too close nor too far.

Once the car was parked, the four of us made our way to the festival. Any fool could find it by just following the sounds of people and music.

When we hit the town square, my breath caught.

I'd never seen the town look so pretty at night before, nor filled with so many exquisite dresses, suits, and supple forms that were shaped and colored so strangely they were a wonder to see.

Glowing white globes hovered here and there like tiny moons, giving the place a moonlit mystique and reminding me of the charm of white Christmas lights. Every booth, dais, pavilion, and gazebo were all decorated with the same white lights. Even the giant water tank with the hot merman was dazzling with tiny hovering globes, and I resisted the urge to go see him again.

"Looks like a good turnout this year," commented Ruth, her smile matching mine as she took in all the people milling in and around the festival. "Gilbert did a good job."

"Yes," agreed Dolores. "Let's not tell him, though. Ah—Tessa. Here they come. Get ready. Just... be yourself and you should be fine. And... I'm sorry."

My gaze shot to Dolores. "Who's coming? And why are you sorry? Sorry for what?" My stomach tightened at the tension in my aunt's voice. And when I followed her gaze, I understood why.

A group of three people, a man and two women, came our way. The man was dressed in an expensive-looking dark suit, and the women matched the quality in elegant dresses. The air thrummed with magic in what I knew was a show of strength and power. They had loads of it and they wanted everyone to know. Witches.

Their magic reached out around us, circling me and echoing different varieties of the craft. Each one felt entirely different from the next.

The female on the far left could've easily passed for my aunts' older sister. Her ninetieth birthday had come and gone long ago, but she stood tall, proud, and strong. Her white hair was cut so short she was nearly bald, but dark eyes pinned me with sharp intelligence. She wore a gown of white silk, which made her pale skin look like the color of new snow.

The female next to her was a bit older than me, with a head full of golden locks that spilled over her front and down her burgundy dress. She watched me with a knowing half-smile. Weird.

The male looked older than the two witches combined—plain, forgettable, bone-thin, and with an age-spotted scalp.

And then there was the goat.

Yes. A real goat with a black and white coat and cute tiny horns walked next to the witches. The sounds of its hooves hitting the pavement pulled my attention to it. Its horizontal, slit-shaped pupils watched me with a strange intensity.

If these witches thought they could intimidate me with the presence of their magic, their plan failed with the goat.

"So, this is Amelia's replacement?" The older male witch wrinkled his nose in distaste, his pale eyes rolling over every inch of me as though he were looking for something out of place to criticize. I hated him instantly. You would have too.

"Her mother wasn't much of a witch," said the witch with the long golden hair. "Your Davenport bloodline diminishes."

"There's probably not even a single drop of magic in her," said the old witch, her dark eyes on me again. I felt like she was trying to see through my skin to the very blood inside me to discern if any magic was hidden in there somewhere.

Dolores turned to me. "Tessa. I'd like to introduce you to the Merlin Group from New York."

Ah-ha. Now I got it. The expensive dress and looking my best made total sense. For these clowns. Part of me wanted to leave. Hell, it was a miracle I hadn't already, but I knew leaving would just make my aunts look bad in front of this coven. It's something my mother would've done. So, I stayed put. I too could play this game. It was on.

"Honestly, Dolores," said the older witch, sunspots peeking through the thin hair on her scalp. "We could have supplied you with the very best. We have many witches trained by us who excel in all manner of spells and magic. All you had to do was ask."

Dolores straightened, towering over the older witch, and I knew she did that on purpose. "Tessa is a fantastic witch. She was the only choice for us. She's a Davenport witch, after all. She's family."

The older witch shook her head. "You cannot choose family over the group. You know how these things work."

Beverly cocked her hip. "But we did. What are you going to do about it, Greta?"

Touché. It took every ounce of effort not to smile or tell these a-holes off. My eyes fell on the goat. It was strangely silent for a goat. Not even a baa or a bleat. Nothing. Odd. Maybe it was mute.

The older male witch rubbed his chin. "The Merlin Groups have a code to follow. You can't just accept members of your family. They must have the witch blood in them. She must have *magic*."

"She does, Travis," argued Ruth, her cheeks flushed. "Tessa's always had magic. She's a very gifted witch." She gave a knowing nod.

Now, this was getting ridiculous. "I'm right here, you know," I said, though none of the witches cared to look my way, even my aunts. "You can ask me anything." I had the feeling this was an old battle between the witches of Hollow Cove and these New York ones, and I was right in the middle of it.

The younger witch with the golden hair kept staring at me with a wide, creepy smile like she knew something I didn't. It was starting to freak me out a little.

"If she's from Amelia's blood," countered the old witch Greta, "she's practically human."

Dolores got right in her face and stared down at her. "She is *not* human. She's a *witch!*"

"And *she's* right here," I mumbled as I crossed my arms over my chest. I was going to give them another thirty seconds and then I was going to split.

"She has to do the trials before she can become a Merlin," pressed Greta. "You know this, Dolores."

I swallowed, dropping my arms to my sides. "Trials? What trials?"

Dolores was quiet for a moment. "She didn't need to. We saw what she was capable of. We didn't see the need to have her do the trials, not when she already excels in magic."

"Hello?" I waved my hand in the air. "What are you talking about?"

Greta gave Dolores a cold smile. "You don't make the rules, Dolores. She will have to do the trials whether you like it or not."

Dolores stared at the older witch, her jaw clenching. I was expecting her to tell the old witch off, but she didn't. What the hell?

"Hey, Tess, how's it going? Wow—you look great."

Ronin came up from behind Beverly to stand next to me. He wore jeans and a black T-shirt, casual and comfortable. Though I loved this dress, I felt overly done and on display. After meeting these witches, I just wanted to go home and take it off. It felt fake somehow. The moment had passed.

"I'll tell you in a second," I told him, noticing how Greta and Travis were looking at Ronin as though they'd just stepped into a pile of horse shit. The younger witch was ogling

Ronin like he was a tempting piece of cheesecake.

The half-vampire beamed. "By the looks on everyone's faces, I'd say I got here just in time to see the witch fight."

Dolores drew herself back. "There is no witch fight, merely a disagreement."

Greta stepped forward. "If you want her to join your group—" she pointed a gnarled finger in my direction, "—she *must* do the trials."

"What's up with the goat?" I blurted with tension pounding through me. I'd had enough of being ignored, and the goat seemed like a good topic of discussion.

Silence. At least now I had their attention. The three witches from New York gawked at me, and so did my aunts. Greta's eyes were wide, and she rocked back a step, her face creased in wrinkles.

Ronin snorted. "Goat? Good one."

Ruth giggled. "There's no goat, silly." She leaned over. "I think it worked. Got them to stop talking nonsense," she added with a wink.

I frowned at her. "No, I'm serious. It's right there. Can't you see it?" I said, pointing at the cute goat as it rolled its ears and blinked its strange, horizontally slit eyes.

"Whatever you're smoking, Tess," said Ronin. "I'll take a kilo."

The three witches from New York exchanged looks. Then Greta turned her dark eyes on me. "You can *see* a goat? Standing here? Next to us?"

"Yeah," I answered, not appreciating her mocking tone. "Why are you all staring at me like I've lost my mind? You're the ones who brought a goat to the festival. Not me." Though it was really cute. What they should have been doing was taking that poor goat to the park so it could graze on some grass.

A horrible thought occurred to me. "If you're thinking of using this goat in some sort of crazy sacrificial ritual," I glowered at the three strangers, "we're going to have a problem." Okay, not smart threatening them. But I drew the line at animal cruelty.

Beverly cleared her throat. "Because, darling, there is no goat. You can stop pretending. I think we all need to relax and go enjoy the festival. I know just the thing," she added, and I noticed her attention was on a tall handsome man in his early fifties.

Fantastic. My temper flared. "I don't know if this is part of these trials you're talking about, and I really don't care. But don't tell me I'm pretending to see a goat. I'm not delusional."

"What does the goat look like?" asked Travis, his wet, pale eyes reminding me of a slug.

My lips parted. "Like a goat? I don't know? It's white and black with cute horns. It looks hungry, by the way. You should seriously think about feeding the poor animal."

Travis's eyes were round, and he jerked back like I'd slapped him. I didn't. Though, I really, really wanted to.

"That's enough, Tessa." Dolores gave me a hard stare. "Enough games."

My smile hardened. "Oh. My. God. What the hell is this?" I pointed to the goat. "It's right there. What's the matter with you people?"

"I think you should stop, Tessa," said Ruth, looking upset like I was making it up.

I opened my mouth. "Look. I don't know what you're trying to prove—"

"Time to go." Ronin grabbed my arm and pulled me away. Which was very perceptive of him since I was just about to lose it on everyone and probably embarrass my aunts in the process. I really didn't want to, but they were all acting nuts.

Ronin led me into the festival. We maneuvered through booths and tables of food lined up along the far edge of the town square. I tripped a few times. Stupid heels. I couldn't even walk in the low kitten heels. I was hopeless, and I was mad as hell.

Fiddles, drums, and other instruments played merry music that normally would have made me smile, but my face was cemented into a frown. The Night Festival was a world of color and sound, but I hardly noticed. Everything was just a giant blur.

"What the hell is wrong with them?" I hissed once we were out of earshot. "You saw what they did? They want me to think I'm crazy. Why were they all pretending like there was no goat?" *Am I missing something?*

"I never saw a goat, Tess," came Ronin's tight voice. "Did you really see one or were you just messing with them? I'm cool with you messing with them. It was *very* entertaining."

I stopped walking as a cold tingle crept up from my lower back to settle around the base of my neck. "You didn't see the goat?"

He shook his head. "No."

I pointed my finger in his face. "If you're messing with me, I'm going to cut off your balls and boil them in Ruth's cauldron." Seeing things that others did not was a very bad sign in the paranormal world, especially when we're the freaks who are supposed to see the bizarre and the strange.

If *I* was the only one who could see the goat... I tried not to think about it.

Ronin covered his balls with his left hand and raised his right hand. "On my vampire's honor. I didn't see any goat."

Crap. My heart pounded in my throat as I spun around and looked back. Sure enough,

Billy the goat was watching me with his horizontally slit eyes—and yes, I had to give him a name too. A Billy goat was a male goat, so it seemed to fit.

I whipped my head back. "This is bad, Ronin. Really bad."

He shrugged. "Why? If you *are* seeing things… at least it's just a goat and not some demon."

"That's just it. It *could* be a demon. Or worse."

"What's worse than a demon disguised as a goat? A demon disguised as a cow?"

I knew Ronin was just trying to make me laugh, but it wasn't working. The truth was, that goat could be several things, and none of them were good. Worse, apparently, I was the only one who could see it. I'd also embarrassed my aunts. They had dressed me up to show me off, and I'd let them down.

Nice going, Tessa.

An icy wave of fear and dread hit me. My stomach clenched, sending acid to coat my throat. What did the goat mean? Why was I the only one who could see it? I wouldn't rest until I figured it out.

"What about these trials I heard the witches talking about," inquired Ronin. "Any ideas what those are?"

Great. Now I had more to worry about. "No idea. But it sounded like a test I'm supposed to pass to become a Merlin."

"Your aunts never made you do any tests. Did they?"

"Nope."

Grinning, Ronin straightened. "Well, let's not worry about that now. Tonight is your first night at the Night Festival, and you should be having a good time. That's what I'm here for. Let's see..." Ronin rubbed his hands together, and his smile turned impish. "What do you want to try first? The faerie quintuplets are doing a belly dance later. I heard whipped cream is used in one of their acts—oh, and there're chains too. What do you say?"

My gaze fell on a purple and white striped tent that would seem at home at the circus. Above the cloth doorway was the sign:

MYSTICAL PROGNOSTICATIONS,
FORTUNE-TELLER.
Charms, Brews, Tarot, Palm, Crystal Ball.
REVEAL YOUR FUTURE TODAY for only
$ 20.00!
No Refunds

Perfect. Pulse pounding, I made a beeline for it.

"Where are you going?" Ronin called after me.

"I feel like getting my fortune told," I yelled over my shoulder.

I needed to make sure I wasn't crazy. Because if anyone could tell me if seeing a goat was a bad omen, a fortune-teller could.

Or so I hoped.

CHAPTER 4

I pushed back the cloth flap and walked in. Three things hit me at once: it stunk of cigarette smoke, *everything* was purple, and no one was in here.

"It's empty," said Ronin as he pushed in behind me.

"I noticed."

The tent was about fifteen by fifteen feet and decorated with plush purple pillows on the floor atop purple carpets and purple throws. A short round purple table sat in the middle of the space with pillows placed around to serve as chairs. A crystal ball, a stack of cards, empty teacups, and candles rested on the table.

Fortune-tellers, mediums, clairvoyants or psychics were all witches who specialized in metaphysical magic, divination, and astral projection. That kind of magic was the foundation for accessing the full potential of your mind, body, and spirit. It was the perception and manipulation of energy, your chi, and worked the subtle energies of the world. It was a brand of White magic, and most witches were capable of doing it. I just never saw the point.

I sighed. The breath that escaped me was tight with tension. "Well, no one's here. Let's go—"

A pop of displaced air was followed by a cloud of purple mist appearing in the middle of the tent. When the mist vanished, a woman stood in its place.

"I am Marvelous Myrtle!" cried a woman dressed in a—wait for it—purple robe etched with lilac-colored stars with a purple scarf wrapped around her head. It was impossible to guess her age with the caked-on purple eye shadow and drawn-on eyebrows, but if I had to guess, I'd say late forties.

She vaulted in the air and landed on the table. "Oldest in experience," she raised her voice dramatically and kicked a candle out of her way with her bejeweled bare foot. "Richest in knowledge and skill."

"Nice," laughed Ronin. "I'll give you twenty bucks if you start dancing."

"Crowned with years of unparalleled success as a Seer," continued Marvelous Myrtle as she waved her gem-covered fingers in the air like she was trying to catch invisible butterflies. "Thousands of happy customers all over the world, begging for a glimpse into Marvelous Myrtle's Master Mind—" her green eyes found us, and she froze like she'd been hit with an immobilizing spell. "You interested?"

Ronin snorted. "If this was a peep show, maybe. Are you going to take off your clothes? Add a couple more of you Myrtles, and then we're in business."

"I'm interested." I moved forward, smiling. This witch was fantastic. If I didn't make it as a Merlin, her gig looked like fun. Maybe we could do a duo act.

Marvelous Myrtle grinned, her teeth smeared with purple lipstick. "Excellent." She jumped down from the table, kicked a cushion out of her way, and froze. "It's twenty dollars. No refunds."

I pulled a twenty out of my clutch. "I know." I moved to hand her the cash, and the woman snatched it up and stuffed the bill down her bra.

"Now it's getting interesting," said Ronin. "I'm getting some serious vibes."

I pursed my lips. "Not to be confused with regular vibes."

Marvelous Myrtle snapped her fingers at Ronin. "Out, vampire. Out! Out! Out! You don't pay. You don't stay."

"Fine." Ronin looked at me and laughed. "I'll be right outside. Enjoy Madame Marvelous."

"It's *Marvelous Myrtle* to you, vampire," the witch shot back.

I watched as Ronin left and then turned back to the witch. "I've never been to a Seer before," I told her, feeling a little nervous.

"Sit!" ordered Marvelous Myrtle. She plopped herself on a cushion facing the round table. She snapped her fingers at me. "What is your name?"

"Tessa."

"Tessa. Sit!" she commanded, like I was a stubborn Labrador retriever.

Stifling a nervous giggle, I did what I was told and sat on the cushion facing her. Marvelous Myrtle placed the candle she'd kicked back on the table next to two others. With a quick nod of her head, each wick lit up with a flame.

I narrowed my eyes. "I think I've seen this movie."

"Shhh!" Marvelous Myrtle threw her hands out over the table, reaching for me. "Give me your hands."

I extended my hands over to her and she grabbed them, her cold skin surprising me. Her gaze was intense as she stared at me for a few seconds without blinking. Now, this was one seriously creepy witch.

"You've got man troubles," commented Marvelous Myrtle, her voice deeper than I would have imagined, and sounding rehearsed. I grimaced as her sour cigarette-infested breath hit me in the face.

I arched my brows at her. "It's not why I'm here—"

"Shhh!" the witch clamped hard on my hands, and I was starting to feel numbness in them. Her painted-on eyebrows rose. "Interesting. Yes... very interesting."

"What's interesting?"

The witch glared at me. "You do have man troubles... but it's not why you're here."

I shook my head in disbelief. "I told you that."

"Shhh."

I glowered at her. The thought that I may have wasted twenty bucks made me cringe, especially being the owner of a gargantuan debt. Great, I'd been duped by a phony witch. Maybe this wasn't such a good idea.

The Seer blinked slowly. "It *is* a good idea, and I usually charge forty so you're saving half," said Marvelous Myrtle as though she'd just read my mind. "Yes. It's what I do. Yes, that's right."

"I'm sorry... what?" I wasn't sure whether I should be impressed or a bit creeped out.

The witch's green eyes snapped to mine, her stare penetrating, and I found that I couldn't look away. "Did you not read the sign over the door?"

"Yes."

"Did it not say mystical prognostications?"

"It did—"

"Shhh." The witch squeezed my hands hard, and my frown reached the bridge of my nose when I heard Ronin's laugh outside the tent.

Marvelous Myrtle let go of one of my hands as she snapped her fingers, and my ears popped. When they popped again, I realized I couldn't hear anything other than the witch's loud breathing and my beating heart. She'd pulled some sort of sound barrier spell.

The witch grabbed my hand again. "Quiet please." She shifted on her cushion. "Now. Empty your mind... and concentrate only on why you came to see Marvelous Myrtle."

Feeling slightly foolish, I did the best I could, focusing on the goat while trying not to think about the witch's clammy, cold hands. Part of me wished I was outside with Ronin and out of this stuffy, cigarette-smelling tent.

"You're not focusing," snapped the witch.

"I am," I shot back. "It's not that simple."

"It is when you can master your mind. You're not disciplined at all. You lack the control of a Davenport witch," she argued, and I wondered if the slip of my surname had been on purpose. Probably. I hadn't told her. But she could have easily researched everyone here days before the Night Festival's arrival.

Marvelous Myrtle's painted-on eyebrows shot up to the rim of her headscarf. "Yes. Oh, yes, yes. I see it now. A dark presence is following you."

Here we go.

The witch frowned, her eyes on my face. "There is a dark presence following you. It's... around you... around your aura."

My pulse throbbed. Nervously, I forced my features to find a confident slant. "You mean the goat. Yeah. I saw that."

Marvelous Myrtle glowered at me. "Goat? There is no goat."

"Of course there's a goat." I fought against the urge to pull my hands away and smack her. "It's the only reason I came here. The only reason why I paid you. I want to know about the goat—ow!" I yelled, as the witch had purposely squeezed my hands hard. The woman had some serious man-hands.

The witch shook her head, letting go of some of her hold on me. "I'm not seeing a goat. If you want to see a goat, by all means, go to a bloody farm."

I gritted my teeth. "There *is* a goat," I ground out, "and if you squeeze my hands again… so help the cauldron… I won't be responsible for what I might do to you."

I tapped into the elements around me, into that well of energy, and directed its power as it spiraled up through me in a tornado of magic that wanted to be released.

I held it and said, "You have no idea who you're messing with, Gypsy."

Marvelous Myrtle gave me an impressed smirk. "Not bad. Adequate control of the elements. But you don't need to threaten me. I'm only revealing what I see. I don't make things up just because it's what you want to hear. I reveal the *truth*. And the truth is, I don't see a goat now or anywhere in your near future. What I do see is an ex-lover with many different women. Including you." Her smile widened. "There is another one… another love interest I see… someone who will be revealed to you later."

Right. I was not here to discuss my love life, and if I chose to do it one day, it certainly wouldn't be with this ashtray-smelling witch.

I leaned forward, my turn to squeeze her hands hard, making her eyes pop. "Listen here, you fortune cookie wannabe." I squeezed harder. "I'm telling you there's a damn goat. No one can see it except for me. Okay? I came here because I need to know what it means. If you can't, if you can't see it, that tells me you're a fraud."

Marvelous Myrtle's mouth fell open in a gasp. "I am not!"

"Prove it. Either give me back my twenty bucks—because I will tell everyone at the festival that you're a joke—or tell me why I keep seeing a goat!" Okay, so threatening another witch was never a good idea, but right now I was desperate.

A few tiny cracks appeared in her frown, and then she shook her head sharply. "Fine. It's your money."

"Right. No refunds. And don't try to make things up either," I said. "I'll know if you're lying. We Merlins have a lie detector spell." I didn't, but she didn't know that.

The witch gave me a sour look, closed her eyes, and took a deep breath before releasing it.

I felt a prickling jolt up my arm, the surge of magical energies rising around me. The air in the tent grew darker and then merged into a cloud of shadows. I knew she was pulling some serious fortune-telling mojo. Within a heartbeat, the cloud deepened and then solidified into a writhing tangle of shapes wrapped all around the Seer witch. The air suddenly filled with hissing and snarling rattles.

Okay, so she wasn't a fraud, but she was a little creepy.

It lasted about twenty seconds and then her eyes flashed open, causing the cloud of shapes to vanish.

Her eyes widened in fear, her gaze distant as she looked at me without really seeing me. It seemed like she was focused on someone or something else sitting across from her. Her mouth twisted into a sudden, vindictive, mad-eyed grimace that made my insides knot.

Yeah. I'd had enough of this. If she couldn't tell me anything about the goat, I'd find out another way.

I yanked on my hands, but the witch had them in her iron-grip and wouldn't let go. "Let go," I yelled, trying to jerk my hands free. "I mean it. Let go. We're done."

And then she let out a scream of naked terror. Scratch that. It was a terror-filling-jump-out-of-your-skin kind of scream. If she wasn't still holding on to my hands with her superstrength, I would have sprinted out of that tent in two seconds flat.

The witch finally let go of my hands, jerking back like I'd hit her with a kinetic spell. She fell back, bounding away in a violent rush. She kept clawing at her eyes with her fingers and scratching at her neck like she was being stung by wasps. She thrashed in a wild frenzy, swinging randomly at anything she touched or bumped into, tearing pillows and throwing candles across the tent.

Then her scream faded into a weeping, gurgling moan, and she fell into a heap of rugs and pillows, her body curling into a shuddering fetal position.

I was torn between going over to her to make sure she was okay and slapping her across the face. Not only had this been a giant waste of my time and money, but the witch had managed to make me feel worse. A lot worse.

There was no doubt in my mind she'd seen something that had to do with me. And judging from her terrified, crazy-ass outburst, it was bad. Worse than seeing a cute goat that no one else could see bad.

I pushed to my feet, rubbing my hands to try and get the blood flow back into my fingers, and took a tentative step closer to the witch. "What did you see?" I hated how terrified my voice sounded, giving away my crumbled composure, but I still wanted to know.

"Get out," mumbled Marvelous Myrtle, still in a fetal position with half her face hidden beneath a purple pillow.

I looked behind me, half expecting to see Ronin rushing in after all the screaming. But I still couldn't hear anything from the outside world, which meant he didn't hear anything coming from inside this tent.

My heart pounded as I tried to control my breathing. "I'm not going anywhere. Not until you tell me what you saw. I know you saw something. Something to do with me. What was it? Tell me!" I ordered when she didn't answer, my blood pressure shooting up.

Kneeling, I pressed my hand on her trembling arm, thinking that kindness was a better approach. "Please, please tell me what you saw? Because right now, my mind is giving me all kinds of visuals and none of them about hot sexy men chasing me on a beach."

Marvelous Myrtle yanked her arm from my touch and glared at me. "Out!" she shouted. "Here. Take it. I don't want it. I never want to see you ever again. Get out!" she threw my twenty dollars back at me, followed by a series of pillows and even a candlestick that missed my head by an inch.

"Crazy bitch," I growled at her as I backed away toward the door. I didn't take my money. I figured she would need it to pay for the shrink sessions she was going to need.

"Out! Get out!" she wailed as she saw me still standing at the door. "O-o-o-u-u-u-t!"

I might have stayed and demanded answers if I wasn't so terrified. Marvelous Myrtle might be a little shady, flamboyant and rude, but I had no doubt in my mind the witch had seen something that terrified the living heebie-jeebies out of her.

And that something had everything to do with me.

CHAPTER

5

"So? What did she say?" asked Ronin as I stumbled out of the tent. "Judging by that frown, I'm guessing she didn't tell you what you wanted to hear? No luck in love or fortune? They're all the same, these fortune-tellers, you know. More like fortune hunters. I could have told you she was a scammer."

I lifted my eyes and found a short woman with a gray fedora clad in a man's suit that would have been in style in the early nineteen-thirties sitting on a stool across from Myrtle's tent giving me the stink eye. The banner above her tent proclaimed: WORLD-FAMED MYSTIFIER. "CAN THE DEAD SPEAK TO

THE LIVING?" A SENSATIONAL EXPOSÉ WITH BEWILDERING DEMONSTRATIONS!

I pulled my eyes away and looked at Ronin, contemplating whether or not I should tell him about what had happened, but I decided to keep it to myself for now. He already thought I was strange and a bit out there with the goat thing. I didn't want him to think I was losing it. Besides, he was the only real friend I had here, apart from my aunts, and I didn't want to lose that.

I sculpted my face into the best fake smile I could muster under duress. "You're right. It was a complete waste of money, but she did tell me I would find a new man in my life, or something along those lines." Which was true, even though at the time I couldn't have cared less.

Ronin pointed to himself. "She was talking about me, baby," he added with a wink.

I laughed. "I need a drink—and food. I take that back. I need *lots* of drink and food."

"Like I said," continued Ronin. "Tonight, I'm your guy. Come on. In a dress like that, people need to see you... because... otherwise what's the point. Right? This way." He grinned and offered me his arm.

Laughing, I hooked my arm with his and walked with the lanky vampire through the cluster of paranormals chatting happily. We passed booths and kiosks as we headed toward a nearby pavilion covered with silken lanterns and sparkling ribbons, toppling with food.

I reached for the bite-sized strawberry shortcake. Once I had eaten two, I tried a piece of apple tart followed by a slice of raspberry pie and washed it down with a tall glass of red wine that Ronin had poured for me. I tasted it, letting the wine swoosh in my mouth. It was bitter, like a young wine that had been bottled before it was ready, but right now, I wasn't the wine connoisseur. I took another sip, hoping it would camouflage some of the bitterness. It didn't. I didn't care.

After a few minutes, the pounding of my heart finally slowed, though the fear was still at the edge of my mind until it became a dull throb. I looked around for the goat but didn't see it. Nor did I see my aunts or the Merlin group from New York. Maybe I had imagined the whole thing. Maybe I was just lying to myself.

I couldn't stop eating. I ate when I was nervous. I wasn't even hungry. But it was more about trying to drive away the darkness from the tent with every bite. Food would help. So would wine.

"More wine?" Ronin tipped the bottle to my glass. Only the best of friends knew when it was time to refill your glass of wine before you did.

"Yes, thank you." The wine would definitely help. I took another sip and sighed as the warm, delicious fruity drink went down my throat and wrapped around my chest, helping me let go of some of the tension as its effects began to soothe me.

"Tonight, we're going to party, baby," said Ronin as he took a swig of his beer. "Tonight, we're getting you wasted."

"Spoken like a true friend." I smiled, taking another large sip of wine and already feeling a little light-headed.

Ronin spread his arms. "At the annual Night Festival, you will find singing and dancing and excessive drinking." He spun like a top. "Did I mention the excessive drinking?"

I snorted. "This wine's not half bad." At this rate, I was going to need help getting into the car.

He put his empty beer bottle on the table, grabbed another, twisted the top, and took a gulp. "Have some more. It'll get better," he added with a wicked grin.

I laughed hard. Laughing felt good, and the more I did, the more I started feeling like my old self again.

Feeling more than slightly light-headed after my third glass, I spotted that same pretty young woman I'd seen Ronin with earlier this morning in a white halter dress that showed off her tan and sculpted shoulders. She kept throwing him smiles and tossing her hair back. Been there. Done that. Now, when I saw it done, it looked pretty stupid.

"I think she wants to talk to you." I reached over and grabbed the bottle of red wine with the label I didn't recognize and poured myself another glass. "You should go over there before she starts to undress herself."

"But I *want* her to undress herself."

I spat some of the wine from my mouth. "I know."

The half-vampire laughed, but his eyes turned serious as he looked at me. "You sure? I don't want to leave you. Not after what happened in the tent. Because I know something happened. You can't lie to a vampire."

I stiffened. Had he heard everything? "Nothing happened," I lied again. I was going straight to hell.

"Right," he mocked, still unconvinced. "You didn't look fine after you left. I know something happened. And you know I'll find out eventually."

I did not deserve a friend like him. "Go. Seriously. Looks like you might get lucky tonight." I winked at him.

Ronin leaned toward me, his eyes flashing. "Not unless you're okay."

I lifted my glass. "I'm in the best company. This guy's never let me down. Ah... here comes Martha," I said having spotted the large witch making a beeline for me. "Unless you want to stay for a chat about perms and Brazilian waxes."

"See ya." Ronin, light on his feet, was next to the pretty brunette in a burst of his vamp speed.

"Tessa! There you are," said Martha as she reached me, slightly out of breath. Her long black and purple dress reminded me somewhat of Marvelous Myrtle's, and I flinched at the memory. I did not want to think about that right now.

Martha rested a hand on my arm. "Gilbert's in such a pickle." She laughed, pushing up her bejeweled glasses with her finger. "He's there arguing with David Gallant, a famous shifter in our circles. Crazy rich. Too bad he's not handsome. You know him?"

"No." I took another large sip of my wine. I wasn't into gossip, but this was so much better than stewing over what had happened with the Seer. Plus, the more I drank, the better I felt.

The witch leaned back, and I noticed how her dark hair was piled on top of her head, like a beehive the ladies wore back in the 1960s. It made her taller, and I was sure that was the reason why she'd styled it that way.

"What do you think of the Night Festival, hon?" she asked after a moment. Her eyes shone with excitement.

I swallowed my wine. "It's—"

"Great, isn't it," expressed Martha and clapped her hands. "Ooh! So much to see... so much to do! I feel like I'm twenty again. I'm beside myself."

"I can tell."

She leaned in and lowered her voice. "Have you been to see Ben?"

"Ben?"

"The merman." Martha fanned herself with her hand. "The muscles on that fella. That chest. Those big, beautiful arms. Makes me want to invest in an inground pool. You know what I mean?" She laughed, touching my arm again.

"I do." Ben the merman was exceptionally handsome. "So, does he grow a pair of legs when he's out of the water? Like Ariel?"

Martha gave me a puzzled look. "Of course not, hon. He's a merman. Not like *The Little Mermaid*."

And there was a difference? "Right. Of course." I took another sip of my wine, wishing Ronin was still here. "Then, how does he.... you know... do the deed?" I couldn't believe I was talking to Martha about Ben's merman penis. That's what wine would do to you. First, it made you insane, and then it made you want to discuss giant fish penises.

The witch leaned forward and whispered, "Hon, you have no idea."

This conversation was getting weirder by the second. I looked over Martha's beehive, and my gaze fell on a handsome, thirty-something man with gray eyes and black, glossy, tousled hair.

Marcus wore his signature black leather jacket, jeans, and a casual black shirt. I was aware of every inch of him, remembering the touch of his hard muscles beneath his shirt. He wasn't dressed for the festival like the others, but I remembered him telling me he was working or rather, making sure no one killed Gilbert.

And just like that, my good mood crashed. What had me nearly growling like an animal was the stunning brunette wrapped around his arm. I thought my dress was beautiful, but hers was spectacular. It was dark gray, metallic-like and short, the hem right across her mid-thigh. Yup, she had spectacular thighs to go with her spectacular dress. And the breasts to fill it in. Whereas the boob fairy had skipped my house. I could never wear a dress like that, not without looking ridiculous.

My intestines twisted like they were trying to French braid themselves together.

He'd brought a date.

But he'd told me he was working. I wasn't sure why I was upset at seeing him with another woman. It's not like Marcus and I were dating. Hell, we were barely in the friend zone as it was. Besides, I wasn't ready for a relationship. The chief was hot. He should be dating, and I should stop spying.

I pulled my eyes away and emptied my glass of wine in one big ol' gulp. Martha was still talking, but I was only vaguely aware of what she was saying apart from the "would look fantastic on a body like yours" and the other "your hair needs another lifting spell."

"Tessa?"

My eyes snapped back to Martha. "Hmm? What?"

"I said," repeated the witch, "it looks like you have an admirer." She moved her eyebrows suggestively.

I spat some of the wine from my mouth. "You mean Marcus? No, we're just friends." *I think*. Heat rushed to my face and I wiped my mouth with the back of my hand.

"Marcus? Oh, no, hon," said Martha, her mocking tone insinuating that Marcus could never like someone like me. The thought of sending a few fireballs into her hair made me feel loads better. "Marcus is handsome. There's no doubt about that. But he's more trouble than he's worth. I'm talking about Adan Williams."

"Who?" Curious, I followed her gaze.

The mystery blond guy I had seen earlier this morning stood at the next pavilion watching me. His crisp white shirt accentuated his tan, and his black pants showed off a pair of muscular legs. Where Marcus was dark, sexy and a little dangerous, this guy was light, model-hot, and mesmerizing. He caught me staring and raised his wine glass.

I smiled at him and raised my own.

"Look at those strong hands," the witch was saying. "I wouldn't mind those feeling me up."

Okay. Enough of that. "You know him?"

Martha pressed her hand on me again. "Everyone knows who Adan is, hon." Her grip tightened as she pulled me closer. "The most popular bachelor in our paranormal circles. He was engaged to some witch for the last year, but they broke up. Apparently, she cheated on him with one of his friends and moved away across the country with him. Can you imagine? He's loaded. Not just with money. No, hon. In power too. His family is one of the most prominent witch families in our world."

I nodded as she spoke. I didn't care about all that. Money was never a goal of mine. If I had enough to live a comfortable life, it was good enough for me. A roof over my head, good meals, and pleasant company was my idea of being rich. The rest was meaningless.

Martha reached out, grabbed a fistful of my dress and yanked it down, exposing a lot more of my cleavage than I was comfortable with.

I jerked back, spilling wine all over my hand and dress. "Oh, my god. What are you doing?" I was seriously going to kill that witch. Thank the cauldron the dress was black, and the wine stains weren't visible.

Martha made a face and shook her head. "There's not much there. But you need to show them off. No worries, hon. Some men like small breasts. It's an anomaly, but it happens."

I gritted my teeth and pulled up my dress. "I'm not talking about my breasts with you." Where was Ronin when I needed him?

The witch put her hands on her hips, still eyeing me like I was a new project for her. "You know… if you would have come to see me earlier… I could have fixed that," she said, still staring at my breasts. "I have an augmentation spell that will increase your cup size by two cups—lasts for five hours. It's one of my bestsellers."

I smacked my forehead, miscalculated due to the wine, and smacked half my forehead half my face—hard. "Ow."

"What are you doing—stop that! You're going to ruin everything," hissed Martha and then lowered her voice. "Your prayers have been answered! He's coming over."

Great. And what prayers? I was about to tell her that I wasn't ready for a relationship, but I stopped myself. Maybe this guy Adan was exactly what I was looking for. I didn't believe in Mr. Right or soulmates anymore. But I did believe in Mr. Right Now. Who knew, maybe he was the nicest rich guy in the world?

"Oh, my cauldron," Martha whispered, "he must be quite the sight naked."

Surprising even myself, I pulled my face into a smile and turned around.

A scream split the night air.

I froze. Adan froze. Martha bounced and squealed.

"What the hell was that?" I spun around toward where the sound came from. A crowd was moving. Then another scream.

I tossed my wine glass, grabbed a fistful of material from my dress, hiked it up, and started after them, leaving Adan and Martha behind. I was a Merlin. When there was screaming, I followed.

Followed, well, it was hard running when you were tipsy and wearing a long dress with heels. I hobbled along, trying to run straight and hoping I didn't look drunk. Who was I kidding? I was drunk. Oops.

The crowd rushed forward and I followed like a drunken idiot. The running stopped as the mass of paranormals crowded around one of the tents.

"What's going on?" Ronin appeared next to me. "Who screamed?"

"No idea." Feeling bold due to the wine, I pushed my way through to get a better look and caught a glimpse of Marcus across from me doing the same thing.

And when I finally made it to the front, my stomach clenched, and all that wine threatened to come out.

I stood before a familiar purple tent, and the cloth door stood open, pulled to the side with a string tie. The smell of cigarette smoke still lingered in the air like a horrible air freshener.

And in the middle of the tent, sprawled on her back above a stack of purple and lilac pillows and soaked in blood lay Marvelous Myrtle.

An angry, deep gash slid across her throat, and blood spilled from her neck and down her chest. Two shards of glass that looked like they had once belonged to her crystal ball punctured both her eyes, leaving a bloody, pulpy mess around them.

Marvelous Myrtle was dead.

Chapter 6

"**G**ives a whole new meaning to the phrase *a killer mind*, doesn't it?" commented Ronin, which made me jump. "Guess you're not the only one who thought she was a fraud."

"I'm not so sure," I added, seeing those chunks of crystal ball glass sticking out from her eyes. Pricks crawled over my body like they were about to jump off and scuttle away with my skin.

The subtle scent of sulfur reached me. Then, I felt a slow, sour tension of magic pulsing and swirling inside the tent with thin traces of energy behind it. But just as soon as I felt it, it was gone as though I had imagined it. But I knew I hadn't. Either this was the remnants of Myrtle's defensive magic, or the person who did this to her had used magic. But why cut her throat and gouge out her eyes when a killing spell was so much faster and less messy?

It was a strange thing to stare at the body of a dead person who'd been very much alive and full of life, who I'd had a conversation with only a half-hour before. The questions were who had done it and why? Had Marvelous Myrtle seen something she shouldn't have?

"Get back. Show's over. Everyone get back," ordered a male voice.

I didn't have to turn around to know who that voice belonged to, but I did anyway.

Marcus pushed his way past me and moved inside the tent, his expression tight and all business as he picked his way carefully around the throws of pillows. His gray eyes never left the dead Seer. He knelt next to her, his shoulders stiff with tension as he took in the state of her. His attention was fixed on the glass shards sticking out of her eye sockets.

I looked over my shoulder to see if his date had followed him, but the pretty brunette wasn't there. The crowd squeezed in tighter around the tent's opening, trying to get a glimpse of the dead Seer or just to get a peek of the action.

Martha knocked a smaller female out of her way with a swing of her hip, her bejeweled fingers pulling at the opening as she peered inside. "Cauldron help us," she said. "Myrtle's dead!" She turned around, knocking me with part of her large boobs.

I tried to jump back to avoid a full-on assault, but my heel caught the hem of my dress and I tripped, only to feel strong hands wrapped around my arms and lifting me up a second later.

"Thanks," I said, feeling a blush work its way to my face as I wiggled out of Adan's grip.

Adan's eyes met mine and he smiled. "No problem." His voice was deep and it thrummed beautifully.

Damn. He was hot *and* had a beautiful voice.

A sliver of heat ran through my body and I pulled my eyes away before my face betrayed me.

Martha waited to get everyone's attention and then wailed, "Someone killed Marvelous Myrtle! Gilbert, come look! You have to see this. Myrtle's dead! Her throat's been cut!"

At that, a murmur began to run through the crowd, just as more excited paranormals came for a closer look. Some I recognized as Hollow Cove residents, who I'd seen around town or at the town's council meeting, but most of them were strangers.

I frowned at Martha's enthusiasm at seeing the dead Seer. It brought a bitter taste to my mouth. Myrtle was eccentric, but she didn't deserve to die like this, nor did she deserve to be stared at like a freak at a circus. But that's exactly what this was.

Gilbert's small, pudgy form squeezed between me and Ronin. His brown eyes widened when he caught a glimpse inside the tent. "Is it demons? The wards have failed us again! I knew it! I just knew it!" he squealed, his face pale in a sudden panic.

"Keep your pants on," I muttered, wanting nothing more than to slap him across the face, just as Dolores had once done. "The wards are fine." Which technically was a lie since I had no idea if that was true. But we'd gotten rid of Samara and her followers. Plus, I wasn't getting any demonic vibes, now that I knew how to recognize them.

And this was not the mark of a demon or a sorceress killing. This was something else. It was personal. I was sure of it. You didn't just stab a person's eyeballs because her blinking annoyed you. No. You did that because of something she said or because of something she *saw*.

Gilbert's eyebrows shot up into his hairline. "I don't like your tone, young lady. Now that you've *conveniently* found yourself a permanent residence," he added, his face sour, "doesn't give you the right to speak to me in that manner."

I stared down at him. "What the hell is that supposed to mean?" I didn't appreciate his tone either, like he thought I had conned my aunts into letting me stay with them.

He pointed a short finger in my face. "You should show your elders some respect."

"You mean little shifters who like to spread panic?" I countered, watching his face turn a shade of red, making Ronin snort.

Gilbert frowned and gestured inside the tent. "There's a dead Seer in there."

"Yeah, we noticed," said Ronin.

"It is perfectly acceptable to panic with a killer on the loose!" Gilbert cried loudly enough for the entire crowd to hear.

"Gilbert's right, hon." Martha's eyes were wide. "People have a right to know. They have to be prepared. No one wants to face a killer unprepared because…" She raked a finger across her neck and stuck out her tongue.

"Killer on the loose! On the loose!" Gilbert shrilled, his voice reaching a level I had no idea a small man could.

I shook my head and looked at Ronin. "We have our own show right here."

"Too bad I'm out of beer," said Ronin. "Popcorn would have been awesome. And olives. Love me some kalamata olives."

Marcus's attention snapped to us and I saw a phone in his hand. Our eyes met and he looked away, his phone angled over Myrtle's face as he began to snap pictures.

Ronin leaned in and whispered in my ear, "Shouldn't you be in there with him? You're a Merlin, remember?"

"Right," I muttered, feeling a little foolish. The job was still very new, and I didn't know for sure what it entailed. But a murder in Hollow Cove seemed to be right up the Merlin Group's alley.

My gaze fell on Marcus who had moved to Myrtle's fingers, snapping pictures. "Be right back." Gathering myself, I made to move forward.

"What's going on here?" came Dolores's voice from behind me, and I stopped and turned toward her.

The crowd parted at one side to let Dolores, Beverly, and Ruth through. And to my utter disappointment, trailing behind them were the Merlin Group members from New York.

And yup. The goat was still there. Yay me.

I pulled my eyes away from the goat as Greta elbowed the younger witch with the golden hair toward where I'd been looking. I would deal with the goat thing later.

"A Seer has been killed," I told Dolores, seeing the look of surprise materializing on each of my aunts' faces. I was careful not to make eye contact with the New Yorkers.

"Cauldron protect us," exclaimed Ruth, as she put her hand over her mouth.

"Damn," expressed Beverly, looking mildly disappointed. "I was just about to go see her."

"Is that what you wear at the Night Festival?" Gilbert was eyeing Beverly's sexy dress like she was a five-dollar whore.

Beverly flicked a silver manicured finger at him. "Don't you start with me, you pocket-sized man."

Gilbert screwed up his face in a sour expression. "You look like a prostitute."

Beverly smiled, tossed her hair, and said, "I was going more for high-class escort."

"Enough." Dolores pushed past them and came next to me. "How? How was she killed?"

"Her throat was cut," I told her, the image of the dead Seer's throat still vividly etched into my mind.

"And her eyes gouged with glass," added Ronin.

Dolores frowned. "There's never been a murder at the Night Festival before."

"Now there has," I said.

"I need to take a look," said Dolores, and just when she poked her head through the doorway, Marcus came out.

"Nobody goes in there," said the chief, making Dolores step back. At her scowl, he added, "Sorry, Dolores. But I can't have you contaminating the crime scene. Not until I know more. I need to get my fingerprint kit to dust for prints. Until then, it's sealed off. I'll share everything I can with the Merlin Group before then."

For a moment, I thought Dolores was going to spell him into a frog. I was still adjusting to the different chains of command between the Hollow Cove Security Agency and the Merlin Group. And I was still unsure who called the shots.

"That would be good," Dolores ground out, though her scowl never left her face as she joined her sisters.

Marcus looked up and whistled with his fingers.

The crowd suddenly parted again, making way for two big burly looking men, which I recognized as Marcus's deputies. I moved to stand next to my aunts with Ronin at my side.

"Shouldn't we be doing our own investigation?" I asked my aunts.

Dolores's dark eyes found mine. "We will. Don't worry. But Marcus is right. With all of us going in there at the same time, we'd be scattering our DNA too and making a mess of things. You know how Ruth's hair sheds."

"Hey," growled Ruth, though she was smiling.

Dolores shook her head. "No. We have to wait."

Ruth squeezed my arm. "Don't worry. Once Marcus and his team have gathered all their evidence, it'll be our turn."

Movement caught my attention and I saw Billy the goat jumping up and down, though no one turned at the sound of hooves hitting the ground. That damn goat. It was a ghost or something. It clearly wanted me to look at it. I glowered at the animal, but that seemed to only make things worse as it started to prance happily around Travis, Greta, and the younger witch.

This night just kept on getting weirder.

"Jeff. I need you to put up a perimeter around the tent," ordered Marcus. "No one goes in without my permission. I want it sealed."

"I'm on it," said the dark one as he pulled out a yellow police tape from his jacket and began to seal off a perimeter around Myrtle's tent.

"Cameron," said Marcus. "I need you to go back to the office and get my fingerprint kit."

Cameron gave a nod of his head and disappeared back through the crowd and into the shadows beyond.

Marcus stood, silent and strong. Despite his cool composure, I could see the tension in his jaw, the way his eyes moved everywhere at once, like he was trying to find who was responsible. That is if those responsible were stupid enough to stick around. I didn't think so. Although some killers did come back to the scene of the crime to relive that killing high.

Ronin nudged my arm. "Shotgun on selfies with the dead Seer later."

"You are one pretty messed up vampire," I told him.

Ronin beamed. "It's part of my charm."

"Did anyone see or hear anything?" called Marcus, and I yanked my attention to him as his eyes searched the crowd. "Even if you don't think it's important. The smallest clues can lead to big breaks."

My gaze traveled over the cluster of paranormals, looking for a guilty face or just something out of place. From the corner of my eye, I could see Billy the goat leaping in the air and trying to get my attention. My eyes settled on Adan. He was staring at Marcus with his arms crossed over his chest and a serious expression on his face.

"This one right here," called a woman's clear soprano. My eyes found the woman in that dark suit and hat I recognized from before who I'd pegged as a Seer or one of the acts here at the festival.

And she was pointing at *me*.

"Tess? Why is she pointing at you?" came Ronin's voice. The tension there didn't help the slamming of my heart in my chest. It made it worse.

Her plain face twisted into a sour expression. "I've been here all night. She was the last one to go see Myrtle. I saw her leave. No one's been in there since her."

Oh. Crap. This was not happening.

The crowd burst into a sudden roar of voices. I heard some yelling in breathless tones, but I couldn't make anything out. However, the sound of it went right to my middle and twisted.

Marcus's gray eyes were on me. "Is that true, Tessa? Did you visit this tent? Did you visit Myrtle?"

My head was spinning, and I forgot to breathe. *No, this can't be happening.*

My throat was parched, and I swallowed hard. "I, uh… yeah, I did. But I didn't kill her, if that's what you think," I added quickly. "You have to believe me. I didn't do this." I searched Marcus's face, but it was blank, and I couldn't tell what he was thinking.

"Now, wait just a minute, here," said Dolores, one hand on her waist and the other moving like a wand at Marcus's face. "You can't possibly be serious? Tessa is no murderer. That witch—" she pointed her long finger at the witch in the suit, "—is a liar."

The witch in the suit dipped her head low. "I'm no liar," she spat.

"Right. A fortune-teller who's not a liar," laughed Dolores. "And I'm the queen of England."

"I think she's confused," interjected Beverly and then pursed her lips at the strange witch in the suit. She took a careful step forward and smelled her. "I smell rum. Cheap too. You've been drinking?"

"No," answered the witch, looking like she was about to spit in Beverly's face.

Beverly laughed, a shocked expression on her pretty face. "Really? And you're wearing *that* sober? Can't be." She laughed as Ruth yanked her back.

"Tessa." Marcus's voice cut through me, and I looked at him. "What did you and Myrtle talk about?"

Everything slowed. Shit. I was not going to reveal to the world that I was seeing goats that weren't there, nor the strange dark cloud that had materialized in the tent.

My blood pressure rose, and I shifted my weight, trying to formulate a plan in my head. "You know… career… love… relationships. Is there a man in my future, that kind of thing." I laughed nervously.

A shiver lifted through me and was gone. I stared at the chief. He couldn't possibly think I could do this. Could he?

Marcus watched me. He seemed to recognize the lie like he could see it in my eyes. His jaw clenched, tension quirking his lips.

"Well, Dolores." Gilbert stood with his hands on his hips. "I never thought I'd see the day when a Merlin was accused of such a horrible deed."

"Shut up, Gilbert," snapped Dolores. "She didn't do this, and you know it."

The little man lifted his chin. "I know nothing of the sort. She was the last one to visit poor Marvelous Myrtle. And there are witnesses, you know," he added with a knowing smile.

Dolores glowered at the short shifter like she was trying to mentally flog his brain. "Witnesses can be wrong. It happens all the time."

I gritted my teeth as I saw his bitter satisfaction that my world was going to be rearranged, and he was going to like it.

"She killed her!" shrilled the witch in the dark suit. "She killed Myrtle." She frowned at me. "An eye for an eye."

I balled my hands into fists. "What? Are you kidding me? We're not in the Middle Ages, lady."

A group of paranormals from the festival had huddled around her. Some had their teeth bared, some had purple and green magic spilling from their hands, and some just stared with open hatred and revenge flashing in their eyes.

Damn. They all wanted to kill me.

Like hell would I let that happen. I tapped into the elements near me, even a slip of ley lines filled my chi. If they moved, I would defend myself.

The three Merlins from New York caught my attention. They were all watching me, even the goat, with their faces grim.

"I need you to come with me, Tessa," said Marcus, and my attention snapped back to him.

I stilled, letting go of the energy. "Come with you *where*, exactly?"

Marcus looked intensely uncomfortable. He paused for a second. "To my office."

Angst rushed through my veins. "You're going to lock me up? Is that it? Are you arresting me?" Now I was pissed. I hadn't done a thing, and I was being blamed for this.

"I need to ask you some questions," answered the chief. "That is all."

Ronin stepped in front of me. "Wait a minute. You can't be serious. Tess didn't do this. She's no killer, man."

"Marcus, no," came Ruth's panicked voice. "You can't do this. You know Tessa couldn't do such a thing."

I looked at the chief, and I could tell he didn't share the same feelings. The truth was he hardly knew me.

Dolores put a hand on her sister. "We'll figure this out." She pinned me with her stare, telling me with her eyes that it was going to be okay.

Sure it was. She wasn't the one being humiliated in front of the whole town.

Beverly let out a puff of frustrated air. "I can't believe this."

Marcus looked at my aunts. "Look. I need to ask her some questions. You know how this goes. She was the last person to see Myrtle alive. I don't have a choice." The chief moved and grabbed my arm, steering me away from my family and friends like a criminal. "Come on, Tessa. Let's go."

And just like that, I was the number one suspect in Marvelous Myrtle's murder.

CHAPTER 7

I'd wanted to spend more time with Marcus, but sitting in an interrogation room with no windows for the last hour was not how I wanted to do it. I was thinking along the lines of coffee, perhaps even dinner.

The chief had put me in here and left. He told me he'd be right back, but from the clock on my phone, that was an hour ago.

At least he hadn't cuffed me and had let me keep my clutch. I felt like an idiot, all dressed up, wasting the exquisite dress inside a room that was starting to feel more like a loony bin. I'd pulled off my shoes, and the cool tile felt nice on my sweaty feet. Now they were sticking to the tile.

My feet weren't the only things sweating. Not if you counted my pits and my lower back. Nervous sweat. The real stinker. By now, I probably smelled like the men's locker room. Great.

My head started to throb, which was my body's way of telling me I'd had too much wine too quickly. I needed some water.

Worse, I had to pee. *Really* had to pee. And no one had bothered to come in and ask if I needed to use the restroom or even to check if I was still breathing. Not that I had seen anyone else here other than Marcus and me. The office was deserted.

Ronin had called five times and texted twenty. I told him not to stress and to please let my aunts know that I was fine. As soon as I knew what the hell was going on, I would call them. They didn't have cell phones (something about the radiofrequency waves disrupting their magic mojo, though I'd never seen any difference) so I was relying on Ronin to be my messenger boy.

I sat in the ten-by-twelve room with white walls on a metal chair. My elbows rested on a gray metal table, which was the only piece of furniture apart from the two chairs. Deep gouges scratched the surface of the table, like some werewolf had run his claws over it.

Maybe he was expressing his artistic side. I spotted some brown stains on the table's legs and a few spots on the wall that the cleaning crew had missed. I was sure some pretty shady characters had seen the inside of this room. Now I was part of that gang. Yippee.

Sitting alone in a strange room for over an hour can start to play games inside your head. I kept replaying the night, over and over again: the Merlin Group from New York, the mysterious goat, the darkness that crept around Myrtle like an evil entity. I rummaged in my head, trying to remember if I saw anyone go in after I'd left Marvelous Myrtle, but I didn't. I was so creeped out by the experience, all I remember was stumbling with Ronin to the nearest pavilion and shoveling food and drink into my mouth.

Let's not forget these trials Greta had insinuated I was supposed to do, or at least, I was supposed to have passed to become a full-fledged Merlin. What was that about? I would have to ask my aunts about that later.

And then there was the way most of the townspeople had looked at me. Like I was guilty.

My pulse leaped, fueled by anger. I shifted butt cheeks. My ass was going to be sore after sitting for so long on such a hard chair. I felt like I was like sitting on a rock. But with a rock, I'd be outside, preferably on the beach below

Davenport House, enjoying the breeze and the sound of the waves hitting the shore.

Yeah. Not happening.

The door to the interrogation room swung open and I jerked. Marcus came in and my breath caught, not only because he surprised me, but I was still stunned by seeing his uber hotness. Those sultry good looks, that hard body, that suave way he moved, part predator part lover. Guys like him only existed in the movies.

"Sorry to keep you waiting," he said. "I had to go back to the crime scene to follow up on a few things." A folder filled with paper hung in his right hand.

I eyed it suspiciously. "Is that my file?" I jolted straight in my chair. Holy shit. I had a file! Never thought I'd utter those words in my lifetime.

Marcus's lips pulled into a tight smile. "Something like that."

I let my hands fall into my lap so he wouldn't see my shaking fists. "You arrested me for a murder I didn't commit. You know that. Right?" Anger made its way into my voice. "Don't you need proof? Not to mention a motive? Why the hell would I do that to a stranger? I'm not psychotic." Yes, I'd contemplated strangling the Marvelous Myrtle a few times, but thoughts didn't count. Otherwise, there would have been a noose over my head long ago with all the murderous thoughts I'd had about my ex.

Marcus grabbed the seat facing me and sat. "I did it for your own protection."

My lips parted. "What? How's that?"

Marcus let the file fall on the table. "The Night Festival attracts a lot of crazies. I run background checks on most of the visiting paranormals, the elite, and the performers. But some just slip through the cracks."

"What does that have to do with me?"

The chief's eyes bore into mine. "They were going to kill you, Tessa. Or they were going to try. I know that look. I have enough experience to know when a deadly fight is about to break loose. And trust me, it was."

My stomach clenched. He did have a point. That witch in the suit wanted to spill my blood. I saw it in her eyes.

I let out a breath and let my head fall into my hands. "How did I get into this mess? I should have never gone to see her."

"Why *did* you go see the Seer?" A smile quirked his lips. "And don't say it was because you were curious about your love life. I know that's not true."

"Oh, really?" I matched his smile, letting my hands fall on my lap again. "And how would you know that, Chief? Are you a shifter turned mind reader? Because I didn't see you with your turban behind a booth giving out five-dollar palm reads."

Marcus's face changed to professional detachment. "Just doing my job. And I don't need to be a fortune-teller to read people. I can tell when they're lying. It's a natural-born talent."

I cocked my head to the side. "Well, my natural-born talent is to give the finger with my toes. Wanna see?"

Marcus's eyebrows shot up, and I wasn't sure if he was impressed or just annoyed. "I need to know everything about the people in my town. It goes with the territory."

"Your town?"

"That's right. My town."

I leaned back in my chair. "So, you brought a date to the Night Festival?" Whoops. I couldn't help it, the words just vomited out of my mouth of their own volition.

Marcus looked at me, his brows creasing. "I didn't bring a date."

"Right." Why was he lying? And why did I care?

The chief looked down at the file and flipped it open.

"That's a lot of paper," I said, my face warming in indignation. "Why is my file so thick?" I leaned forward, trying to get a glimpse of what was written, but my skills of reading upside-down were nonexistent.

The chief's gray eyes met mine. "Have you ever met Myrtle before tonight?"

I shook my head. "No. Never. Tonight was the first time I'd even met a Seer before." I pressed my lips tight. "I'm not lying."

"I didn't say you were." He laced all his fingers into a single fist. "What did you and Myrtle talk about?"

Here it comes. My Oscar-worthy acting chops. If Marcus indeed had some built-in, supernatural lie detector ability, I was screwed.

I leaned back in my chair. "Nothing that would merit me killing her," I said, my voice carefully bland to match my blank features. "Are you going to tell me what's in my file or do I have to guess?"

Marcus exhaled through his nose, and a frown creased his forehead. "It would be a lot easier if you started to tell the truth."

I swallowed. "You calling me a liar?"

Something stirred in his eyes. "Right now… yes. I know you're holding something back. I can see it in your eyes. You're not that good a liar, Tessa."

Magic built around me, drawn from the elements in the room. It weaved into my core and pulled from my emotions. Emotions were an added boost when you were weaving magic. And right now, I was the holy grail of emotions. I couldn't settle on one. I kept flicking between guilt, fear, anger, attraction (damn hormones), and betrayal.

And yet anger always seemed to be the winner.

Marcus frowned, having sensed the build-up of magic. "What did you talk about with Myrtle?"

I thought about coming clean and telling him the truth. About the mysterious goat that no one but me could see, and the Seer's freak-out at something she'd seen about my future. The thought of seeing Myrtle clawing at her eyes and twitching like a dying animal still haunted me. But could I trust Marcus? If I told him, he'd keep me here. I was certain of it. He'd probably think I was crazy too.

Maybe I was being an idiot, but I didn't want him to see that side of me. Not until I figured out what the hell the goat was.

I took a breath and said, "When do I get my phone call?"

Marcus's face was stone. "Why are you avoiding the question?"

"Why are you denying that you brought a date?"

Marcus sighed and shook his head. "What are you hiding, Tessa? I can't help you if you don't tell me what it is. It's my job to protect this town. If you know something, you have to tell me."

I crossed my arms over my chest. "I think I need to call my lawyer. Isn't that how it works?"

A twitch ran through Marcus's face as if the gorilla in him wanted to claw its way out. "I'm not kidding around, Tessa," he said, his voice rough and strained like he was trying to control his beast.

"Is this the gorilla talking? Does it want a banana?"

Marcus let out an exasperated breath and rubbed his face with his hands. Such pretty, strong hands. "Why are you being so goddamn difficult? What is it with you?"

"Maybe it has something to do with being wrongfully accused of a crime I didn't commit."

A muscle twitched along the chief's jaw. "Witnesses put you at the scene. I know you were in there for at least five minutes."

"Spying on me now. That's wonderful." And strangely, I kind of liked it.

"The two of you talked," continued the chief. "I need to know what about."

My eyes narrowed in annoyance. "I don't see it as any of your business. That was a private conversation. Hell, Myrtle put up some sound-blocking spell so no one could hear what was happening inside her tent." Shit. I shouldn't have said that.

"She did. Why's that?"

"Because Ronin was trying to eavesdrop," I said quickly, which was totally true. But I could already see the doubt simmering in those fine gray eyes of his. He was beginning to think I was guilty.

It struck me hard, like I'd spelled one of my own power words at myself. "I didn't kill her," I said softly. My voice shook, and I hated it.

He leaned forward, letting the light play on his handsome features. "Then tell me what happened in there. Tell me what she told you." He hesitated. "Why won't you help me?"

"Help you?" Rage poured into me like a fever. "It's all about you. Isn't it? Forget about how you embarrassed me in front of my aunts and the entire town."

A muscle shifted on Marcus's jaw. "You did that to yourself."

Oh. He was going down. "I'm finished talking. I want my lawyer." I had no idea if the paranormal justice worked the same way as the human system. I'd never had the incentive to ask before now.

A vein throbbed on Marcus's neck. "Do you want to spend the rest of the night in here? Because it looks like it might happen if you don't start talking."

My eyes fell on the file. I moved my hand to grab it, but Marcus snatched it up.

He tightened his jaw, clearly angry. "Don't you see how this looks?" he asked.

"Pray tell," I said bitterly.

"It looks like you're guilty," he said, his face hard. "The entire town was there. I had no choice but to take you in. It's my job."

"It's your job to arrest innocent people? Then, man oh man, you excel at your job. Good for you." I gave him a thumbs up.

Marcus shook his head. "You're worse than your aunts."

"You do realize the killer or killers are still out there while you're wasting your time with me." I could see my fantasy of me possibility dating the chief pop like a burst soap bubble. My heart thrashed in my chest, and I hated it. "You think I did this?" I asked, my throat tight. I wanted to hear it from him, see the word come flying out of his mouth. When he didn't respond or meet my eyes, I had my answer. It was far worse than being accused by the entire town. Whatever delusions I'd thought up about him evaporated.

Fury singed along my skin and I stifled my anger. I plopped my arms on the table. "Go on then. Arrest me."

Marcus's face jerked. Anger flooded him and then, with a single enormous struggle of will, he regained control. The effort was almost physical. "You're free to go," he said finally, "but don't leave this town."

Right. Like I had somewhere else to go.

He'd said it conversationally, all matter-of-fact and flat, but in his eyes, I could see a simple certainty. If he had to, he would lock me up if I was behind this.

Furious, I stood up, grabbed my clutch and phone, pulled open the door, and stormed out.

Only when I hit the street did I remember I'd forgotten my shoes.

CHAPTER 8

I sat at my desk, a dark mahogany makeup vanity that used to belong to my mother, trying to ignore my pounding head as I searched the net for everything I could find about Marvelous Myrtle. I'd been at it since seven this morning. After five hours of intense searching, I'd discovered a few things. Her real name was Myrtle LaVine, she was forty-eight years old, never married, no kids, and lived in twelve different cities in the past ten years. Her employment was listed as Psychic Detective. Her name had appeared in the papers a few times. She'd worked alongside human detectives, helping them in solving crimes with her psychic abilities on cold cases. Her last address was an apartment somewhere in Boston.

I couldn't find anything on her personal life. She didn't have a personal Facebook page, just her business one. She didn't have a social media presence. No friends. No family. Nothing.

But someone hated her enough to slice her neck and gouge out her eyes.

"Where are you?" I said to my laptop. "I know you're there somewhere."

I'd been in a foul mood since I woke up. Scratch that. I barely slept at all. Who could blame me? Not after my giant fiasco with the chief. I went from thinking he could be potential dating material to utterly loathing him in the space of just a few minutes.

I had forgiven him for the incident about my mother, which had turned out to be totally legit after what she'd pulled. She'd abandoned her partner on the job, which got him killed in the end.

But this? Dragging my ass to an interrogation room in front of the town and my aunts? Yeah, not cool. He could have taken me aside and done it differently, away from everyone. But he didn't. He chose to humiliate me.

I hit my fingers on the keyboard hard, feeling the tension in the tendons of my wrists and fingers. If I kept this up, I was going to need a new laptop. And the cauldron knew I didn't have the money for it. I was dirt poor. If it weren't for my aunts, I'd be wrestling a homeless person for a park bench.

Speaking of money, after my humiliation, who was going to hire me? The Merlin witch accused of murder? Yeah. I didn't think so. Or worse, what if my aunts' own business suffered because of this? I couldn't live with myself if that happened. I'd have to leave. There was no other way around it.

I was angry as hell, but the betrayal ran deeper, twisting through my core and gushing through my veins until it seeped out of my pores.

Whatever happened to innocent until proven guilty? Or giving the person accused the benefit of the doubt? Seemed like in Hollow Cove you were guilty by claiming you were innocent.

The chief hadn't *technically* arrested me or charged me with anything, but he might as well have done it. It felt like it, anyway.

The fact was, if I wanted to stay and keep my position in the Merlin Group, I needed to clear my name. And to do that, I needed to find Myrtle's true killer, even if Marcus was on the case. *I* would find them.

My aunts had been avoiding me too. I didn't blame them. I was in a devilish mood this morning—Tessa-Godzilla. Ruth had been kind enough to bring me up some raspberry pancakes and coffee for breakfast. I barely registered her presence and scarcely heard anything she said as I stared at the computer screen.

Dolores and Beverly had popped in as well, but they never said a word. Either they didn't know what to say or they did but had preferred I not freak out. Which meant that whatever they wanted to say—it was bad.

I closed my laptop, popped two Tylenol into my mouth, swallowed them dry, and headed toward the staircase. I wouldn't get any more information about Myrtle on the net that I hadn't already discovered. Plus, I was being rude to my aunts, cooped up in my room like an angry teenager.

But I'd been dying to ask a question on my mind. And now seemed like the best time.

I hit the bottom of the staircase and made my way to the kitchen. Voices carried to me—angry, heated voices.

"...I've had enough with this town," came Dolores's deep-toned voice.

"...after everything we've done for them," I heard Beverly say.

"I'm going to borrow Janet's poodle Killer and have him urinate all over Gilbert's perfect front lawn," said Ruth with resentment in her voice. "Bet he's going to hate that."

"I think I'll invite Gilbert for a tour of the basement," said Beverly, her voice harsh and laced with metal. "He's been bugging me for a house tour for years. Looks like it's his lucky day."

And then I heard the sound of plates or something banging together.

Oh, dear.

I stepped into the kitchen and halted.

Dolores, Beverly, and Ruth sat at the kitchen table facing the biggest strawberry cheesecake I'd ever seen.

They each had a whopping serving that spilled over the edges of their dessert plates.

"Maybe you should get bigger plates." I couldn't help my smile.

Ruth licked a chunk of cheesecake from the corner of her mouth. "We eat cheesecake when we're anxious. When something is bothering us." She tore into her piece of cheesecake with her fork.

Dolores let her fork fall on her plate with a clank. "Like having our niece wrongly accused and brought in for questioning! It's a festival, for cauldron's sake. Not a hanging. You're supposed to explore the different venues. It's what they're there for!"

"Come, sit, Tessa," said Beverly. "We set a plate for you." She gestured next to her toward the clean plate. "Trust me. You don't want to miss out on this cheesecake."

I did as she instructed and sat, realizing only then how hungry I was. After Ruth cut me a generous slice, though considerably smaller than any of theirs, I tore into it with my fork and took a bite.

Delicious fruity, sugary cheese exploded around my taste buds. My eyes widened. "Wow. You weren't kidding."

"It's better than sex," informed Ruth, a knowing smile on her face.

Beverly screwed up her pretty face in a thoughtful expression. "I don't know what kind of sex you've been having... but this cheesecake is *not* better than the sex *I've* been having," she said with a wicked smile. "And I've been having a lot of it."

"I'm with Ruth," I told them, taking another bite. "I've had lousy sex for five years because this cheesecake is probably the best thing I've ever tasted in my entire life."

Ruth laughed and hit my fork with hers in solidarity.

"Did you see the look on Greta's face?" growled Dolores, scooping up the last of her cheesecake from her plate with her fork. "That damn witch enjoyed every minute of it. It's what she's always wanted. To prove that her Merlin Group was better than ours."

I shrugged. "Who the hell cares what she thinks."

The three sisters dropped their forks.

"It matters a great deal, Tessa." Dolores had gone rigid in her chair. "I know some of our ways are new to you. This place, especially. But our reputation with the other covens is of great importance. We Davenport witches have always been the most envied of the Merlins. Because... *we* are the best."

I suddenly didn't feel hungry anymore. "So, you're saying I've ruined it. I've ruined your good name. Great. I feel awesome."

"Wasn't your fault." Beverly shifted in her seat. "It was that damn Marcus Durand's fault. I should have never slept with his father."

I choked on my cheesecake. I did *not* want to go there. "What were these trials they spoke of?" I asked instead. I'd been dying to ask about them ever since Greta had mentioned it.

I cast my gaze around my aunts. They'd gone silent on me again, and for a moment I thought they weren't going to answer.

"The Merlin trials," informed Dolores. She pushed her empty plate to the side and clasped her hands on the table. "Usually, to get your Merlin license you must perform the trials and pass."

"But I didn't." I looked at Beverly. "You even gave me my own cards."

"Our situation was unusual," continued Dolores before Beverly had a chance to answer. "With the attacks on the town from Samara, we took it upon ourselves to promote you without the trials."

"No rules say we can't," interjected Ruth.

"But Greta seemed to think so," I added. "She doesn't recognize me as a real Merlin. Not sure how that's going to play out for my future here."

Beverly speared her cheesecake with her fork. "Greta can shove her broom up her ass."

I laughed, but I still felt a little uncomfortable, like I didn't merit the title or didn't get all my girl scout badges. "So, I'm still a Merlin?" Either way, I didn't need the title to keep investigating Myrtle's death. I could still do that on my own. But having that title had filled me with a sense of purpose and pride, something I thought I'd lost years ago. I didn't want to lose it.

Dolores flattened her fingers on the table. "In the event of an emergency, we had every right to elevate you to Merlin—without going through the trials. And, you proved to everyone that you were capable of some serious defensive magic. In a way... fighting Samara... the demons... the dragon... those were real trials too. And let me tell you, my dear, you passed with flying colors."

I smiled, gratitude swelling in my chest. "Does it merit another piece of cheesecake?"

Ruth let out a hearty laugh, reached over the table, and cut me another slice of that marvelous cheesecake. She dumped it on my plate with a thump.

Speaking of marvelous. "Did you have a chance to check out Myrtle's tent?"

"Yes," answered Dolores, her features pinched in what looked like worry. "We went over the crime scene while you were... *incarcerated*."

"And?" I perked up, hoping they'd found something.

Dolores pressed her lips into a thin line. "We didn't pick up any unusual traces of magic or anything else that would suggest she was killed with magic or anything paranormal. Just Myrtle's magic."

Weird. "So the killer or killers didn't use magic. Why? Maybe to conceal their true selves."

"It's possible." Dolores dipped her head like she was thinking about it. "Unless Marcus pulls some prints or has more evidence, we can't know who did this to her."

"Or why they did it in the first place," interjected Ruth, her blue eyes sad. "Such a shame."

I wasn't going to let it go. "Did any of you know who Marvelous Myrtle was? I found out a bit more on the net but nothing that would help me figure out who killed her."

"Well," started Dolores, "I remember seeing her at every Night Festival for the past ten years. But I didn't know her personally, I'm afraid. I mean, it's not like we needed to have our fortune told." She laughed.

"I did."

We all looked at Beverly.

"What?" She shrugged as a slow smile appeared on her face. "I was having a hard time choosing between Harry and Stephan. Both sexy, both with hard bodies, both incredible in bed."

I took a bite of my second piece of cheesecake. "So, who did you choose?"

"I didn't." Beverly giggled. "I kept seeing them both."

I laughed hard and took another bite of my cheesecake.

"Tessa."

I looked up at the tension and concern in Dolores's voice. "Yes?"

A worried expression pinched her features. "Last night you said you could see a goat. What did you mean by that exactly?" She pointed a spindly finger at me and added, "And no lies... I can tell if you lie."

Just like Marcus, huh? My stomach clenched. Crap. I knew this was coming. I knew they wouldn't let it go. Hell, I couldn't. If I could trust anyone with this strange freakshow that was my life, it would be my aunts.

"I saw a goat," I said finally, making Ruth snort. "I know how crazy it sounds. Especially because *I* was the *only* one seeing it. But there was a goat. I swear it. A black and white goat with cute little horns and tail. It was standing next to Greta and the others."

Ruth let out a sigh. "I've always wanted a goat. And chickens, ducks, and a pony. Oh, and a cow. I've always wanted a cow." Her eyes widened. "A moo-cow."

Beverly pointed her fork at Ruth. "The next time you pray to the goddess, pray for brains."

I took a breath and said. "Does that mean I'm going crazy?"

"No." Dolores's eyes pinned me. "But it means something." She leaned forward in her chair. "Tessa. I'd like you to keep that to yourself until we figure out what seeing a goat means. It can mean different things. And not all of them bad."

"And not all of them good, either." I sighed through my nose. "I can keep my mouth shut about the goat."

Hopefully, Ronin could keep his mouth shut. But I wasn't going to sit here and do nothing while my reputation and my aunts' were soiled. Not that I even had a reputation, apart from being a Davenport witch and having Amelia Davenport as my mother, who had mastered the reputation of being a "flake."

Beverly pushed back her chair and stood. She had on a pair of black pants in a slim cut that hugged her curves and didn't leave much to the imagination. She'd paired them with a lowcut periwinkle blouse that accentuated her green eyes.

"You look fantastic, Beverly," I told her truthfully, wishing I'd look that good at her age.

Beverly beamed and brushed back her golden locks with her fingers. "Thank you, darling," she said, moving her hips. "It's my lucky outfit."

I raised a brow, thinking she didn't need any luck. She was stunning in anything she wore. "Really? Why's that?"

Dolores snorted. "She's not wearing any underwear."

My jaw dropped as Beverly shrugged and laughed it off, like it was her wicked little secret. Loved my aunts.

"Thanks for the cheesecake." I stood up and moved toward the wooden peg rack on the wall to grab my bag. My heart was pounding, and I wasn't sure if it was from the excitement of what I was about to do or the sugar rush from those two slices of cheesecake.

"Where are you going?" came Dolores's voice behind me.

I turned around. "To the festival," I said as I slipped on my black flats. "If anyone knows anything about Myrtle, they'll be there." Maybe I could even get the witch in the suit to talk. I wanted to know why she'd pointed at me in the first place.

I hoped someone knew something. Because if they didn't, I didn't know where to turn next.

CHAPTER 9

High as a kite on a cheesecake the size of a large pizza, I rushed down Stardust Drive, took a right turn on Shifter Lane, and headed for the festival.

The Tylenol had numbed some of the pain in my head, and my thoughts—though exhausted and slow—seemed to be firmly connected to my body again.

Most of the festival's performers and members were sleeping in their trailers, getting some shuteye before tonight, but I spotted a few mingling with the townspeople. *Gotcha*.

I checked my bag to make sure I had my copy of *The Witch's Handbook*—I never knew when it might come in handy—and I moved deeper into the celebration. Though the real festivities were at night, there was still some music playing and lunch was displayed below some of the pavilions.

"I've told you once and I'll tell you again," Gilbert was saying to a man with a baseball cap. "The bottom line is that the lights go *around* the streetlights in a counterclockwise pattern. And I daresay that you seem to be doing the opposite on purpose."

I ducked behind a portable potty ('cause all those half-breeds needed to go somewhere) and hurried as far as I could away from Gilbert. That little owl shifter was a menace, and if he wasn't careful, I was going to pluck him like a chicken.

I had no real plan, except for the part that I needed to find someone—anyone—willing to answer some questions. I wasn't intending on threatening them with my magic either, but I was going to do what it took to clear my name. If that meant spelling a few reluctant paranormals from speaking, then so be it. At this point, I didn't care anymore.

Besides, most of them thought I'd done Myrtle in, so I was going to use that as a scare tactic. Why waste such powerful incentives?

Still, someone *had* killed Myrtle, and I wouldn't rest until I figured out who.

My gaze found my first victim—a young guy, maybe twenty, sporting a light brown manbun and matching beard that spilled over his chest. The younger ones were easier to break. I really didn't get the trend, though. To me, beards carried a plethora of bacteria.

"Excuse me!" I called as I hurried over. "Yes. You. Hello there. I thought I might ask you some questions. I—" The rest of what I was going to say vanished from my mind. "Huh. Are those breasts?"

The paranormal I first thought was a dude had some very obvious breasts. Either that, or his pecs were abnormally large. Obviously, not the right thing to say either by the scowl on her face, and yes, I mean *her*. How did I miss that? Those?

The bearded lady pressed her left hand, which was covered in tawny fur, on her hip, making me think of Dolores, while the other held some sort of green drink. "Excuse me?" said the woman in a very womanly voice. "Oh, my god. Stop staring at my breasts! What kind of freak are you?"

I lifted my gaze to the large sign behind her that proclaimed MEET BAMBI. WORLD FAMOUS BEARDED WOMAN.

I looked at the woman, sipping that green drink from a straw. "You're a shifter stuck between her breasts—I mean beast?"

Bambi rolled her eyes, yup definitely a girl. "What do you want? Make it quick. I have to get my beard shampooed and my nails clipped."

I bit down on my tongue as I pulled out my pen and notepad from my bag. "Did you know Myrtle LaVine? Can you tell me if she had any enemies?"

Bambi stopped slurping, her light eyes round. "You," was all the warning I got before she tossed that vile drink at me.

But at least I had the instinct to jump out of the way. "Hey!" I yelled, my right leg and shoe having been the only things she caught. I flicked my leg to get some of the green goo off my jeans. "What's the matter with you?"

Bambi's bushy eyebrows lowered to the bridge of her large nose. "You killed her. You killed Myrtle," she seethed. "She was my friend."

This was going *so* swell. "I didn't kill her. I went for a reading. That's it. I wish everyone would stop accusing me of something I didn't do."

Bambi stared at me for a moment and then made a contemptuous noise in her throat. "I'm not telling you anything." And with that, Bambi spun around and disappeared between two trailers.

I sighed. "Well. That went well."

With the green drink seeping through my jeans like pond scum and making them stick to my skin, I hobbled on, heading in the direction of voices. Someone here had to be willing to tell me something about Myrtle. Someone would see that I was only trying to help and, in turn, would answer some of my questions. I hoped.

Frustrated—and now with a slop of green goo plastered to my jeans, so I could forget about making a good first impression—I kept going.

A dozen small humanoids were sitting on a bench, eating what looked like sandwiches and salads on paper plates. Their hair was all different colors, varying from blue and orange to bright pink, and drifted around their heads like dandelion down. They were dressed in light, silky looking tops paired with tights like you might see at a ballet. Wings similar to a dragonfly's hung from their backs like iridescent cloaks.

Sprites.

Sprites were another race of half-breeds or paranormals, rarely taller than two feet. They were more reclusive than the other races and preferred to live away from the human population, sticking mostly to forests and islands. The best part? They were nasty little buggers.

No one looked twice in my direction as I approached. Hell, it was almost like I was invisible.

I planted myself in front of them, smiling to try and disguise my unease. "Hey there. I'm digging the tights, very Peter Pan. I was wondering if I could ask you some questions about Myrtle LaVine?"

The largest of them—maybe two foot three inches, young and athletic—that I pegged as their leader, stood on the bench as to give him more height. But he was still a lot shorter than me. He was dressed in bright blue tights that matched his hair and wings.

I waited for him to speak, but all he did was glare at me, like that would scare me off or something. "So, did you know her?" I pressed. "Anyone? Hello? You do speak English, right? My Spriteglish needs some work." I laughed.

The leader hissed at me, and his wings buzzed behind him in irritation. "Boo." Was all he said to me.

"Boo?" I laughed again, relaxing a little. This wasn't so bad. "Is that your name? Boo—Ah! What are you doing?" I screamed as he threw his half-eaten sandwich at my head. "Stop that! Stop!" I jerked as another sandwich hit the side of my head.

It wasn't enough that I was soiled by some green drink. Now I was being attacked by sandwiches. Yay me.

"I said stop!" I ducked, throwing up my hands to protect my face, but too late. I could feel something cold and slimy gliding down my cheek. Let's not even start with my white T-shirt. Note to self. Never wear white when going to speak to sprites or a bearded Bambi.

"Boo! Boo! Boo!" they thundered at me, and I was assaulted by another volley of sandwiches.

I spun, hands on my head, and rushed in the opposite direction. I hit the sidewalk with rapid momentum but somehow managed not to fall on my face. Using a parked car as a shield, I stood and yelled, "Next time, use whole wheat bread! You little shits!"

The leader gave me the finger. Pfft. I was no lady. So, I gave him the finger back, with both hands.

I walked away feeling more frustrated and hopeless and looking like I went rolling in this week's town garbage. I peeled the cold meat slices from my notepad and shoved it in my bag.

And on and on it went.

It was the same case whenever I met someone new. They scurried away like I was a carrier of a plague. No one would tell me anything apart from the spew of curses that flew from their mouths. They all thought I'd killed her.

Thanks, Marcus.

Just when I'd decided this plan of mine was hopeless and was on my way home, a shape stood in my way. "Scouting out your next victim?" asked a woman wearing a man's suit I recognized as the same one who'd accused me last night.

Oh, this was going to be fun.

I molded my face into a smile. "Yeah. And if you're not careful, it'll be you." Okay, a little overkill and definitely *not* the best thing to say when the town thinks you're a murdering psychotic bitch. But she was asking for it. And she was wearing a butt-ugly suit.

She smiled wickedly, her short dark hair oiled back with not a single strand out of place. "You might have fooled some of your people, but we're not fooled. We know you killed Myrtle."

I raised a brow. "Is that the same suit you wore yesterday? That's kind of gross." I pulled my face in mock surprise. "Are you wearing the same underwear too?"

Her face didn't move, not even a flinch, like she was a wax figure. Creepy.

"We're watching you," suit-lady warned.

"We?" I laughed. "You, me, and all your friends inside your head? Stop sniffing that hair balm. It's messing with your brain."

Several forms hurried out behind her.

"Oh, you mean *those* friends." My heart thrashed as I stared at four men, their eyes hard and faces unyielding as stone. What had I gotten myself into?

Suit-lady smiled, enough to show a slip of teeth, but there was no warmth in it. "Things are going to change around here. Starting with your attitude," she warned and glanced at two of the four men behind her.

Then the air shook with energy. Suit-lady flicked her wrists, and coils of red magic wound around her hand. "You're gonna pay for what you did to Myrtle."

I opened my mouth to protest but slammed it shut. Another five paranormals, witches by the magic dripping from their hands, came to stand next to her.

Okay. That was my cue to leave.

"Love to stay and chat," I said as the others moved in closer. "But it's like they say. No rest for the wicked."

I gave them a finger wave and walked backward. No way was I going to show suit-lady and her minions my back. Never turn your back on your enemy, right? Or something along those lines. Heads whipped my way, disapproving frowns from the faces of other members of the festival as I shuffled in a backward motion. They could gawk all they wanted. I wasn't about to duel with a bunch of pissed-off witches. I was still technically a trainee.

I was walking backward surprisingly well. Until I hit something solid.

"Tess? You're one strange chick."

I spun around. "That's the best compliment I've had all day." Relief welled into my chest, happy to see Ronin. But there was still an underlying rage rippling through my veins. These strangers loathed me, wanted to harm me, that I was certain. And all for something I didn't do.

Ronin's face quirked into a smile. He reached out a hand over my head. "Why were you walking backward? And why do you have lettuce in your hair?"

"The sprites. They attacked me with their sandwiches."

Ronin flicked the lettuce from his fingers. "I'm not sure how I'm supposed to respond to that."

I looked over my shoulder and let out a breath of relief. Suit-lady and her minions hadn't followed. But they were all still staring at me with open hatred.

"Hey. You never called me back," accused Ronin. "If I wasn't so narcissistic and happily secure with my half, uber-hot vampire self, my feelings might have gotten hurt."

"I know." I exhaled some of the pent-up tension from my body. "I'm sorry. I've been busy all morning trying to get a better idea of who Marvelous Myrtle was. I came here to see if anyone could help me out with that."

Ronin dipped his head. "And how did that go?"

"I've got lettuce in my hair. How do you think it went?" I shook my head. "No one wants to help me. They all think I did it."

"Idiots." Ronin lost his smile. "I'm sorry the chief did that to you. That was a dick move. He shouldn't have taken you in."

I shrugged. "He was just doing his job," I answered, surprised that I was actually defending him. He had said he'd done it to protect me, though I wasn't sure I believed him. Still, I didn't want to talk about Marcus right now. He'd been invading my head for hours, and I needed a break.

Ronin shoved his hands in his jeans pockets. "How can I help? Give me a job. Anything. I'm all yours."

I smiled warmly at him. Ronin was a great friend. "Well, for starters. I need to find out if Myrtle had any enemies. I have to find out who did this to her. It's the only way to clear my name."

Ronin clenched his jaw. "I know. And we will. I promise."

"How?" I said exasperated as I laughed bitterly. "No one will talk to me. They want to *kill* me, Ronin. They're all very protective of

Myrtle, and I get it. I would be too if someone killed one of my friends. But I didn't do this."

"I know you didn't. Especially not while wearing that dress."

"It was messy. Personal. The murderer knew her. I'm sure of it." I cast my gaze around the crowds, looking at individual faces and wondering if they were the ones who'd done it.

The clanking of hooves sounded somewhere near.

I stared out at the crowd, sweeping my gaze slowly around in the direction of the sound and flinched, biting my tongue.

That same goat poked its head out from behind a tall half-breed who looked like his ancestors could have been a tree at some point. The goat stared at me with those big, horizontally slit eyes, stretching its neck in the hopes that I would notice it. Nope, I was not making eye contact.

I turned back around. "Looks like this was a giant waste of time. No one wants to talk to me. If only I knew how to get someone to talk."

"Torture?" Ronin perked up. "You do realize I have some pretty compelling vampire mojo. No one can resist… *The Ronin*."

I laughed, thinking of all of those women who jumped into bed with him. "I'm sure you do. But a lot of them are witches who I'm pretty sure can repel your vampire compelling charms." What I needed were the dirty secrets Myrtle was hiding that had gotten her killed.

The hairs on my neck rose as I felt eyes on me. I swept my gaze over to the gazebo. Marcus stood next to it, speaking to a tall man with a hat. Though he was talking to the man, his eyes were focused on me.

An idea formulated in my head, wickedly evil, and all kinds of bad. I was practically beaming.

I pulled my eyes away and turned my back to Marcus so he couldn't read my lips. Who knew? The shifter had some serious hearing skills, so I was willing to bet he could read lips too.

"Ronin. I've got an idea on how we can get more info on Myrtle."

The half-vampire rubbed his hands together. "You've got that wicked gleam in your eye, like you're about to say something naughty... or rip off your clothes. I'm good either way."

My pulse raced at what I was about to say. "Apparently the chief keeps files on everyone. Hell, even *I* had a file. I'm willing to bet he has one on Myrtle."

Ronin stilled, the whites of his eyes showing. "Are you out of your witchin' mind? He'll never give it to you."

I couldn't help my smile. "I know that. And I wasn't planning on asking either. I'm going to sneak in and take it." Yes, I was. It was perfect. Take that, Marcus.

Ronin watched me, trying to stifle the panic I saw in his eyes. "How are you gonna do that? Marcus is always in his office. And let's not forget his secretary, Grace. She won't let you in. Not after what happened the last time."

The thought of me barging in that time with my grocery bags made me giddy inside. "He's not *always* in there."

The half-vampire made a face. "You're going to go in there when he's on the can?"

"No."

"Then how?" Worry etched Ronin's brow. "How do you know that for sure? Can you foretell where he's going to be at any time? Marvelous Tess?"

"Because, vampire," I answered, my excitement growing at this new plan of mine. "I *know* where he's going to be tonight."

Ronin's eyebrows rose, and a smile curved his lips. "You going on a date with him? You naughty witch?"

"No, you idiot," I teased, smiling despite myself and hating how that idea made butterflies flutter around my insides. "At midnight tonight, the chief will be patrolling the festival. Which means…"

"The office will be empty," answered Ronin.

I nodded. "Exactly. Because he'll be at the festival." This was going to work. I was going to get my hands on Myrtle's file and it gave me a burst of hope.

"And here I thought you were just another pretty face," laughed the vampire. "You are a naughty little witch, Tessa Davenport. Marcus has no idea what he's getting himself into."

I ignored that last part and stared at one of the few people in this town who believed in my innocence. "You with me?" I asked, tense, edgy, and excited all at the same time.

Ronin smiled. "Like a bad habit."

I flashed a smile. "Good. We do this tonight."

CHAPTER 10

Breaking into the town chief's office was pretty high up there on my stupidest-things-I'd-ever-done-in-my-life list.

But at least I wasn't doing it alone.

My faithful, half-vampire friend crept along the dark hallway of the HOLLOW COVE SECURITY AGENCY with me. Though you could hear my shoes flap against the hard-tiled floors, Ronin's were nonexistent like the soft pads of a cat. Damn that vampire stealth.

"Thanks for coming with me," I whispered, truly touched that he was helping me.

"You can thank me once we're out of here with the file." Ronin's face was a little pale, but he was part vampire, so I didn't think much of it.

So far we'd been lucky. The front door wasn't locked, so no alarm to worry about. But it also meant Marcus was planning on heading back to his office sometime during the festival. We had to do this quickly. Easy peasy, right?

My pulse was fast as we headed down the dark hallway, past the front desk where Grace had given me a hard time, and toward the dimly lit main room to Marcus's office. All the main lights were off except for a few nightlights along the walls, which gave us enough light to see where we were going, at least for me. I suspected Ronin didn't need extra light to see in the dark.

I reached Marcus's office first. MARCUS DURAND with the words CHIEF OFFICER under it was stenciled on the window in black letters. I had a spell ready if the door was locked. I'd prepared it hours before and memorized it. Thanks to *The Witch's Handbook*.

I knew I was breaking all kinds of laws. Marcus would never forgive me if he caught me in here snooping around in his stuff. I wasn't thrilled with the way that made me feel, like a constant pressure on my chest. It wasn't that I felt guilty breaking in. It was that I actually cared about Marcus's impression of me. But he wasn't leaving me many choices. As far as I was concerned, this was payback for bringing me in for questioning.

With my heart hammering against my ribcage, I reached out and turned the doorknob. It opened easily.

"Here we go." I swung the door open and moved inside.

Marcus's office looked exactly like I remembered it, except now everything was in shadow. A single desk, stacked with papers next to a laptop, sat in front of the only window in the place. To the right of the door was a wall lined with filing cabinets. Rows of bookcases occupied the wall next to the desk.

"Where do you want to check first, boss?" Ronin moved in next to me.

My eyes moved to the filing cabinets. "There. He must have a hard copy of Myrtle's file."

The two of us rushed over. I pulled out my phone and switched on the flashlight. Holding it with my left hand, I yanked open a cabinet drawer and started flipping through the files with my right hand. "These are sorted alphabetically," I said, my fingers on the name of the file that read Alan Hicks. "Look under M for Myrtle and I'll look for L for LaVine." I kept thumbing through files as Ronin yanked open another drawer.

I rolled out another drawer with the surnames starting with L. "There's nothing here," I said, after a moment, disappointment loud in my voice. "You?"

Ronin pushed back the drawer. "Nothing."

Frowning, I looked back at the desk, seeing the cluster of papers. "Maybe on his desk."

Moving quickly, I reached the desk and shined my phone's flashlight over it. I grabbed the first pile of paper and started flipping through it. Ronin did the same but without the flashlight.

"These are just bills," I said as I checked the last page of my stack of papers with the name CENTRAL HOLLOW COVE POWER written on the top.

"This isn't." Ronin handed me a file. "This is *your* file, Tess."

"What?" I snatched it up and stared at the copy of my driver's license on the first page. "I've always hated that picture. I look drunk." The file was thick and held together by clips.

This was the file Marcus didn't want me to see. So, for obvious reasons, I flipped it open.

It's a weird feeling going through your own file, actually *having* a file and seeing it displayed before you in pieces of paper and photocopies.

"What does it say?" Ronin cocked his head.

I looked up at him. "Just basic stuff. Where I've lived. My past employment—oh, my god. He even has a copy of my bank statements." Great. Now he knew the enormous debt I had.

"Huh? It says White witch next to my name here on the half-breed class ID. But it's crossed out with a pen and someone scribbled *Dark* above it."

Ronin snorted. "Marcus thinks you're a Dark witch. Guess he doesn't know about the Shadow witch thing?"

"Guess not." I'd shared with Ronin what my Aunt Dolores had told me about being able to weave White and Dark magic. I was a Shadow witch according to her. I could still conjure up Dark magic, like summoning and controlling demons, though I was still more inclined toward White magic—magic of the elements and even ley lines.

I resisted the urge to grab a pen and cross out Dark to put Shadow witch instead. Bet Marcus wouldn't like that. If I did that, he'd know someone was in here, and who else would write in my file than little me? He'd know it was me.

I kept reading down the file. The blood left my face as I spotted something else that caused me to shiver despite the heat. "Uh... there's something else here," I said, my voice sounding faint in my ears.

"What?" Ronin leaned closer until I could smell his musky aftershave.

I lifted the file and pointed with my finger. "My father's name's been crossed out... and there's a question mark next to it. What the hell? This has to be a mistake." I wasn't sure if those last words were spoken aloud or if I'd said them in my head.

A dull ache formed in the pit of my stomach as I stared at the question mark. I rubbed my eyes. It was still there. It was obvious what it meant, and a nauseating mix of dread twisted my gut.

No. It couldn't be true. It just couldn't. My mother would never cheat on my father... would she?

Ronin grabbed the file from me and brought it closer to his face. "It doesn't mean anything," he said, giving me the file back with a frown on his face. "This is just what Marcus thinks. This is *his* file on you. It doesn't mean what you think it does."

"But what if it does?" My heart raced and I felt a panic attack on its way, which would be totally inappropriate when one is trying to steal a file from the chief. I needed to be calm, collected, and focused, but I was none of those things.

I was freaking out.

The half-vampire put a gentle hand on my shoulder. "Tess. Don't do this to yourself. It's not worth it. It doesn't mean anything."

"It's not like I can help it. This isn't your file. It's mine."

Ronin let out a breath. "Well, you can freak out later. Right now, we still need to find what we came here for. And we've already wasted too much time."

He was right, of course. I couldn't let my emotions get in the way of this case—which was to clear my name. If I was found guilty of this crime, it wouldn't matter who my real father was. I'd be locked up in some paranormal prison to live out the rest of my life. I'd worry about the question mark later.

"Okay. Okay. You're right." I dropped my file on the desk, trying to calm my beating heart but failing miserably. The damn thing wouldn't stop.

Focus, Tessa.

I cast my gaze around the room. If Marcus had a file on me, he had one on Myrtle. I just had to find it.

My eyes landed on his laptop computer. "Let's check his laptop." I moved over and sat in the chief's chair, stifling the urge to moan at how comfortable the leather was around my butt. My trembling fingers hovered above the laptop, and I had a brief moment of guilt. Then I lifted the laptop's display screen. The screen flashed, revealing a few icons and apps over a landscape image of a lake surrounded by trees.

I took a steadying breath. "Lucky for us he didn't shut down his computer." Otherwise, we would've had to hack his password, which I doubt we could have done.

At first glance, his operating system was Windows—my loyal friend over the years. This would be a breeze.

I interlaced my fingers and cracked them. Because, why the hell not. Using my index finger, I moved it around the touchpad and then double-clicked on a file explorer icon. A window popped up with multiple files. "Here we go," I said as I double-clicked on the folder icon.

Ronin leaned forward, his breath on my cheek as he asked, "How do you know?"

"Cause it says Myrtle LaVine on it."

The vampire grinned. "You clever witch."

The file opened revealing one Word document, a PDF file, and another file containing pictures. I went through the pictures first. Seeing Myrtle's murder on digital images was just as upsetting as when I'd seen it in person. Okay, worse now that I saw a closeup on her neck and then what was left of her eyes once the glass had been removed. Yikes. I'll do you all a favor and skip the description.

"I think that's the autopsy report," informed Ronin, pointing at the PDF file named Autopsy-ML-HC-10009.

"Just says that she died from extreme loss of blood due to the slash across her neck," I said after reading the pathologist's report. "Says that she was alive when they gouged out her eyes and slit her throat. Probably so she couldn't call out." Myrtle must have been in excruciating pain. And no one heard her cries or her struggles. I felt a bitter, metallic taste in my mouth. We were dealing with a true monster.

Ronin whistled. "Well, we can establish that we're looking for some seriously demented wackjobs," he said, echoing my thoughts exactly.

I clicked on the last file. "This is from Marcus's office," I said as I read the letterhead HOLLOW COVE SECURITY AGENCY. Pricks of excitement shot through me. If we were going to find anything important, it would be here.

Ronin leaned forward until his chin was practically resting on my shoulder, and we both began to read.

"No fingerprints were found," expressed the vampire. "Means they used gloves."

"Or they used magic," I said. "I didn't feel any residual magic at the scene and neither did my aunts. But it doesn't mean it wasn't used. Maybe they're just really good at covering their tracks. Magical and non-magical."

My gaze moved down to the area called "List of Suspects." I blinked at the name I saw there. My own. "Mother f—"

"He probably had to write that," laughed Ronin, sending my anger to another level.

"Given the situation he was in. Hey? Don't look at me with those big judgy eyes. I didn't write it."

"I'll give him a situation." I glowered, imagining strangling the chief. I let out a sigh. "What does it matter anyway? The whole town thinks I did it." My gaze flicked to the witnesses section. Two names were written—mine and someone called, Winnie Wilde. Bet that was the suit-lady Seer witch.

"He has 'inconclusive' written in the motive section," informed Ronin with a snort. "Means the dude has no idea."

My pulse jerked as my eyes moved to the large paragraph under the "additional comments" section. "Look here," I said as I began reading. "Myrtle's from a long line of Seers. She was tested in 1985 by the Board of Magical Seers and Oracles. Wow. She scored 99 out of 100 in accuracy." I looked at Ronin. "Holy shit. She was for real."

It meant whatever she'd seen when she'd looked into my future that made her scream in utter terror—was very real. Fantastic.

Ronin glanced at me. "And someone went in after you and killed her. Because she saw something they didn't want her to see."

"And they killed her to keep her quiet." I leaned back. It made sense. I was right. Someone had killed Myrtle to keep her mouth shut. So who? Who would kill her like that?

Voices came from the hallway outside Marcus's office followed by the unmistakable tread of two or more people walking.

Time to go.

My breath caught. "Marcus!" I whispered, my pulse rising.

"Quick, where's your invisibility cloak!" Ronin looked behind me as though I was hiding a cloak.

"I don't have one! I'm not Harry Potter!" I hissed.

"Oh, yeah." Ronin vaulted to the doorway and then ran back. "It's Marcus and his two thugs. They're coming right this way."

Crap. We could forget about using the front door as our exit. If they found us here, it could lead to some serious damage to my already damaged reputation. So, what do you do?

You find another exit, or you make one.

"Window." I rushed over to the window, pushed the vertical blinds out of the way, and turned the lock with my thumb. I lifted the window and stood staring at the small opening. It had seemed bigger a second ago.

"Ladies first," insisted Ronin, though I had a feeling he wasn't being gallant. He wanted to see if I could actually fit through.

I didn't even look down, I just clambered over the windowsill, pulling myself out, while Ronin pushed on my butt. I landed with a thud and a grunt on my side on some soft patch of grass. Ronin landed expertly on his feet next to me without a sound.

I glowered at him. "Hate you."

With a smile, the half-vampire pulled me up, and then we were running.

We kept to the shadows. The music and the sounds of people mingling at the festival reached me, but we didn't stop. When we passed a pink Victorian house with a flashing sign that read HOT MESS WITCH, BEAUTY SALON, I remembered we'd left the window open.

Damn. Marcus would know someone had snooped around in his office. But I couldn't worry about that now. I had bigger things on my mind.

Said things were that Marvelous Myrtle had been killed because of her innate talent to read the future. Something in my future had made her scream, and let's not forget the question mark next to my father's name.

Was my father really my father? And if not, who was he?

Chapter 11

Breaking into Marcus's office hadn't been a total bust, but it didn't give me that much more to go on. The killer or killers had worn gloves as to not leave any fingerprints or had used magic to manipulate the objects used to kill her. Then they had conveniently covered their magical tracks.

But it still didn't explain *why* she was killed. The only thing we knew for sure was Marvelous Myrtle had been a true Seer.

And yet, it begged the question. If she was legit, couldn't she have predicted her own death? Couldn't she have *seen* it coming? And if so, why didn't she run?

Maybe Seers couldn't see their own futures. Maybe it was the downfall of being one.

I'd waited most of the morning to ask my aunts the burning question that had kept me awake all night. I sat, my fingers curled around my cup of coffee that had gone cold, trying to come up with the proper way of asking if my mother had cheated on my dad.

The sleeping around didn't bother me (the fact that it *didn't* bother me bothered me more than the actual act). What concerned me was not knowing if the man I'd been calling dad for the past twenty-nine years was really my daddy dearest after all.

"Out with it." Dolores dropped the newspaper she'd been reading and set her glasses down, her dark eyes pinning me from across the kitchen table.

My lips parted. "I'm sorry, what?"

"The question that's been burning a hole in your head," giggled Ruth, stirring a large stainless-steel pan on the stove. The scent of onions wafted from it. She turned to look at me, her pink apron with the words, "This witch can be bribed with chocolate," printed in big bold letters. "It's written all over your face."

"It is?" Damn these witches were perceptive.

"So?" pressed Dolores. "What's going on?" She leaned her elbows on the table and pointed a finger at me, her brows pinched. "If this has to do with Marcus putting you in that interrogation room… let me tell you… we're not finished with him. He's going to get another earful, right after I'm done with my paper."

I shook my head. "It does have something to do with Marcus, but not in the way you might think. It's about something he wrote."

"Something he wrote?" Dolores's voice had a tinge of worry to it.

"He wrote you a love letter!" Ruth clapped her hands together, sending a spoonful of yellow glob splatting on the nearest cabinet.

My face flamed. "Not even close."

"What's going on, Tessa?" pressed Dolores.

My gaze went from Ruth to Dolores. I braced myself and said, "I broke into Marcus's office last night."

Silence.

Wait for it—

"Are you out of your mind!" roared Dolores, grabbing her head like she thought her brain might explode.

Ruth, though, was staring at me with a confused expression on her face. "Was he there?"

"No, you idiot," cried Dolores. "That's what breaking in means! You do it when no one's there. That's the whole point."

"Oh." Ruth laughed. "Was it fun? I bet it was. I've always wanted to try breaking and entering." She said it like it was a new type of car one might take a ride in.

"Don't you encourage her," snapped Dolores. She turned her icy stare on me. "Why?"

I knew better than not to answer if I didn't want to end up in the basement. "I needed to find more information on Myrtle. I know. I know," I said, lifting my hand. "Not smart. But it's not like Marcus gave me a choice. He treated me like I was a suspect." I thought leaving out the part that Ronin was with me was a good idea. Besides, it had been *my* idea to begin with. He shouldn't have to be blamed if things went sour.

Dolores rubbed her eyes. "We remember."

"Well, I found his report," I went on, "his report on me. And get this—*I'm* his number one suspect." The memory of seeing my name in the file sent tiny tendrils of fury through my body.

"Can't be." Ruth let herself fall in the chair next to me, still hanging on to the wooden spoon like it was a big pencil. "He knows you can't do something like that to a person. He has to."

I shook my head. "That's just it. He doesn't really know me. Does he? I'm still practically a stranger to him."

Ruth's eyebrows joined in the middle. "But he brought you home. He had you in his arms. He put you to bed!"

"I know. I remember." Guess that hadn't meant the same to him as it did to me. Maybe I'd made it all up in my head. Wouldn't be the first time I'd been wrong about a man.

Dolores rubbed her temples. "I feel a giant migraine on its way. And we're all out of Tylenol."

I swallowed and added, "There's more."

Dolores let out a howl like she was being eaten alive by a pack of wolves.

I gripped my cup tighter. "I'm telling you because… when I was making my getaway… I forgot to close the window behind me. Anyway, I thought you should know, just in case he brings it up."

Dolores's eyes rolled over my face. "There's something else. Something that's bothering you… and don't say no. I can see it in your face. Go on. Spit it out."

I took a breath and released it. "I think I should wait for Beverly."

"I don't know when she'll be back," answered Dolores. "Probably rolling around naked in some man's bed."

"With oils and whipped cream and cherries," said Ruth, nodding her head like this had been a conversation between the sisters. I did not want to go there.

Dolores smiled to show the barest hint of teeth and leaned back in her chair. "I swear. That witch has a mattress strapped to her back."

On cue, the kitchen's back door flew open.

Beverly sauntered in, wearing a dark pair of skinny jeans, a black blouse, red ankle boots, and a man on her arm.

"Hi, girls," said Beverly as she steered the man through the breakfast area and toward the basement door.

Once again, the man on her arm had that dazed look in his eye, like he was either sleepwalking or under some mild sedation. His dark hair was peppered with grays and whites, and he wore some purple tracksuit that would have been popular in the early nineties.

"Who's this?" I asked, waiting for the narrative. I knew from experience that he was one of her victims and definitely *not* a date.

"This here is Harold," said Beverly as she reached over and pulled open the basement door. "Harold gambled away all of his wife's savings at the casino. Didn't you, Harold?"

Harold gave a slow nod. "I did." His voice was sluggish, like he was talking in his sleep.

Beverly placed both hands on her hips. "Well, you shouldn't have."

She kicked him in the ass, and Harold fell through the threshold, just as Beverly slammed the door shut behind him.

There was no surprised yelp this time, just the familiar sound of someone hitting the stairs all the way to the bottom. Next came the shaking of the kitchen, as though a small earthquake had hit us. I lifted my coffee mug off the table and waited for the tremors to stop.

With a final rumbling that erupted from the basement, the house settled.

"Well, then," said Beverly, smiling happily like she was facing a panel of judges at a beauty pageant. Her green eyes sparkled. "Girls! I've got some great news!"

"What?" drawled Dolores, an eyebrow cocked. "They have a sale on condoms this week?"

Beverly smiled and her eyes widened. "I got the part I wanted in the *Macbeth* play." She raised her chin dramatically. "Oh, girls. I'm going to be *fabulous*. I'm going to be the most gorgeous, sexiest actress the Night Festival has ever seen. Everyone is going to be there. It's tomorrow night, so be sure not to miss it."

"I have to check my schedule," said Dolores. "But I think I'm booked for a colonoscopy."

Ruth clapped her hands together. "Which part? Lady Macbeth?"

"The sexy weird sister, silly," laughed Beverly and crossed the kitchen to the half-full pot of coffee.

Ruth made a sour face. "The old witches weren't sexy. They were withered and wild. I remember reading that they had warts. And lice."

Beverly waved a hand dismissively. "Oh, that's just a rumor. Everyone knows the second witch was the sexy one."

I bit back a snort. If anyone could play a decrepit and withered old warty witch as a sexy one, that was Beverly.

"I need some coffee." She poured herself a cup. "So, what did I miss?" she asked, turning around with her back on the counter. "You all look flustered like you've been arguing."

"Tessa was about to tell us what's been bothering her all night," expressed Dolores, giving me a pinched look like I was hiding some dark secret she was about to yank out of me.

"She hardly slept," added Ruth, and I cut her a look. How the hell did she know that?

Beverly took a sip of her coffee. "Well, go on, darling. Tell us." She took the empty chair facing Dolores and sat.

I drummed my fingers around my cup.

I had been walking on eggshells around my aunts all morning, afraid to say anything lest I make things worse. I crossed my ankles under my chair. I'd thought about how to put it into words all night. I mean... how do you ask if your mother was cheating on her husband to her sisters?

You just come out and say it.

"Did my mother have an affair?"

Beverly spit out her coffee right into Dolores's face.

Ooops.

"What in the cauldron!" cried Dolores as she grabbed a paper towel from the center of the table and dabbed at her face.

"She asked if her mother had had an affair," expressed Ruth, a bewildered expression on her face like she'd never seen me before.

Dolores glowered at her sister. "I know what she said. I was referring to my sudden coffee shower."

"Sorry." Beverly wiped her mouth and set her coffee mug down. She looked at me and asked, "What makes you say that?"

Silence fell on me again, and I felt my face go hot. Not because I was embarrassed but because I feared what they might say.

I gave Beverly a recap of my break-in. "Why would he put a question mark next to my father's name? Because it's questionable." I looked at each aunt in turn. "Marcus isn't an idiot. I don't think he was made chief on the account of his good looks. If he put that there… it's because he knows something or found out something about my father." I leaned back in my chair. "So, did my mom cheat on my dad?"

"Of course not." Dolores scrunched up the coffee-stained paper towel in her hand. "That witch worships the ground he walks on. She would never. Never. I'm absolutely certain of it."

"I'm not."

We all stared at Beverly. "What?" she shrugged. "The witch wasn't a saint. We can't know for sure she didn't have a fling."

Somehow I couldn't see my mother having an affair with someone other than the man she idolized. "So, there's a possibility?"

Ruth tapped the table with her finger. "There were rumors…"

"Ruth," snapped Dolores.

I stared at Ruth. "What rumors?" She looked at Dolores as though waiting for approval. "What rumors, Ruth?" I pressed.

Beverly let out a sigh. "That she was already pregnant when she married your father."

My gaze flicked across each aunt's face. "That just means they were having sex before they got married. Last I checked, that wasn't a crime." I waited for Ruth or Beverly to elaborate but they didn't. "This isn't the nineteenth century. You don't grab the first man who gives you some attention because you got knocked up with someone else's kid."

"You know what?" Ruth reached out and covered my hand with hers. "Why not call Amelia and ask her yourself?" she said, her smile kind and warm.

I made a puff of air. "Right. Like that's a conversation I want to have with her," I said.

"Not really. I'll think I'll pass." I cringed inwardly just at the thought. Maybe Marcus wrote that because he'd heard the rumors too, and he too thought that perhaps my father wasn't my biological father?

A buzz sounded in the kitchen pulling my attention to the toaster. There was a sudden pop—and a white card the size of a cue card came flying out. In a blur, Ruth's hand moved to snatch it up. With reflexes like that, she should have been a softball player.

I perked up. I could really use a job to clear my head. I had finished all my freelance work with the last website design, so I had nothing else for another week.

Ruth's blue eyes expanded as she read the card. Her head snapped up and she looked at me.

"What?" I let go of my cup. "What's the job? Ruth?" Damn. I knew it. This was about me breaking into the chief's office. Marcus had found me out.

Dolores leaned over and grabbed the card from Ruth. Her eyes narrowed. "Well, well, well. It is a job. From Gilbert. Seems like the safe was broken into last night. All the jewelry, money, and gold are gone."

"Gold?" That was news to me. "I had no idea there was even a safe. Why is there one, exactly?"

Dolores looked up at me. "The Night Festival relies on donations. It wouldn't exist without them. The performers and special guests didn't come out of the goodness of their hearts. We have to pay them. Hosting the event is very expensive but worth it. We all give what we can afford. Some more than others."

Ruth made a pout. "Which wasn't much this year."

"So, someone robbed the safe." I leaned forward, excitement fluttering through me at the prospect of working on a new case. "You think it has something to do with Myrtle's death?"

Dolores shook her head. "I don't see how the two are connected."

I pushed my chair back and leaped to my feet. "Well, we should go check it out." I put my cup of cold coffee in the sink, and when I turned back around my aunts were avoiding my eyes.

"Okay. What's going on?"

Dolores let out a breath. "Gilbert specifically asks that you not be there."

"What? Give me that." Temper flaring, I moved to the table, grabbed the card from her hand, and read:

Notification alert.
Attention: Merlin Group. Services required.

Problem: Safe broken into. Night Festival funds were robbed. All valuables were stolen.

Location: Gilbert's Grocer & Gifts. Hollow Cove, Maine, USA.

Amendment: Requesting that murder suspect Tessa Davenport not be involved or in the vicinity.

"Murder suspect? That little bastard," I hissed. A seething anger warmed my face. "I'm going to kill that little shit."

"Language, please," scolded Dolores. But I'd won a smile from Ruth.

Beverly cocked her hip. "She's not wrong. I couldn't have put it better myself. He is a little shit."

"So, that's it then," I growled, giving the card back to Ruth before I ripped it up, pretending it was Gilbert's face. "I'm finished? I can't even work on any cases anymore?" I could feel my blood rage rise from the tip of my toes to settle around my scalp.

Dolores stood as a slow smile appeared on her face. "Of course not. Gilbert doesn't control the Merlin Group. We do. If he's requesting our help, he will get it." Her smile widened. "And that means *all* of us."

CHAPTER 12

It was half-past noon by the time we reached Gilbert's Grocer & Gifts. We'd all piled into the old Volvo station wagon because Beverly made it clear that she did not want to walk in her new ankle booties. I really didn't mind driving if it meant we got there faster. The sooner we arrived, the sooner I could see Gilbert's frustrated face at the sight of me, and the sooner I could strangle the little shifter.

It made me all warm and fuzzy inside.

I was feeling slightly better at the prospect of Gilbert's angry face when Dolores pulled up on the curb of Shifter Lane and cut the engine. We all clambered out.

When something went amiss in Hollow Cove, naturally, the entire town knew about it. And naturally, they all wanted to take a peek.

And that's exactly what it looked like.

A crowd of over a hundred paranormals, residents, and Night Festival participants all clustered around Gilbert's store, their voices high in excitement. Jeff and Cameron stood by the front door with their large arms crossed over their wide chests. Their domineering postures made them look like beefy bouncers at some night club. If they were here, it meant Marcus was here too.

"Let's go, girls." Dolores shut her car door with her hip and headed for the front door, pushing onlookers out of her way with a quick shove of her arms. Beverly was right behind her followed by Ruth, who waved at a couple of people. I brought up the rear.

"…look… that's her! It's her!" I heard a woman say, making me cringe. I put my head down and kept walking.

"…the one who killed the Seer," came another voice, a man this time.

"…why did they let her go free?" asked the same woman.

"… she shouldn't be here. She should be locked up," came another voice.

My skin tingled with magic, feeding off my fury and coiling around my fingers before I could control it. I was going to hurt somebody.

But then Ruth turned around and gave me one of her smiles, one of the infectious ones that said, "Everything will be okay."

I felt some anger diminish, and with that, so did the pent-up magic. I had to learn to control my temper. Either that or live with the consequences of hurting a few ignorant people. Yes, they were ignorant *and* stupid. Besides, I was already labeled as a murder suspect. I didn't need to add a *real* murder to the list.

Gritting my teeth, I kept my head down and followed my aunts through the glass door into the store.

The small grocery store was empty of customers. On a normal afternoon, especially on a bright sunny day like this, it should be packed. Voices trailed from the back. I looked past the aisles to where a door stood open at the back of the store. Apparently, Dolores was leading us there.

When we reached the door, we stepped into a small office-like room that looked like it acted as both an office and storage. It housed a desk littered with papers squeezed in between boxes that were piled to the ceiling.

My eyes found Marcus first. His stupidly handsome face always seemed to get in the way of the others—no idea why. When his eyes found mine, his brows inched up knowingly, and a sharp understanding laced his gaze. Either he was expecting me to show up or he knew I'd broken into his office last night.

I couldn't care less what he thought of me at the moment. I was a professional. I was a Merlin, and I had a job to do.

And yet that question mark next to my father's name sent sparks of my anger anew. The thought that Marcus knew something about me that I didn't really annoyed me.

Next to him stood Adan, and he turned around at the sound of our approach. The frown on his face vanished at the sight of me, pulling his features in a spectacular smile.

Oh. My. Goodness.

I gave him a tight smile back before looking away, my face flaming.

Control yourself. You are a professional.

With his hands on his hips, wearing a pair of khaki pants, a polo shirt, and the scowl of the century, the other occupant needed no introduction.

"What is *she* doing here?" growled Gilbert, spit flying out of his mouth and his face deepening in color along with his wrinkles.

I glanced at the clock on my phone. "A whole five seconds before your freak-out. Must be a new record," I said and dropped my phone in my bag.

Adan laughed. The sound was deep and genuine, and it eased my anger. I liked him immediately. It didn't hurt that he was easy on the eyes, too. More like eye-filling-candy-hotness.

Dolores turned and gave me a pointed look, and I shrugged. Yeah, I know, that was a bit much, but the little shifter rubbed me the wrong way. I couldn't help myself. It was like asking the cat not to play with the mouse. Not going to happen.

Gilbert and the others were all gathered around something, so I stepped to the side to get a clear view. A large metal safe the size of a dishwasher sat in the only corner of the space that wasn't littered with boxes. The door to the safe lay open. From what I could see, only a folder and some papers sat inside. There was no sign of the gold, no glittering jewels, no stacks of Benjamins. The safe was empty.

With his face in a sour expression, Gilbert pointed a short, grubby finger at my aunts. "I asked that *she* specifically *not* be involved. Have you all gone illiterate since this morning?"

Dolores towered over the small shifter. "You asked for the Merlin Group. We four are Merlins. Here we are." She lifted her arms and gestured to the four of us. "We are the Merlin Group—not singular Merlins. We come together..."

"Or not at all," finished Ruth, giving Gilbert her best stink eye. Loved her.

"Marcus!" Gilbert whirled around and faced him. "Do something. You have authority over them as chief and councilman. Tell her to leave."

My heart pounded in my throat while I waited for the chief to answer. I had no idea what he'd say. Did Marcus have authority over the Merlin Group? The truth was, I wasn't entirely sure how the laws operated here in Hollow Cove. And yet, in his report, Marcus had named me as their number one suspect, but he hadn't arrested me. Which meant he had nothing on me.

A muscle twitched along Marcus's jaw. His eyes met mine and he said, "Tessa is free to go anywhere she wants. She's not a prisoner, and she's not under arrest."

Huh? That was unexpected. "There," I told Gilbert. "Can you shut your beak now so we can get on with our work?" You miserable little chicken.

"But you arrested her!" wailed Gilbert, outraged. "We all saw it."

"She was brought in for questioning. She was... one of the last people to see Myrtle alive, so she had important information." Marcus was still watching me. A faint smile quirked the corner of his lips, which I wasn't sure was for me or Gilbert. "She was never charged."

"I was never charged," I repeated like an idiot. Marcus, though, was still watching me with an intensity that made me uncomfortable. I didn't know what he was playing at, but if he thought defending me in front of Gilbert would somehow smooth out his taking me in for questioning... Well, it didn't.

"So what is she then?" argued Gilbert, clearly not able to let this go.

"She's under... revision," said Marcus.

"Under revision?" snapped Gilbert, shifting uneasily with his hands clenching at his sides. "You just made that up. You can't make up rules whenever you want. Who do you think you are? The king of Hollow Cove?"

Marcus's eyes narrowed. "Don't tell me how to do my job, Gilbert. I'm the chief. I can do whatever I want."

I snorted, wishing Ronin were here. He would have loved this exchange.

Gilbert's eyes were round, looking like they might pop out of their sockets at any moment. "I will not have it. For all we know—" he pointed at me, and I hated how he continued to discuss me as though I wasn't standing in the same room, "—she killed Myrtle and stole all the contents in the safe for an easy getaway."

Oh hell no. "Shut your beak before I roast you in my cauldron, owl," I shot at him, taking a few steps forward. "You are *not* going to blame me for this too. I had nothing to do with this, and you know it." Energy spindled in my head and around me as another influx of magic soared. I exhaled, forcing it down.

I was going to barbecue this bird. *I know it. You know it. We all know it.*

Gilbert made a face. "Fine. We can clear this up right now."

"Good." I rolled my shoulders, letting go of some of the tension. He wanted to fight? Fine, I was going to kick him in the throat.

The small shifter gave me a knowing look, the kind that said he had some information on me that I would rather not have revealed. He straightened and said, "Where were you last night from midnight to two a.m.?"

Oh. Shit. "Why?" I kept my face blank, not liking where this conversation was headed. The fact that everyone's attention all snapped to me didn't help either.

Gilbert smiled at something he saw on my face. "I don't remember seeing you at the Night Festival. Care to elaborate on your whereabouts?"

Like I said. I was going to deep-fry this bird. But I too could play this game.

I pulled my face into a Colgate smile. "I thought I'd stay home, seeing as the Festival's brought me only misery."

"Ha!" shrieked the little man, shooting his hand in the air like he'd caught me in a lie, which he did. "Well, I have it under good authority, that you and that miserable Ronin were seen running away on Shifter Lane."

My pulse hammered, and I strained to keep my guilt from showing. "Is running a crime now?" Damn. This was not happening. "Why am I always the one blamed for everything? Blame the new girl in town, is that how it is here? I'm sorry someone broke into your safe. But I had nothing to do with it."

Marcus still watched me with a serious intensity, like he was trying to read my mind or detect a slip of composure that would show my guilt.

Yes, I was guilty of stealing information but not stealing from a safe.

Gilbert made a rude noise. "Tell him that." The shifter hooked a thumb at Adan. "His family donated thousands of dollars to the Night Festival, and now it's all gone. How are we going to pay for everything? The town doesn't have the money."

"The town has emergency reserves, Gilbert," shot Dolores, her eyes hard. "You know that."

Gilbert grumbled something in response, but I couldn't quite catch it.

My eyes found Adan, but he was looking down at the safe. "I'm sorry about your money," I said, just as Adan moved his gaze to me, "but please know I didn't take it."

"Hello, Adan." Beverly put herself next to the tall, handsome witch. "My, my. It seems every time I see you, you get even more handsome over the years." She laughed. "Makes me wish I was… five years younger." Dolores cleared her throat in warning. Beverly giggled and said, "Have you met my niece?"

That's my aunt. Always working the room.

Adan's soft hazel eyes rolled over my face. "I haven't had the pleasure." His voice was deep, meticulously educated, and beautiful. Damn. I was a sucker for beautiful voices.

Adan moved to shake my hand, but Gilbert stepped in the way.

"This is all very polite," he mocked, and I dropped my hand. "But it doesn't solve anything." He glared at my aunts. "You're supposed to be working the scene. Trying to solve this crime, not match-making."

Heat flared to my face. That's it. Before the day was over, I was going to roast this little owl.

"Then get out of our way," ordered Dolores and pushed the smaller shifter none too gently with a swipe of her long arm. Gilbert muttered a few angry curses, but he gave the sisters room to work.

Together, the three aunts stood before the safe. I stepped in beside Dolores, not wanting to be left out, but I was really curious about what magic they were going to use. Even though I had my Merlin card, there was still so much I needed to learn.

"Ruth," said Dolores.

From her large tote bag, Ruth pulled out a small container the size of a jar of jam, twisted the top, and sprinkled some pink-colored powder over the safe. The powder fell like pixie dust, glimmering as it settled around the safe and covered the floor like pink, shimmering snow. It was quite beautiful.

"Show me the path I cannot find," chanted Ruth, her voice clear and melodic. "Let magic reveal what can't be seen and restore what was left behind."

Power surged all around and through me, and I held my breath as I felt my aunts tap into their wills. The outpouring of energy from their auras united, chiming and resonating.

It was fantastic.

With a sudden burst of energy, two things happened. First, a blast of blinding light flashed before our eyes as energy rushed through the room. Second, Ruth's pink dusk burned a dark blood red.

"And?" Gilbert slipped in between the aunts. "It changed color. What does all this mean? Does it say who broke into the safe?"

Good question. I wanted to know too. So did Adan, if I read the tension all over his wide shoulders. It was nearly palpable. Poor guy. I felt sorry for him.

Marcus, though, snapped a few pictures with his smartphone. His expression remained unreadable.

Dolores's face was a dark cast. "It means whoever broke into the safe left a concealing spell that countered Ruth's revealing spell. Unfortunately, we can't tell who did it. Unless—which would really surprise me, considering the amount of effort that was put into this spell—Marcus lifted some fingerprints?"

The chief shook his head. "No fingerprints. Nothing."

"It's why I requested the help of the Merlin Group," growled Gilbert. "You're supposed to *see* and *feel* things beyond mundane fingerprints."

Crap. "So, we're looking for a witch," I blurted, ignoring Gilbert's glare that I dared to speak.

"Yes." Dolores took another look at the safe. "Someone with enough skill to pull off a complex spell like this one. Definitely someone who knows their way around magic."

Adan crossed his arms over his chest. The frown on his face said it all. He was pissed, pissed that his family's money had been lost and pissed we couldn't figure out who'd done it.

"Tessa?" Ruth dipped her head. "You look like you want to say something."

I shook my head, feeling Marcus's eyes on me. "No. Just thinking." I don't know why, call it my witch's intuition, but I had the feeling this break-in and Myrtle's death were connected. But with the way both Gilbert and Marcus were watching me, I was not going to share any of that now.

Beverly let out a breath. "A lot of out-of-town witches are milling about with the Night Festival going on. Do we have a list of all the witches? Maybe we can start there. See who's new and who we don't know."

My gaze flicked to Marcus. I was pretty sure he had some sort of list. The guy had said he'd checked out everyone at this year's festival.

Gilbert stuck out his chest proudly. "As a matter of fact, I do. I have a list of all those attending. Everyone was requested to register online on the town's website. And I have a guest book that everyone participating in the festival must sign." Well, that solved the mystery of where Marcus got his list.

"Good. We're going to need that list," demanded Dolores. She stuck out her hand, like she was expecting Gilbert to have it on him. Maybe he did.

A tiny thrill of excitement washed through me. Good. Something I could do. "If we split the list between the four of us, it'll go faster."

Marcus cleared his throat. "I think you should sit this one out, Tessa."

Oh. No. He. Didn't. "What did you say?" With my hands on my hips, I stepped in closer. "I thought you said I wasn't under arrest. That I was free to go wherever I pleased?"

The chief sighed, his entire body moving as he exhaled. "I said you were under revision."

Sparks flew—real sparks from my fingertips—but I had enough control to keep my magic as just sparks. I bit my tongue before the unholy curses flew out of my mouth.

"I can't believe you'd do this. After everything..." I left it out in the open like that. I was pissed. He narrowed his eyes, the anger showing on his face, but my anger won.

"Marcus is right." Dolores looked at me, and a sad expression crossed her face. "Some of the witches might feel a little... *uncomfortable* around you. They might not want to talk to us with you there."

I lifted my arms. "Great. That's just great. Fine. I'll do my own investigation." Marcus didn't say that I couldn't, and it's not like I needed his permission.

Dolores gave me her infamous raised brow look. "There's no need for dramatics. That's Beverly's job."

"Hey," said Beverly, though she didn't look upset but rather like her sister had complimented her.

"I need some air." I spun around and headed out, back through the rows of aisles, straining from the urge to knock a few items off the shelves. That would have made me feel much better.

I wasn't mad at my aunts. Hell. They were right. The witches on that list would probably bolt the other way if they saw me coming. My aunts would get better results without me.

Plus, I didn't mind going about this on my own. I liked working alone. All my creative work was done with just me and my laptop. It got my introvert juices flowing.

Big questions needed answers. If I was right about the two crimes being connected, I was going to need the proof to back me up.

I crossed the store to the front glass windows. The crowd of onlookers was still outside Gilbert's store, some with their gazes glued to the glass, trying to catch a glimpse of what was happening inside.

I braced myself for the insults as I reached out and grabbed the metal door handle.

"Tessa!" called a male voice behind me that wasn't Marcus's.

I stopped, only because it wasn't Marcus. Dropping my hand, I turned to find Adan coming my way.

"I know this must sound crazy and forward," said the handsome witch. He laughed, scratching the back of his neck. "Maybe even totally inappropriate… but… would you have dinner with me tonight?"

My lips parted and I hoped I didn't look too shocked. "You want to have dinner? With me?" Yes, I know how that sounded, but I had to make sure he knew what he was asking. He did just lose lots of his family's money, and that could mess with someone's head a bit. Or maybe he was just looking for a distraction. It didn't bother me. A distraction might be just what I needed.

Adan grinned, his perfect white teeth showing around his full lips. "Yes. I do."

"Okay," I answered, surprising myself. Too late to take it back. Besides, this could be really good for me. To get out and have a bit of fun with this sexy witch.

"I'll pick you up at seven." Adan gave me another one of those brilliant smiles before turning back and heading toward the others.

Movement caught my eye and I looked past Adan in time to see Marcus walking away from one of the aisles and disappearing into the back of the store.

He'd been standing there the whole time.

Chapter 13

"I can't believe I'm going out on a date," I told my reflection. "I haven't been on a date in what? Five years? More?"

I rubbed my sweaty hands on my jeans again, for the fourth time in less than twenty minutes. My body twitched with nerves and uncertainty. I started to second-guess myself, more like I'd started to second-guess myself the moment I'd said yes to a dinner date with Adan.

A part of me didn't want to go. I didn't even know the guy. What if he was a real bore and talked only about sports and cars? I'd kill myself if he started to talk about golf. No, I'd excuse myself and escape through the bathroom window. Yeah, that's what I'd do.

Of course, I was acting like a sixteen-year-old and not a soon-to-be thirty-year-old woman. What the hell was wrong with me? It was just a date. It's not like I was going to jump into bed with him later. Casual sex wasn't my style. But I'd been lonely for a long time, so best keep the wine away from me. Just in case.

I matched my dark jeans with a light burgundy top and finished the look with my black flats. No way was I wearing heels. If I wanted to ridicule myself, I would wear heels. Plus, if I needed a quick getaway, flats were a must. Or I could just go barefoot, but I doubted my aunts would approve. My long, skinny toes would have Adan running in the opposite direction.

The moment my aunts had arrived back at Davenport House, I'd told them about my date with Adan. The three of them burst into a brood of excited hens.

"Don't forget to wear clean underwear," Ruth had so amicably pointed out.

"And don't prattle on about *Star Trek* and *The X-Files*," Dolores had added, a hand on her hip while she directed me with her other hand. "You'll sound too nerdy. You don't want to scare him off. Men want to believe they're smarter than you. But most have their brains in their pants, and they sit on them all day—so there you go."

"Don't put on anything that screams desperate either," Beverly had told me. "You don't want to show too much cleavage. Not that you have much to show. Still, men need a challenge. If it's too easy, they'll look the other way."

"If that's true, then how do you get dates?" Dolores had replied, making Ruth laugh.

I was glad they were having such a good time. You'd think they were going on the date with Adan and not me. I didn't understand what the fuss was about. It was just a date. I guess being from a prominent witch family meant a lot to my aunts. To me, that meant just as much as a rock.

After pulling my long brown hair back into a low, messy bun, I applied some eyeshadow, liner, mascara, and some lip balm. I stood back and inspected myself.

"So, how do I look, House?" I asked the mirror. And then I quickly added, "Magic Mirror, on the wall, who now is the fairest one of all?" I laughed.

The mirror on the dresser wavered, removing my reflection and replaced it with the image of a potato.

I made a face. "Nice. Thanks a lot." It seemed House had a sense of humor.

I sighed and rubbed at the space between my eyebrows. My headache was back. Not only was it back, but the pain was getting worse. Not taking any chances, I downed a couple more Tylenol.

Resolute, I headed downstairs, trying to convince myself this was a good idea, but the twisting in my gut said otherwise. I hit the last step just as the front doorbell rang.

"He's on time." True to his word, Adan showed up at exactly seven p.m. The witch was punctual. I had to give him that. And sexy as hell. This could mean trouble.

"See you witches later," I howled toward the kitchen where I heard my aunts congregating.

"We won't wait up," came Dolores's shout, followed by a series of giggles from the other two. There was a sudden hush of conversation followed by the distinctive clink of glasses hitting together. Were they toasting something?

I shook my head. You'd think they were sixteen-year-olds.

I pulled open the front door. Adan stood on the front porch, his smile bright and illuminating though the light was getting dim with the setting sun. He wore a black shirt with a pair of designer jeans if I were to guess. I'd have to sell ten book covers to afford a pair like that. Lucky for me, I wasn't a label whore like my ex. I stuck to the classics, which were mainly anything in black, and hoped I didn't need another wardrobe for at least ten years.

His blond hair was damp, and the pleasant scent of soap and aftershave drifted from him.

Cauldron help me, but he looked great. He looked like a cover model for *GQ*. He had every quality a woman could ever want: handsome, powerful, confident.

And yet, I was glad he wasn't dressed too formally. I had no idea where we were going. Wearing a dress had never entered my mind. Jeans were my go-to comfort clothes.

Adan's lips twitched. He knew I liked what I saw. I'd have to be blind to not appreciate beauty when it was smack in front of me. Plus, I was single, which meant I was allowed to look. *Yay me.*

The sound of a car door slamming pulled my attention behind Adan.

Marcus was walking up the stone path toward the porch, his gray eyes hard and icy as he glanced between me and Adan. He looked... he looked *angry*.

He wasn't wearing his signature leather jacket. Only a gray T-shirt—a *tiny* gray T-shirt, stretched tightly over the hard cords of muscle. My thoughts went to that hard, golden chest I'd felt once. How safe and comfortable and natural it had felt. Damn.

My heart did a little backflip, and I hated it.

The chief looked me over slowly, judging me, and taking measure of my clothes. His brows moved up as if in approval that I hadn't gone too sexy, like something Beverly would have done. I pushed away the blush that threatened to paint my cheeks and chose to glare at him instead.

"What are you doing here?" I asked, my voice level. "Come to arrest me? Are you going to tell me I can't go on dates, now? Is that it?"

The chief's expression smoothed into a casual one. "I'm here to see Ruth." He reached the first porch step, his eyes on the male witch. He gave a nod of his head. "Adan."

"Chief," said Adan, a strange smile on his clean-shaven face, and I swear I saw him puff out his chest.

I rolled my eyes. Men.

My stupid heart was still pounding even harder as Marcus stepped up and reached the landing. His broad back, corded with muscle, showed the power and strength of a man you didn't want to mess with. I knew then he'd left his jacket on purpose. He was showing off his strength to Adan. I didn't doubt in a physical fight, Marcus would beat the witch to a pulp. But Adan was a witch, from a long line of powerful witches, which meant he could hurt the chief with a single spell. Though Marcus was somewhat resistant to some magic, he couldn't repel everything.

"Ah, yes," I said, trying to keep my pulse under control. "That blue stuff she's been preparing for you." I still had no idea what the blue substance was that Ruth prepared for him, on what looked like a regular basis. Seeing him like this now, all territorial and posturing (because that was the only way you could describe it), I was even more confused than ever about how I felt...

Marcus watched me a beat too long. "Where are you going?" Again, with the casual voice, but the hardness in his eyes betrayed him.

I huffed at him. Like that was any of his business. "I'm not one of your deputies. I don't report to you—"

"Fabio's in Elizabeth Town," said Adan, that same smile on his face, puzzling over the chief as though he were an odd-looking insect.

The chief pursed his lips. "Hmmm. So you're taking her *out* of Hollow Cove."

What the hell was his problem? Elizabeth Town was the neighboring town just after Hollow Cove bridge. You could walk to it. "Sounds great. I'm starving. Let's go." Why was he doing this?

Marcus frowned, his attention going from an unapologetic Adan to me. "I told you that you couldn't leave town. Not when you're implicated in an ongoing murder investigation."

Now it was my turn to frown. "Are you freaking kidding me? You're going to stop me from going to dinner?" Was it me, or did he seem happy to do this?

"Don't worry. I'll drive her back," laughed Adan with the smug glee of a kid tattle-telling on his older sibling. "But your restaurants are more like diners, and I wanted to treat Tessa to a special evening with great food and ambiance."

Question high in his expression, Marcus shook his shoulders and stepped in beside me. I couldn't help but notice how close his chest was to me. "We've got loads of ambiance and great food in Hollow Cove," said the chief, a vein throbbing on his forehead as his jaw clenched. "You've just got to know where to look."

Adan shrugged. "I looked. Nothing nearly good enough. Small town. Small expectations."

Whoops. That was the wrong thing to say to the chief, who grew up here, but he was asking for it.

"Small expectations," repeated Marcus slowly, but I had the distinct feeling he wasn't referring to the town.

Adan's smile was slow and lazy. "Have you found out any leads about my family's fortune?"

Marcus gave him a cryptic smile. "I'm not at liberty to say." Oh boy, did he enjoy saying that. I could picture him doing cartwheels.

If I didn't know any better, I'd say Marcus was acting territorial like a jealous boyfriend, and I wondered if the beast in him was acting out. But why would he do this? There was nothing between us. He'd made that very clear—to me and the entire town when he'd brought me in for questioning. Why the hell should he care who I dated? Was it because Adan wasn't from here?

The two men stood glaring at each other, like two alpha males waiting for one to submit. I wasn't sure if I should be furious or flattered. I chose neither.

Finally, after the macho staredown, Adan stepped in beside me and gave me his arm. "We should go. We don't want to be late for our reservations."

I stood still for a second, contemplating if I should take his arm. I decided I would and slipped my arm in the crook of his. Why the hell not, right? We *were* on a date.

The moment I took his arm, I felt the pulse of magic along with the mixed smells of pine needles, wet earth, leaves, and wildflowers—the scent of White witches—wafting toward me.

I didn't know why but at that instant, I glanced at the chief. A small muscle twitched on his cheek, as if his face wanted to twist into a feral snarl. It looked as though he was struggling to keep his beast from coming out.

Okay. I was getting some seriously mixed signals right now. I did not understand him. I needed to get away and clear my head.

With my arm wrapped around Adan's, he pulled me with him, and we stepped off the porch to the flagstone path. He led me to a gray Mercedes Benz sports sedan, a model I'd never seen before. The witch opened the front passenger door for me and I slipped inside, part of me wondering if this was just a show for Marcus's sake.

As soon as Adan shut the door, I immediately felt claustrophobic, which was not a good sign as having just officially started the date. Telling myself this was just nerves, I let out a sigh through my nose, letting go of some of the knots of tension in my gut as Adan pulled open his door.

The tall witch slipped in behind the wheel, started the ignition with a push of a button, and pulled the car from the curb.

I should have been excited about the date, but I couldn't stop thinking about Marcus. What the hell was that about?

And when I turned in my seat to grab my seatbelt, I looked out the window.

Marcus stood on the landing of the porch, watching us, his face a mask of stone.

Chapter 14

It turned out, Fabio's was a very nice Italian restaurant with a modern interior of gray and orange seats and tables in an open-concept style room with fourteen-foot ceilings and exposed pipes. The tall windows at the front let in the last of the evening light. It was a comfortable place, and as soon as my butt hit the soft, gray leather of the booth next to the window, I felt myself relax. But I'd also chugged my freshly poured glass of red wine in two giant gulps.

"That good, huh?" Laughed Adan, sitting across from me in the booth. He picked up the bottle of 2016 Mazzei Concerto di Fonterutoli and filled my glass halfway. Never heard of the wine, probably because I couldn't afford it and it didn't come in a box.

Gulping down my wine wasn't going to win me any points in the first impression category, but knowing I'd feel the effects of the lovely wine in less than a minute, I didn't care.

I grabbed my menu and started to go over the list of appetizers and main courses. My eyes blurred for a second and I blinked until my vision was clear. My head had started to pound again, only much worse. I needed something stronger than Tylenol. It could also be my body's way of telling me it was running on empty. I needed to fuel it back up with some lovely carbs. And, oh boy, this menu was all about carbs. It was carb central. And I loved it. Carbs. Carbs. Carbs.

Having made my decision, I folded my menu, grabbed a slice of warm, homemade bread, piled on the butter like it was cream cheese, and took a bite.

I moaned. "Wow," I said, chewing and letting the salted butter explode over my taste buds. "Good bread. Really good bread."

Adan laughed again. He was easy to please. I liked a man who thought I was funny. Maybe this wasn't such a bad idea after all.

As I buttered another slice of bread, a pretty woman about my age dressed in a black shirt and matching black pants stood at the edge of our table. A pad of paper and pen were clutched in her red painted fingernails.

"Have you made your choices?" Her dark eyes were on Adan, and lust flashed in them. She gave him a lazy smile that was way too intimate to give a stranger. When Adan didn't answer right away, she leaned over, her hip touching his shoulder.

"The Costoletta di Vitello is very popular," she purred, batting her fake eyelashes at him. She was practically undressing him with her eyes.

Okay, lady, control yourself I told her with my eyes, not that she noticed. Yes, Adan was hot, but this was just plain rude. I wasn't a jealous woman, nor was I insecure about my looks, but the tramp had to go.

"I'll have the Sicilienne Pizza," I blurted loudly. "Thanks for asking. And some more bread would be nice."

The waitress gave me a sour look, but she moved away from Adan, jotting down my order. Yup, she was going to spit in it now. I was certain of it.

Adan cleared his throat. "I'll start with an order of fried calamari. And then I'll have the Costoletta di Vitello." He took my menu with his and handed them to the waitress, who took them and flashed him a dazzling smile before she sashayed away from our table.

"Love a woman with an appetite," said Adan as he took a sip of his wine.

"Well, you're going to *love* me 'cause I'm *ravenous*." I finished off my piece of bread, remembering that only a few months ago I only ate carbs on Sundays. Stupid, stupid girl.

"So," began Adan as he set his wine down. "I heard you recently moved back to Hollow Cove from New York. What made you decide to move there?"

Oh boy. I did not want to talk about my ex, especially not on a first date.

"I lived with someone in New York," I began, finding it hard to choose the words as my headache intensified like someone had taken a jackhammer to my skull. "Things didn't work out." I took a breath. "I thought a change of scenery might be good."

Adan squeezed his light eyebrows together and leaned forward. "Are you okay?"

"Fine." I reached for my glass of water. "Just a headache. I shouldn't have drunk that wine so fast," I said, laughing, though every word sent jarring pain in my head. "I'm sure I'll be fine when the food comes. So," I shifted in my seat, trying to keep the throbbing pain from showing on my face, "tell me about you. I'm told you're famous."

Adan laughed. The sound was so beautiful. Too bad I could barely hear it over the pounding in my head, which was the same with his conversation. I could barely make out the words, my head hammering away as my vision blurred with pain until I could see two Adans. That was not good. I'd gotten migraines before, from lack of food, but this one was the migraine of the century—of the universe.

The food didn't come for another half hour. Whether that was normal or the waitress was trying to get back at me, I had no idea. And when it did come, I couldn't eat. I picked up my fork and it kept slipping from my fingers.

"You need some help?" Adan's voice pulled my attention up to him, or should I say, both of them, seeing as there were still two of him. Hey, two Adans were better than one, right?

"Shupid forg," I mumbled, the words barely audible even to me. What the hell did I just say? I dropped the fork again as a series of cold shivers took over. A hard mix of pounding headache and nausea shook me, and I held my breath so I wouldn't be sick.

Okay, this was definitely not a normal migraine. Food poisoning? Maybe. But not from the restaurant, and the only thing I ate for lunch was a banana.

My senses were assaulted with a myriad of reactions: the sharp scent of the bile, the rippling scratch of hundreds of pricks along my skin, the sensation of pressure behind my eyes.

The last thing I needed was to throw up all over our table. I'd probably hit both Adans too, as my luck would have it. Nope. Not going to happen.

And then the worst thing that could happen on a date happened—cramps.

Oh, no, not the monthly ones... the *other* ones... the intestinal failure ones.

"Eghooze me," I ground out, as I stumbled out of our booth.

"Tessa? Are you okay?" came Adan's voice.

I would have loved to answer him, but if I opened my mouth, it wouldn't be words flying out.

Stumbling like a drunk, I moved between tables, and faces blurred past me as I made my way toward the back. *God, please don't let me puke.*

A picture of a woman on a door came into view and I hurried through it. I didn't even bother to lock the door as I made a beeline, well okay, maybe a zigzagged drunk-like beeline, for the toilet.

I threw up, not once, but three times. The strange black substance at the bottom of the toilet wasn't what had me freaking out a little as much as the fact I didn't feel any better.

In fact. I felt worse. Much worse.

My body felt like it was being pulled in every direction while my head never stopped pounding. Dribbles of sweat fell into my eyes, and I felt like I was dying.

What's the matter with me?

I stole a quick peek in the mirror and wished I hadn't. My skin was pale and pasty with dark circles under my eyes. I looked like a zombie. I couldn't face Adan like this. I didn't want to see anyone. I just wanted to go home.

I stumbled out of the bathroom and made for the kitchen area, holding onto the walls as I went and concentrating on putting one foot in front of the other.

"Hey. You can't be in here," a male voice shouted at me.

I really didn't care. I could barely move, let alone open my mouth and start a conversation. He kept yelling. I kept moving, my eyes on what I thought was the back door.

By the miracle of miracles, I made it through the back door and out into the alleyway behind the restaurant without leaving a trail of black vomit behind me.

The fresh air seemed to give me a bit of energy, and the pounding of my head eased a little so I could think beyond the feeling of dying.

It was a thirty-minute walk back to the Hollow Cove bridge. I could call my aunts to pick me up, but then I'd have to explain what was wrong. I didn't have that kind of energy right now. I just wanted to walk it off. Walking was good.

"Okay. You can do this." The words were easier now that I'd emptied most of what was in my stomach.

And if I puked my guts out on the way, well, at least it was dark, and I was only giving the earth a bit of fertilizer.

With my legs feeling like cement blocks, I willed them forward and headed toward the sidewalk at the end of the alleyway. I made it to the corner and turned east. If I could make it to Ocean Side Road, I would be fine.

My head pounded, and tears filled my eyes at the pain. I couldn't feel my legs anymore. Was I even still walking? Maybe I was floating? My body was damp and cold, and the come-and-go flashes from the streetlights and cars burned at my eyes. My head thumped harder and stronger. My mind muddled over until nothing was in there but the feeling of pain and wanting it to end.

Cars honked and my eyes snapped open. I hadn't even realized I had shut them. Okay, so this was bad. It was time to call my aunts.

I grabbed my bag, thanking the cauldron it was still attached to my shoulder somehow. Breathing hard I searched my bag for my phone, but I couldn't find it. The bustling traffic around me made it twice as hard to concentrate.

The pounding in my head intensified. A dizzy spell hit and I fell to my knees, not having the energy to stop the fall or to stand anymore. My hand grazed something slick and hard, and I pulled out my phone. Blinking through the tears, I swiped the screen. Only it was completely black. I pressed the side power button. Nothing.

Fear hit. Shit. I'd forgotten to charge it.

My head swam. I was so tired. *Maybe I'll just lie down for a moment, and then I'll get up and start again.*

I felt myself fall sideways, and then my cheek hit the cold hard surface of the sidewalk. My muscles hurt. Hell, everything hurt.

And then numbness. Not good.

Okay. I was dying. I was dying on the goddamn sidewalk. I couldn't call out for help. I couldn't even call 911.

Thoughts were a jumble in my mind, and all I could think about was why? Who had done this to me?

Darkness pulled at the edges of my mind, my vision going dark. I knew what was going to happen next. If I closed my eyes, I might never open them again.

My lids felt like lead, pulling themselves down, but I could barely keep them open.

I heard the sound of clopping on pavement approaching.

And when I looked up, a goat stared down at me.

CHAPTER 15

I blinked into the horizontally slit eyes. On any other day, I would have thought I was hallucinating, but seeing as I'd seen this *particular* goat before, I knew I wasn't. But why was it here? And why now?

With tremendous effort, I opened my mouth. "You? Why?" was all I could manage.

The goat's eyes widened, and its ears flattened on its head, like a dog would when sad or caught stealing food from the table. I didn't know goats could do that. Then again, this was a ghost goat or something, so maybe it did things differently.

The goat opened its mouth. "Baaaa!"

I stared. "Don't. Speak. Goat."

"Baaa!" said the goat again and then it started to hop around, moving its head to the side.

Okay, so this goat was crazy. But I was dying, so who cared. Right? If I had the energy to laugh, I would have. Seeing as I didn't, I just blinked.

"Meeeh!" said the goat, and it started to frantically scratch at the pavement with its front leg. Next, it moved a pebble toward me, kicking it with its front hoof. Okay, not a ghost. It could actually move stuff, so definitely not a ghost.

"Baaa!" it bleated again. And then it did something really weird. It bent its head and put the pebble in its mouth. "Meh!" it said, as it spit it out.

I shook my head, my cheek scraping the cold pavement.

The goat shook its head, clearly frustrated that I didn't understand goat speech. Again it picked up the pebble in its mouth, its eyes staring, pleading. "Baaa! Baaa!" it bleated, spitting out the pebble once again.

I rolled my eyes over to the nearest small stone next to my knee. I looked at the goat. "Stone. Mouth?" If it thought I was going to put that dirty, god-only-knows-where-it's-been stone in my mouth, it was a stupid goat. Cute. But stupid.

"Meh! Meh! Heh!" The goat started to bounce again like it had springs in its hooves. It picked up another pebble from the sidewalk with its mouth and looked at me, its short tail wagging like a dog.

I sighed. I was dying anyway, so what did it matter that I caught a gazillion diseases? I just wanted it to go away.

"Fine." I stretched my arm towards my knee and grabbed the tiny pebble between my fingers. I brought it closer to my face and popped it into my mouth.

Yes. Yes, I did.

As soon as the cold stone touched my tongue—something happened.

No, I didn't throw up. I didn't even spit it out.

The first thing I noticed was the throbbing in my head vanished, as though a switch had gone off. Next, my vision cleared, and I felt better, lighter, like whatever illness had taken over me washed away. I blinked in shock, the cramps, the nausea, the feeling of death, and all the pains of my body disappeared as renewed energy came flooding back into me. My brain reeled for a few seconds, trying to shift gears and make sense of it all.

I sat up, staring at the goat. "No way?" I said, moving the stone around with my tongue and trying not to think about where it'd been. "How did you know?" I stared at the goat, really stared at it this time. It looked like a regular, normal, black and white goat, and it was a female—not male. Clearly, nothing was normal about the goat. The animal knew a stone would alleviate my illness—if you want to call it that. I still didn't know what had happened to me. But I *would* find out.

First, I needed to find out more about this supernatural goat, ghost or not.

The goat cocked its head. "Baaa… baaaaa."

"Right. We've got this communication thing down. Haven't we?" Having the feel of my legs again, I pushed myself up and brushed some of the dirt from my jeans and my face. "Thank you for saving my life," I told the goat, seeing its intelligent eyes widening in understanding while reflecting the streetlight.

It dipped its head. "Meh."

I took that as a "you're welcome." When I'd first realized that no one but me could see the goat, I'd taken it as a bad omen. Clearly, I was wrong. "How did you find me?"

The goat pursed her lips, her jaw gnawing like she was chewing grass.

I looked over my shoulder. The street was now deserted for a Thursday night. Everyone was either out eating or staying home. If the goat hadn't found me, I'd most certainly have died, only to be found rotting by some poor early bird the next morning.

I tucked the small stone inside my cheek like I would a mint or hard candy. Now that I was better, I contemplated whether I should go back and see Adan. I'd been gone a while, so he was probably worried. But then I'd have to explain to him about the goat and the pebble. I barely knew him, so talking about a goat that no one else could see didn't seem like a good idea.

I'd text him later to explain. If he didn't want to ever speak to me again after that, I wouldn't blame him. But this was the right decision.

My eyes found the goat again. "Are you a witch's familiar?" It was the only logical explanation I could think of. Cats were generally the creatures of choice when it came to selecting familiars, but not always. I'd heard owls, lizards, squirrels, even snakes and beetles could be a witch's familiar. Depended on the witch, and the familiar.

"Baaa," said the goat, shaking her head. "Meh. Baaa!"

I sighed. "What am I going to do with you?" She was so cute. I couldn't leave her here. She'd obviously followed me for a reason. Plus, she'd somehow managed to save my life. Why? Standing here in the middle of the night talking to a goat that no one else could see wouldn't solve any of my problems.

I had an idea.

"Okay, Billie," I told the goat, mentally changing the spelling now that I knew she was a girlie goat. "I'm calling you Billie because I don't know what else to call you. But you're coming home with me. Okay?"

At that, Billie started to bounce up and down excitedly, swinging her head and kicking out her legs. God, she was cute. I had to refrain from reaching out and squeezing her.

That was a start.

"All right, then. Let's go."

With the small stone still tucked inside my cheek, I adjusted my bag's strap higher on my shoulder and headed south. Billie walked alongside me, my head ringing with questions.

There was still Myrtle's murder to solve and the recent break-in to Gilbert's safe. But first, I *was* going to find out what the hell had happened to me because that was no food poisoning.

No, this was something else.

CHAPTER 16

By the time I'd made it back to Davenport House, it was almost ten at night. I found the three sisters gathered around the kitchen table, enjoying a bottle of wine and some late-night snacks before getting ready to head out to the Night Festival in two hours. One look at my disheveled appearance and they all jumped out of their seats.

"What happened? Did Adan do this to you?" Ruth was the first at my side, inspecting me for more serious injuries. Guess I must have looked dreadful.

"I'm going to kill that bastard witch," growled Dolores. Red blotches marred her face, her long fingers clasped into shaking fists.

Beverly brought me a glass of water. "Let House deal with him. That's what I would do."

I shook my head and raised my hands. "It's not Adan," I told them, and assuming it was safe now, I pulled out the stone from my mouth and watched the surprise and shock mirroring on my aunts' faces. "He didn't do anything wrong."

Ruth giggled. "I used to suck on rocks too. Like the earth's mints. Kind of cleans your teeth, doesn't it?"

I didn't know what to answer to that. "Uh… sure."

Dolores put a hand on her hip. "Start talking. What the hell happened to you?"

I took a sip of water and then another, and told them everything—from the intense headache that started at the Night Festival to the events of my date.

"Did you call Adan to let him know where you are?" asked Beverly. "He's probably worried sick."

"I couldn't. My phone died. Did he call?"

Beverly gave a nod of her head and picked up her glass of red wine. "He did. The handsome fool thinks you ditched him."

I sighed. "Great." Crap. I was going to have to fix that.

I pulled out my phone, walked over to the kitchen counter next to the fridge where I'd left my charger, and plugged it in. I was not looking forward to that conversation. I'd really screwed up things with Adan, but I couldn't think about that right now.

I turned around, putting my back on the counter, and saw Dolores eyeing me, her dark eyes calculating. Billie was nibbling on Dolores's skirt, but not hard enough for my aunt to notice.

Dolores gestured with her free hand. "So, you were deathly ill and then you happened to know that putting a rock in your mouth would cure you?"

Here it comes. "Not exactly."

Dolores shot me an alarmed glance. "Then how did you know the stone would remove the curse?"

My mouth fell open, fear rising anew. "I was cursed?" Damn, guess there was a first for everything.

"Yes," said the three sisters together.

"And a very bad one at that," informed Ruth, her blue eyes round and filled with worry.

Fear spun liquid strands through me, and I tried to control my emotions. "What kind of curse?" I asked, though somehow I already knew.

Dolores sighed. "This was the worst kind of curse you can weave." She paused and said, "It was a killing curse."

My pulse hammered. "I figured that. But why would someone want me dead? Why me?" You'd think I'd be scared, but I wasn't. I was mad as hell. Why would someone try to kill me? I hadn't done anything to anyone, if you excluded ditching Adan tonight. I wasn't a Saint by any means, but I didn't deserve this.

"It was Myrtle's friends," said Beverly. "It's the only thing that makes sense. They think you killed her. They've been spreading all kinds of rumors about you at the Night Festival. You should hear how they talk about you. It would make the hairs on your arms stand up."

"Great." I closed my eyes and rubbed my temples as I felt another giant headache that had nothing to do with the curse creep inside the walls of my skull.

"You still haven't answered my question," pressed Dolores, and I flicked my eyes open to see her raised brow. "Not many witches know about the effects of some natural elements in curing a killing curse, and it wasn't in any of those books I gave you. How did you know?"

My eyes found Billie, and a smile quirked the corners of my mouth. "She saved me."

"Who saved you?" asked Dolores. "Who else was with you?"

I took a deep breath, readying myself for what I was about to say as well as the onslaught that would come after.

"The goat," I breathed. "The goat saved me. She told me to use the stone... well, not in so many words. But enough for me to understand that putting a stone in my mouth was the right thing to do."

Dolores frowned at me. "The same exact one you saw on your first night at the Night Festival?"

I sighed. "The very same."

Ruth snorted and looked around blearily.

Dolores smacked her forehead, a moan escaping her while Ruth gave me a warm smile like I'd just told her muffins were the very best things on earth. Beverly threw back her head and chugged the last of her wine.

"She's not a figment of my imagination," I continued. "She's real. She's right here... in this kitchen."

Dolores cast her gaze around the kitchen before her dark eyes settled on me. "You're telling us that a goat is standing here... in my kitchen." Her brows raised in disbelief.

"Yes. That's exactly what I'm saying," I told them, and I glanced down at Billie who was still working on the bottom of Dolores's long skirt, nibbling at the hem. Cute goat.

Dolores gave me a sour look. "I know you've had a long night but enough with the goat. Are you trying to give us a heart attack? There is no goat—ah!"

Dolores jumped backward and hit the kitchen table with her butt. "Something just yanked my skirt!" she screamed, her eyes wide.

I smiled. "That was Billie."

At that Ruth screeched like a little girl and ran around the kitchen with a spatula in her hand, like she was trying to swat some flies. "Oh, I just love goats. Where is she? Is she near me? I'm I hot or cold? Ooh… this is so much fun!"

"Cauldron help us," said Beverly lazily and poured herself some more wine.

"Look, the thing is," I began and moved to stand next to the goat, trying not to laugh at the horror on Dolores's face. "I thought maybe she was a witch's familiar, but then it wouldn't explain why no one can see her. I still don't know why *I* can, but I have a feeling… if she is a familiar… I think this is a spell or a curse. I think someone did this to her. Made her invisible to everyone."

Billie's attention snapped to mine, and then she began jumping up and down around the kitchen again, knocking one of the tables, which made Dolores try to flatten herself against the table.

"She's saying I'm right," I said, seeing Billie's reaction.

"Who's saying?" asked Dolores, her eyes looking everywhere at once.

"The damn goat, that's who," said Beverly, her speech a little slow and her cheeks red.

"I know how we can help her," said Ruth as she locked eyes with me. "Wait right here." She bolted out of the kitchen, past the hallway, and vanished into the room just off to the left, which was the potions room. Something crashed to the floor, and then Ruth was back.

She grabbed my hand and put a small container in it. "This is the same stuff we used on the safe. You need to sprinkle some on her. I would love to do it, but I can't see her."

"I bet you would," grumbled Dolores, but she managed to move away from the table and take a step closer to us.

Doing as I was instructed, I pinched my fingers around the pink powder and sprinkled it over Billie, who stood still like she knew exactly what we were doing. Her horizontally slit eyes stared up at me expectantly.

At first, I thought I'd see the shape of the goat, but the pink powder disappeared as soon as it landed on her, which told me she was still invisible to everyone.

"Good." Ruth took my free hand and said, "Now. Since you're the only one who can see her, that means you're connected. Only you can remove the spell."

"If there is one," said Dolores.

Ruth ignored her sister, her body shifting nervously. "Say the revealing spell, Tessa."

I looked down at my aunt. "Uh... I don't know it."

Ruth giggled. "Oh, that's right. Just repeat after me. *Show me the path that I cannot find*.

"Show me the path that I cannot find," I repeated.

"Let magic reveal what can't be seen and restore what was left behind."

I exhaled and said, "Let magic reveal what can't be seen and restore what was left behind."

Just as it was in Gilbert's store, power soared all around the kitchen and through me in an outpouring of energy from my aura. With the sudden torrent of energy, a flow of blinding light flashed before our eyes. The air shifted, and then the magic settled.

Standing in the middle of the kitchen wasn't a goat but a young woman. And she was completely naked.

Chapter 17

"It's a girl!" Ruth clapped her hands, jumping on the balls of her feet, as though one of us had just had a baby. Yes, my aunt was a little odd, but I loved her just the way she was.

"A very naked girl," commented Beverly who was still sitting at the table with her fingers wrapped around a glass of wine. "Nice rack, but mine are perkier."

Dolores moved to the wooden peg rack next to the back door, grabbed her black raincoat, and draped it around the young woman.

The young woman. Holy crap.

Now that her nakedness was covered, I looked at her face. Silky, straight black hair fell just past her jawline, and her large brown eyes accentuated her sharp features and pretty heart-shaped face. She looked a few years older than me, maybe thirty-two? It was hard to imagine, but not impossible to think that only a few moments ago this pretty black-haired woman had been a goat.

"Hi," I said. "I'm Tessa. But you already knew that. What's your name?" She was shorter than me, around Ruth's height, five-five, five-six.

"How come you were a goat?" Ruth bumped her shoulder against my arm. "Did a witch do this to you? Or did you do this to yourself by accident? Or maybe you were hiding from someone? Did you drink something you weren't supposed to?"

I put a hand on Ruth's shoulder. "Ease down, soldier," I told her. "Let her speak." I watched her closely, and for a horrible moment, I thought she wouldn't or maybe couldn't.

The woman blinked, her eyes moving from me to each of my aunts, and then back to me. Everyone was staring at her now that they could see her.

"I'm Iris," she said. Her voice was soft and faint, almost as though she wasn't sure she'd uttered those two words out loud.

I waited for her to say something else, but she didn't. "Let me get you some water." She was most likely dehydrated from the effects of transforming back into a human form from a goat. But what did I know? And I mean *human* form because clearly, she was a half-breed. I just didn't know which one.

And then, just like that, the mixed scents of vinegar and earth came wafting toward me along with a strong pulse of demon magic.

She was a witch. But not just any witch. She was a Dark witch.

I knew my aunts could sense it too, but no one said a word. We all had one thing on our minds—helping this poor witch.

I turned toward the fridge, but Dolores beat me to it and gave Iris a tall glass of water.

Iris took the glass and held it for a long moment, enough for me to see the dirt packed under her fingernails, and one look at her toes was like she'd gone barefoot for years on the farm. She took a sip of water. "Thank you. Wow. I'm drinking from a glass. Can't remember the last time I held a glass." She went silent again, her eyes focused on the water.

"The poor girl looks traumatized." Beverly had appeared next to me. "What she needs is something *stronger* than water. Like vodka..." A smile appeared on her lips as she added, "... or Jake Collins."

I was not going there. "Iris. Can you tell us what happened to you? Who did this to you?"

The Dark witch took another sip of her water and shook her head. "I... I don't remember." Again, her expression went blank.

"I've got a potion that can help retrieve memories," said Ruth happily. "I can have it ready in a jiffy." Humming to herself, Ruth pulled a small cauldron from one of the bottom cabinets and plopped it on the stovetop.

"Why don't you sit here." Beverly steered Iris to the kitchen table, and we all followed. "You must be tired from your... *journey* back into a woman's body."

I took the seat next to Iris, questions bouncing in my head like a ping-pong match. "Thank you for saving my life."

Iris blinked at me. "You've already thanked me. I'm the one who should be thanking you." She pulled out her hand and wiggled her fingers, like she was trying them out for the first time.

"Well, thank you, again." I watched her for a moment. "Tell me, Iris, how come I was the only one who could see you in your goat form?"

Iris put the glass of water on the table. "Well, that's simple. You did some Dark magic."

"What?"

"Didn't you weave some Dark magic spell recently?" asked Iris. "It's the only way you could see me. Only someone who'd conjured Dark magic could see through the Dark curse."

Dolores leaned forward in her chair. "But how would you know this? You said you don't remember who did this to you. How do you know for certain it was Dark magic?"

Iris looked at Dolores. "You're a White witch, right? All of you, except for Tessa. I could tell. A goat has a very strong sense of smell."

"I agree," said Beverly, wrinkling her nose at Iris. "Very strong."

"I could sense the White magic on you all," continued Iris. "Just like I could sense that this curse was Dark and weaved by someone skilled in Dark magic." She looked down at her glass of water. "I just... I just don't remember who did this to me."

My heart ached at the emotion in her voice. "So, it's possible that whoever cursed you also put some sort of memory spell on you," I said. I wasn't an expert, but at the nod from Dolores, I knew she agreed with me.

"Working on that!" came Ruth's voice from over the stove. She sprinkled some dried leaves into her cauldron and stirred. "I should have it ready in about an hour. The first batch won't be as potent. The next one will be better." She nodded her head.

The smell that wafted from the cauldron smelled like rotten eggs. I hoped for Iris's sake it wouldn't taste like it smelled.

"You're a Dark witch?" I asked Iris, knowing there weren't any Dark witches in Hollow Cove, but I'd heard of a few covens right here in Maine. I'd never met a Dark witch before, and my pulse leaped in excitement at the prospect of picking her brain about demons. How many had she conjured, and which ones were her go-to-demons? You never knew. Might come in handy someday.

The Dark witch nodded, a tiny smile on her lips. "Hmm-hmm."

"What's the last thing you remember?"

Iris looked up at me, her smile gone. "I… I remember the sound of traffic… then just darkness… then me as a goat." Emotions flashed over her face—fear, anger, confusion—and I felt sorry for her.

"Iris?" Dolores watched the young witch intently. "Where are you from? Do you remember? Can you tell us anything about your family? They're probably worried sick about you. We should call them."

Iris shook her head, a frown on her pretty face. "I don't know. I can't remember." She pressed her lips into a thin line, her features set in concentration. "For some reason, I can only remember my name. But I do remember being in New York City after it happened." She glanced down at herself. "After I turned into a goat. Bit of a shocker."

I laughed. "Bet it was."

Iris smiled. "I realized quickly that no one could see me. And after a few hours of freaking out, I found my way to Central Park... and then I developed a craving for grass. Can you believe it? I couldn't stop eating it. It tasted... it tasted good... like I was eating chocolate."

"Nothing wrong with eating grass," commented Ruth. "I still do it. Helps with my constipation."

Iris's eyes widened, but she said nothing about Ruth's grass comment.

Beverly saluted Iris over her glass of wine. "Welcome to our madness."

I laughed, Iris laughed, and I saw the visible tension easing from her shoulders.

"I decided my best chance was to find another witch," continued Iris. "If anyone could help me, it would be witches. So, I went out looking for them. I couldn't remember who I was, but I could still sense magic." She sighed heavily. "I followed my senses and it brought me straight into a coven of witches. But they couldn't see me either. No matter how loud I yelled—"

"Baaa," I corrected, seeing a tiny smile reappearing on her face.

"Yes, that," Iris said. "I was invisible to them."

I tapped the tabletop with my fingers. "But how did you get here? It's a really long walk from New York. And in hooves."

Iris tilted her head and stared at her toes. "I heard the witches talking about the Night Festival. So I got on the bus with them. I figured there'd be lots of different witches there. A substantial group of really powerful witches. There had to be at least one who could help me." Her eyes met mine and she grinned. "And I was right."

I laughed. "I'm not powerful. If I was, I would have figured out that someone had cursed me." The memory of the pain I felt from the sickness sent a wave of dread rippling through me, but my anger squished it.

"Curses are tricky, Tessa," said Dolores, having read my mood. "Even the best of witches sometimes are taken by surprise by curses. You can't blame yourself for not noticing."

But I did. I should have. If it hadn't been for Iris, I would be dead.

"Well," Iris went on, "I put two and two together and realized the witches I'd followed here were White witches. As were most of the witches at the festival. But when you saw me—when I realized *you* could see me—that's when I made the connection between Dark magic and the Dark curse. No one at the festival could see me except for you. I figured you'd dabbled in the Dark arts a couple of times."

"You were right." I looked at my aunts. "Any new leads with Myrtle? Or the safe?" Maybe going out with Adan hadn't been such a good idea. I should have been here, working the cases, because now it seemed we had three: Myrtle's murder, the break-in, and a killing curse on yours truly.

Dolores made a sound in her throat. "Nothing. We couldn't find any evidence that would give us a clear indication of motive or suspects."

"The motive is that they wanted the money," said Beverly.

Dolores shot her sister a glare. "And what about Myrtle? Where does she fit in? And now Tessa?" Dolores's voice rose dangerously high. "I don't like this one bit." She hit the table with her hand, making us all jump. "Something smells bad."

Ruth spun around, "Oh, sorry, that was me. I didn't think it would reach you over there."

"I think I'll call Helen Morgan," said Dolores and then added at my questioning brow, "she's part of the Merlin Group in Boston where Myrtle is from. If Myrtle was dabbling in anything untoward, she'll know about it. Well, it's a start."

I nodded. "Anything that can help." Because right now, we needed it.

Beverly shot to her feet. "Well, it won't do us any good arguing about it. We need to get out. The Night Festival is about to begin in about an hour. What better way to find clues than with drink and loose tongues?"

"She's right." I stood up, just as Ruth disappeared from the kitchen again. "This whole mess started when this freak show came to town. Someone at the festival knows something."

Beverly pulled down her already low-cut blouse. She caught me staring and said, "It's a party, darling, and I plan on showing cleavage."

"You need to be extra careful, Tessa," said Dolores, pulling my eyes away from Beverly. "Folks at the festival think you killed Myrtle. And now, someone tried to kill you too."

Anger overpowered my fatigue. "I know. But you see, whoever tried to kill me probably thinks I'm dead. Right? Which gives me the advantage."

"How so?"

"If they're surprised to see me, they know something." It wasn't a great plan, but it was all I had. Until I figured out my connection to Myrtle and the safe, I didn't have much to go on. But someone at that festival wanted me dead. Why? No idea. But if it was the suit-lady,

Winnie, the look of surprise upon seeing me tonight would be proof enough for me.

"House!" commanded Beverly. "Please prepare the spare bedroom for Iris." She looked at the young witch. "And you, my dear, need a nice long shower."

Iris stood up slowly, her thin pale arms wrapped around the raincoat. "That bad, huh?"

Beverly flashed her a brilliant smile. "Worse."

"Tessa?" Ruth's voice came from behind me.

I spun around. "Yes?"

Her hands were a blur, and then I was hit in the face with a mist-like spray that smelled strongly of oranges, urine, and something else I couldn't guess.

I jerked back. "If that was skunk pee… I'm going to kill you, Ruth," I cried out, rubbing my eyes and hearing Iris laugh. "Why the hell did you do that?"

Ruth's eyes were wide with a frenzied glee. "It's my new counter-curse spray. I added some orange peels for a little citrus scent. You like it?"

"Not really." I pulled my fingers from my face. They were sticky like I'd just peeled an orange.

Ruth gave me the once-over and then, seemingly satisfied, said, "Whatever you do… don't shower for another eight hours." The witch turned and skipped back to her boiling cauldron.

I stifled the urge to go over there and dunk her head in it. Peeling a sticky strand of hair from my eyes I watched as Beverly led Iris out of the kitchen and up the staircase. The poor witch had had to live like an animal for god knew how long. Looking at her fingers and feet, I was guessing months.

Who was evil enough to do that to Iris? And why? Iris had saved my life. I owed her. I *would* find out who did this to her, and there'd be hell to pay.

But first, I needed to find Adan and apologize. And that was *not* a conversation I was looking forward to.

Chapter 18

After I'd freshened up, which was brushing my hair and changing my clothes since I was not allowed to shower, I headed to the downtown core of Hollow Cove and the Night Festival with Iris, who, after her fabulously long shower had been assaulted as well with Ruth's anti-curse spray. Why had Ruth decided to spray me before my shower? I had no idea, and I didn't have the patience or the energy to start up with that argument.

Iris had also succumbed to a large cup of Ruth's "memory refresher elixir" as she'd called it. And though Iris had drunk it all down, she still couldn't remember who had cursed her or anything else, much to Ruth's dismay.

"Hmmm." Ruth had observed the Dark witch closely. "You're going to need a triple dose."

"That was disgusting," Iris had said as soon as the front door closed behind us.

"That was just the beginning." I laughed and gave her a few mints as we headed into the crowd. The aunts had stayed behind, for now, something about Ruth's cauldron catching fire. They said they would find us later.

Iris had borrowed my black blouse and matched it with a pair of Beverly's jeans (Dolores and I were Sasquatches in terms of height and build, so she would be floating in a pair of our jeans) and some of Ruth's black flats. Beverly had also supplied brand new panties and bra, which for some odd reason, she had stacks of.

Beverly had laughed at the expression on my face. "When you have to leave in a hurry, you don't always remember your underwear."

It didn't matter what she wore. Iris looked stunning. Looking at her now, you'd never guess only an hour ago she was a four-legged animal with hooves and covered in fur. But she'd been a cute goat.

The Night Festival opened up to us with an array of lights, music, food, and the paranormal. It was like stepping into fairyland or something similar. Though just as lively as every other night, the Night Festival had lost its appeal to me, and I was looking forward to it ending.

"Stay alert," I told Iris, keeping my voice low as we hit the crowd of spectators. We started picking our way through booths and half-breeds. "See if anyone recognizes you. We'll start with that." The Merlin Group from New York was here somewhere. Maybe they'd recognize Iris. If she was in New York when the curse hit her, I had a hunch maybe that's where she was from.

There was still a killer on the loose, and now with the attempt on my life, that was two killers. Or could it be the same person? A tiny voice inside my head said yes. But I wouldn't know anything for sure until I dug a little deeper.

"So, who's this guy Adan?" asked Iris, matching my strides with her short legs. "Is he a potential boyfriend?" She winked.

I sighed. "If he was… I ruined my chances. I sorta ditched him to go puke my guts out by the expensive restaurant he took me to. That's when you found me."

"I'm sure he'll understand if you tell him."

I shrugged. "Maybe." I cast my gaze through the crowds in search of the tall, handsome blond witch, but all I got were glares and the occasional sour expression.

We moved deeper. A round of nervous whispers and quiet comments went through the throng of paranormals. Some of the older half-breeds turned and shuffled away as though one glance from me would turn them into stone. Most of the crowd just stared, but one grizzled old man growled, "Killer."

I cocked my brow at Iris. "The crowd loves me." She laughed as we continued walking in silence for a little while, both lost in our thoughts.

Before I realized where we were going, a purple tent with yellow police tape came into view. Myrtle's tent. Shit. I did not want to be seen near there.

A pair of eyes glimmered next to a white light in the dark. Next came the figure who owned the eyes accompanied by the scowl of the year.

"Who's that?" asked Iris, having followed my gaze.

"That's Winnie Wilde." I glared at the witch who was still in a man's suit, though this one was red and pinstriped, with as much hate as my face could muster. I had every reason to believe she'd cursed me. The bitch wanted me dead.

The flicker of surprise that moved across her features, the slight widening of her eyes, and the parting of her lips were my answer.

Winnie Wilde had cursed me.

I smiled at her and gave her a finger wave. "I have to say, Winnie… that was a pretty stupid move you pulled. But seeing you now wearing *that* suit… I'm not so sure which is more stupid."

I waited for a reaction, but Winnie kept staring at me, her face a mask of anger.

"Let's go." I grabbed Iris's elbow and steered her in the opposite direction. We didn't get far because a familiar gray-eyed person stood in our way.

Iris leaned over and whispered. "Is that Adan? He's hot."

My face warmed watching his wide shoulders sway as he approached. "No. That's Marcus. He's the town's chief." He wore the same clothes I'd seen him in earlier today, though a short, black leather jacket was over his shoulders now.

"Who's your friend?" Marcus eyed Iris with his familiar cold stare, his face wrinkling as I was certain he was taking in her scent as a Dark witch.

"This is my cousin, Iris," I blurted the first thing out of my mouth. "She's here for the festival."

Marcus turned his eyes on me. "Two days late?"

"Cramps," said Iris as she put her hand below her belly button. "Worst cramps ever. I couldn't move for days. You know what I mean?" She cast her smile at him.

Even in the dim glow of the white hanging lights, I saw Marcus's ears and face redden. He scratched the back of his neck, looking uncomfortable. Men.

I glanced at Iris and smiled. Smart witch.

"What happened to your date?" asked the chief, seemingly recovered from the whole cramp thing. The tiniest of smiles curled the corner of his lips. "Shouldn't he be here to escort you?" His eyes grew intense as he watched me for a moment. "Was the date that bad?"

My lips parted. "The date was fine."

"Really?" Marcus folded his arms over his chest. "What did you talk about?"

I frowned. Where the hell was he going with this? Had Adan told him that I'd ditched him?

"Why do you want to know? What's it to you, anyway?"

Marcus watched me, and his gaze lingered on my lips. "Does the Merlin Group have anything new on the break-in?"

"Not that I know of." I swallowed, my heart pounding just a little faster than it should.

His eyes met mine, mesmerizing in their gleam. "Nothing?"

"That's what I said," I told him. "We're still working out some theories. Why?"

The chief made a disapproving sound in his throat. "What time did you get back from your date?"

I pressed both hands on my hips and glowered at him. "Are you interrogating me?"

Marcus's wandering attention lighted briefly over me, from my shoes to my hair before rising to my eyes. I think he recognized that something had happened to me but decided not to mention it. Or maybe he was just reacting to Ruth's counter-curse spray.

"Just, don't leave Hollow Cove again," he said, amused by my sudden reaction. He turned away, moving with the liquid, animal grace that only a shifter could achieve. I watched his confident pace as he made his way through the crowd, his jeans fitting his firm ass way too perfectly, so of course, I kept looking. Couldn't help it.

"Wow. He's intense," said Iris. "He's like a mix of a panther, a wolf, and a bear, all in a tight, sexy package." Iris's face cracked into a smile. "I like him."

"He's irritating," I growled. "He knows how to get under my skin. I think he likes to infuriate me. Turns him on or something."

"The sexual tension between the two of you is off the charts."

I shot her a look. "What? It is not." Was it?

Iris laughed. "Yeah. It is. I wasn't sure whether I should leave you two alone so you could get it over with in one of those tents." She cocked her brow and looked at me. "Is he single?"

"I think so."

"So why aren't you two having crazy-hot sex?"

Good question. "It's complicated." Because mostly, he thinks I'm involved somehow in Myrtle's murder. At least that's what I used to think. Now I wasn't so sure anymore.

"Tess! There you are." Ronin stepped around an older half-breed who glared up at him and then continued walking over. "I've been calling you all night. I thought…" He glanced over at Iris, his eyes widening as he stared at her. His mouth hung slightly open with whatever he had planned to say but had seemingly forgotten.

Oh, boy. "My phone's dead." A smile crept on my face. "Ronin. This is Iris. Remember the goat I told you about?"

"Yeah…"

"She's it."

Ronin's attention snapped to mine. "No way."

"Way." I quickly recounted the events of my date, the killing curse, the goat, and how with Ruth's help, I had managed to remove the curse from Iris.

The half-vampire gave Iris one of his infamous vamp smiles. "You look good as a woman."

Iris gave him a scowl, though her lips were smiling. "I was always a woman. The goat was like a glamour—a furry, smelly glamour. And I'm more than happy to be rid of it."

"Well," continued Ronin, leaning closer. "You still look hot. Ouch!"

I pulled my fist away from his arm. "Stop that, or I'll punch you again. She's still brand new—in a matter of speaking—so give her some space, you horny vamp."

I caught a few glares aimed our way, even a few curious looks coming from three middle-aged faeries who were standing close enough to eavesdrop on our conversation.

Ronin's eyes were locked on Iris. "You have such pretty hair—"

I yanked Ronin forward. "Come on, Casanova. Let's go find somewhere more private so we can talk." The last thing we needed right now was for Ronin to work his vampire mojo on Iris. The poor witch had been traumatized enough.

Ronin moved out of my grasp. "What's that smell?" He leaned in and sniffed. "Oh. It's you. Damn, girl. Did you get sprayed by a skunk?"

"No." I sighed as I heard Iris snort. "It's one of Ruth's counter-curse sprays." Great. Is that what Marcus had smelled too? "She's still making adjustments. But if it smells bad, it means it's working." Total lie, but what else could I say? And why hadn't he said anything to Iris? She'd been sprayed too.

We walked to the end of the town square, past a few of the parked motorhomes and trailers across the street from us. The small park next to it, with the fountain that had intoxicated hundreds of pixies with a spell from the sorceress Samara only a few weeks ago, was the perfect place to chat in private.

I headed for the nearest bench, only someone was already sitting on it.

The said person was hunched over, a bottle of honey-colored liquid, half-drunk, hanging in his hand. Unintelligent mumblings uttered from the drunken figure, and then I heard a couple of words I could understand the closer I got.

"Stupid, stupid," slurred the person. "How could I be so stupid."

I recognized that voice. I glanced at Ronin before I walked around the bench and faced the drunk.

"Gilbert?" I asked, taking in the dribble on his chin and the tears on his cheeks. "Wow. You're drunk."

"You know him?" Iris was staring at Gilbert with open curiosity and just a little bit of mistrust, as though he might be the one who had cursed her.

My gaze traveled over the shifter. "Unfortunately. He's our mayor."

Ronin let out a low whistle. "More like our drunken little Yoda."

"I'm not drunk!" grunted Gilbert, sloshing his drink all over himself. "I'm the soberest shifter in this town. A mayor knows his limits. A mayor does not get drunk. A mayor has control."

I laughed. "Yes, well, I get all tingly inside when you take control like that."

Gilbert's head lolled to the side until he finally managed to keep it straight, though his eyes rolled all over the place, never settling on me than half a second. "What do you want?" he spat. "The Merlin Group is here to arrest me!" he shouted.

I glanced over my shoulder. A few half-breeds stared our way. "Shhh! Gilbert. Knowing you. I doubt you want to attract attention in your state." I didn't know the shifter well, but I knew he wouldn't want his townspeople to see him like this. Which could only mean something horrible had happened to knock him off his rocker.

The shifter put the bottle to his lips and took a swig. Half went in, and half went down his chin. He swallowed and said. "Doesn't matter. It's all over for me."

The sound of pictures snapping pulled my attention to my left. Ronin had his smartphone out and was clicking away at Gilbert.

"Seriously?" I glared at the vampire.

Ronin took one more picture and then slipped his phone into his jacket pocket. "Leverage. You never know when they might come in handy."

I pursed my lips. "Sounds more like blackmail to me."

Iris was staring at Gilbert with a sad look on her pretty face. Then she surprised me when she sat next to him on the bench. The shifter, though, never noticed.

I stared at him for a second. "Gilbert. What do you mean *it's all over*? What's all over?"

Gilbert moaned, his face pasty with sweat and tears. "I told them it would be safe. They trusted me. I failed them."

That piqued my interest, so I moved closer. "What would be safe?" When he didn't answer, I pressed. "I can help you, Gilbert, but you need to tell me what's bothering you," I soothed, as gently as I could to someone I loathed. He accused me of murder, among other things. I despised the little shifter, but something had happened, and I needed to know what.

Gilbert strained to lift his head and meet my eyes, like it was three sizes too big for his body. "I'm a fool."

"When he's right, he's right," commented Ronin.

I let out a breath. "Why? What did you do, Gilbert? Remember. I work for the Merlin Group. If something happened in this town, I need to know."

Gilbert picked a spot on my chest, seemingly trying to focus, and said, "The ring."

I raised my brows. "Okay, good. The ring. What ring?"

At that, the shifter started to sob like a baby. Huge, disturbing sobs were soon followed by an eerie, keening wail. Damn. I didn't feel sorry for him. It just made me really uncomfortable.

"Is he crying?" Ronin stared at Gilbert like he wanted to punch him. "Make him stop. The dude's leaking. Dudes don't leak."

"Why do *I* have to make him stop?" I cringed as Gilbert's sobs turned into gasps and twitches. If he didn't stop soon, the entire town would hear him.

Iris leaned closer and inspected Gilbert. "I know a few Dark spells that can sew a man's mouth shut. Work like a charm," she said and winked. "Want me to give it a go?"

At that, Ronin's mouth twisted strangely, and he stared at Iris like she was sex on two legs.

Okaaaay. "Uh, thanks, but I think I still need him talking." With my hands on my hips, I straightened. "Now. You're going to tell me about this ring, Gilbert. Don't make me repeat myself," I said, doing my best Dolores impersonation, voice and all. I even lifted myself onto the balls of my feet to give me a few extra inches. I knew it had worked when the shifter started to blab.

"The Elder ring," moaned Gilbert, and he took another mouthful of his bottle. "It was in the safe in my store. I told them it would be safe. That nothing could break it open."

"Someone did," snorted Ronin, and I shot him a look and told him to shut it.

"Now it's gone because of me," slurred Gilbert. He tipped his head back and finished the last of his drink.

"Is this a magic ring?" I guessed. "Had to be if it was locked away in a safe. Right?" From my readings, and what I'd known about magic rings most of my life, all magic rings had supernatural properties or powers of some kind. Some magic rings could endow the wearer with a variety of abilities including invisibility and sometimes immortality. Others could grant wishes, but most of the time, magic rings were used as a conduit for magic spells, charms, hexes, and curses to help the wearer direct their magic.

Sometimes magic rings were just a family heirloom without much magic properties. But the way Gilbert was acting told me this ring was special. Either the owners were rich and powerful, or the ring was.

My heart pounded. "Gilbert," I started, hearing the fear in my voice. "What's so special about this ring?" Unease wove a knot in my belly, and it was tightening.

Gilbert tossed his empty bottle on the ground. "The ring makes the wearer all-powerful, that's what. If they're a werewolf, they'll become the most powerful werewolf that ever was. If they're a witch, the ring will make their spells a thousand times more effective, stronger, and more powerful. They'll become... invincible. In the wrong hands, the ring could inflict devastation on the world."

Ronin let out a few jaw-dropping curses. "Why the hell would anyone bring something like that here?"

"It was part of the exhibition," garbled Gilbert. He sniffed and said, "I was to present it during the festival's last night as part of the show."

"Does Marcus know? Did you tell him you put it in there?" If my aunts knew, they would have told me by now, or they would have mentioned it the moment we arrived in Gilbert's store.

Gilbert shook his head. "No. He doesn't."

Thought so. "Who owns this ring, Gilbert?"

Gilbert frowned at me, a tiny part of his drunken state lifted. "No one *owns* it, you idiot.

It's too dangerous. No. It's kept at the Institute of Paranormal & Magical Objects with all other magical artifacts. Someone had mentioned to add it to the display this year."

My heart pounded. "Who? Who asked?"

Gilbert grimaced and shook his head. "I can't remember."

I reached out, grabbed him by the shoulders, and shook. "Think. This is important! Who asked? Tell me!"

"Get off me, you murderess!" he shouted, and I let him go, stepping back. "I'm next on your list of victims! Is that it!" Then he tipped over the side of the bench, landing with a thud and an "oof."

I resisted the urge to kick him. Dubious little man. But he had given me loads of useful information. Whoever made sure this Elder ring would be moved to a less secure environment was likely the same person who stole it, and I had the nasty feeling they'd used the ring to put that killing curse on me as well.

And then it hit me. The break-in with the safe had never been about the money.

Fear flashed through me. It had always been about the ring.

And now it was gone.

Chapter 19

I stood silently for a moment, letting all this new information settle around my big brain. Although some of the pieces of the puzzle now fit, they didn't explain why Myrtle was killed or why someone had tried to kill me.

Loud snores interrupted my thinking, and I stared down at a sleeping Gilbert. On his knees, he had his face splattered in the grass while his bottom was in the air in a very compromising position.

I smiled. So tempted to kick...

My thoughts went to a familiar Seer in a man's suit, and the pieces fell into place. "I think I know what happened," I said as the jumbled thoughts started to make sense. Iris and Ronin both looked at me.

"Are you going to share? Or do we have to bite it out of you?" asked the lanky vampire. "Please say bite."

I nodded, knowing I was right. "This is all Winnie. All of it."

Ronin jammed his hands in his pockets. "And you think she stole the ring?"

I opened my mouth to answer, but I was thrown off by Iris, who had kneeled next to the snoring Gilbert. With her hand, she plucked a few of his hairs and slipped them into her pocket.

She caught me staring and said, "You never know when you might need these to curse him."

I didn't know what to say to that, so I chose not to speak.

A smile blossomed over Ronin's face as he stared at Iris. "I think I'm in love."

I let out a long breath. "Winnie stole the ring. My guess is because she wanted it to become more powerful as a Seer. To *see* more, maybe? I don't know how their magic works. But it also makes sense that Myrtle—with them being close—got wind of Winnie's plan."

"Maybe they were in it together?" mused Ronin, rolling his shoulders.

"Maybe. And then something must have happened," I continued, the words spilling out of my mouth. "Myrtle didn't agree to steal the ring. So, Winnie killed her."

"I like where you're going with this," agreed Ronin. "I think you might be onto something."

My pulse throbbed as everything came to light. "And then she tried to frame me for the murder. And when that didn't work…"

"She used the ring to curse you," answered Iris as she straightened. "It fits."

"It does." The surprise on her face at seeing me cemented my belief. A flutter of excitement and nerves rushed through me. "It also means I have to tell Marcus."

"The hot chief," smiled Iris, raising her eyebrows suggestively. "I bet you do."

Ronin lost his smile. "He's got good hair. That's it. I'm the sexy guy. Right?" He pointed to himself. "Hello, vampire here. Ladies? Hello?"

I pulled my phone from my bag, and seeing that I had three bars of power left, I called Marcus. "He's not picking up," I said as the phone went straight to voicemail. "I need to find him."

"I saw him heading towards his place before I found you guys," offered Ronin with a slightly irritated look on his face.

"His office?" Maybe Marcus had found a new lead and had gone back to file some paperwork.

Ronin's eyes were on Iris. "No. His place. His home."

Somehow I thought it better that I speak to Marcus in person. "Where does the chief live?"

Ronin shrugged. "Upstairs from his office. He owns the building and has an apartment on the top floor. I offered to buy it from him." And at my raised brow he added, "more square footage than my place."

I had no idea how Ronin made a living. That was a conversation for another time.

I looked over my shoulder and spotted the chief's building. "Ronin," I said, turning back around. "Can I trust you to take Iris back to Davenport House? I need to speak to Marcus. If my aunts are there, do me a favor and tell them what I've just told you."

Ronin's smile turned devilish. "I can take her to my place—"

"No," I said, seeing Iris laugh. "Davenport House. I mean it, vampire. Don't test me."

Ronin clicked his heels and gave me an army salute. "Yes, captain." Then he stepped next to Iris and offered her his arm, which she took happily.

I watched the couple move through the crowd of paranormals, winding their way around the Night Festival. Ronin's head was high and proud like he was escorting the most beautiful woman in the world. I didn't have time to think of what might be happening there. I had more pressing matters to take care of. Like stopping Winnie from cursing me again because I had the feeling she wouldn't stop until I was dead.

When I couldn't see Ronin and Iris anymore, I turned and made my way across the street toward the gray stone building with the large letters—HOLLOW COVE SECURITY AGENCY.

I'd been to this building multiple times and I'd never once noticed the second floor. The last time I was here, I'd been too busy worrying about whether the front door was locked or if anyone was headed our way when Ronin and I broke into Marcus's office to even realize there was another floor to the building.

Now that I knew, I saw the side entrance to the left. Shadows stretched out long and dark on either side of the building. The streetlight gave me just enough light to see where I was going. I reached for the side door, pulled it open, and stepped into a small entrance with a tall staircase that led to another platform. Dim yellow light spilled from the single ceiling fixture.

I hurried up the stairs to the landing and faced the only door. I glanced at the numbers stenciled above the door—295B. I listened, but I couldn't hear anything. He might not even still be here. My heart thrashed in my chest, probably from going up all those stairs.

Making up my mind, I lifted my fist and knocked three times.

Nothing.

I knocked again—

The door swung open, and lo and behold—a wet Marcus—with only a white, itsy bitsy towel wrapped around his trim waist.

Holy.

Moly.

Guacamole.

All my thoughts evaporated from my head. Instant brain-freeze. Yes. Seeing a half-naked Marcus would do that to a person.

"Uh…" I said, still suffering from my brain-freeze, or rather, brain fart. And yet, I was always so articulate in times of seeing uber-sexy, half-naked men. In my head.

Though my brain might have been experiencing a temporary malfunction, heat spiraled through the rest of my body as though I'd just walked into a sauna as I reacted to this nice piece of man-flesh. He was perfectly proportioned and muscled like a Greek statue. His dark hair fell around his square jaw in wet, messy strands, making me want to run my hands through it. He did have amazing hair.

To add to the sexiness, Marcus leaned on the threshold. "Tessa? What are you doing here?" His voice was smooth, a deep mellow tone, and rolled over my skin as though he were touching it.

I blinked and then swallowed. And blinked again. "Why are you only wearing a towel?" When in doubt, go with the obvious.

The chief cocked a brow, a smile tugging his lips. "I was in the shower when you knocked."

"Oh. Right." *Oh, right?* What the hell was wrong with me? My eyes drifted to his tanned, no fat, just lean muscle chest, my pulse throbbing in my throat. Did I mention it was hairless? With rows of tanned, really pretty muscles?

I jerked my gaze up when I realized I'd been staring a bit too long. Marcus caught me gawking and his smile widened to show a slip of teeth. Great. Just freaking great.

"You know, you shouldn't greet people at the door half-naked," I said, wishing I had one of the festival's pamphlets to fan my hot face. "What if I was Gilbert? Or Martha?" Martha wasn't a good example. The witch would have probably thrown herself at him.

Marcus crossed his arms over his chest, biceps bulging. "Why? Does it bother you?" He leaned on the doorframe, unashamed in all his half-naked, golden glory.

Nervous laughter bubbled up. "No. I mean, yes. Yes, it does." When did I become a blabbering fool?

He eyed me with that smile again. "What happened to your cousin? Iris, was it?" By his tone, I could tell he didn't buy that Iris was my cousin. Right now, it didn't matter.

"Look," I exhaled. "I have some news about Myrtle's death, the break-in, all of it."

"Which break-in? The one from the safe or the one from my office."

Oh. Shit.

"The safe," I said, playing dumb, but my nonexistent poker-face probably betrayed me. "I know who's responsible." I should have asked about his office break-in. The fact that I didn't made me look guilty. Too late.

A muscle jerked in Marcus's face. "Who?"

"Winnie Wilde."

Marcus stared at me. "Winnie Wilde? One of the Seers at the festival? The one who accused you?"

"Yes, yes, yes," I dismissed him with a wave of my hand. "I know how this sounds. But listen." I told him quickly about Gilbert's ring. All of it. I even found myself blabbing about Iris. Might as well. Seeing as he was a chief, he would have connections and contacts about missing witches. He could help find more about where Iris was from and who she was. And it felt… right that I was telling him all of this.

"Winnie tried to kill me," I told him after a moment. "She used the Elder ring and did a killing curse. She's going to try again. I might not be so lucky anymore."

Marcus had listened attentively the whole time without saying a word. "This is what you were hiding from me. Is there anything else I should know?"

"No," I shook my head. "That's all of it."

Marcus's gaze fixed on me. "Where's Gilbert now?"

"Passed out next to a park bench. He doesn't remember who asked for the ring."

A slow, lazy, predatory smile touched his lips. "I've got my ways to make people give me what I want."

I had the faintest impression he wasn't talking about Gilbert. "I'm sure you do. But... shouldn't you be looking for Winnie?"

"Why?"

My eyes widened in exasperation. "Why? Haven't you heard a word I've said? Or did I waste my time coming here? You need to arrest her. That's what you need to do."

Marcus raised a brow. "Arrest her? Based on what? A hunch?"

I frowned, remembering all too well how quickly he'd dragged me in for questioning. "Well, if you won't, I will." I had no freaking clue if the Merlin Group arrested people. Though I could push Winnie down the basement stairs. Yeah. That brought a smile to my face.

"Why are you smiling?"

Whoops. There went my face again, betraying me. "What? Nothing." I sighed. "So, you're really *not* going to do anything about Winnie?"

His eyes flicked over my face as though he liked what he saw. "I didn't say that. I'll look into it."

"You'll look into it?" Why was I repeating his words like a halfwit?

Marcus's brows came together. "I will. But first I want to know more about this ring and where it came from. And Gilbert's going to tell me."

"Fine." I guessed that was good enough for now. "Okay, then. Ummm. I guess I'll leave you to it. Gotta go." I half turned and said, "If you do get Gilbert to blab, make sure to pass it along to the Merlin Group." I blinked. "Please." Thought I'd add that in there, just in case. I gestured with my finger at his body. "And make sure you cover up next time. The next woman might think you're coming on to her, looking all sexy and wet." What the hell was wrong with me. "What? Why are you looking at me like that?"

A light danced in his eyes. "There are two more nights left to the Night Festival."

"Exactly, so we need to move fast—"

"Are you going to go on another date with Adan?"

I stared at him, shocked. "I'm not exactly sure." Why was he asking me this?

He raised a brow. "You're *not* sure. So if he asked you out again, you're not sure if you'd say yes?"

Where the hell was this going? Did he just inch closer? "No," I said, realizing I *didn't* want to go out with Adan again. Not that he wasn't nice. He was very nice, just, the "it" wasn't there. I didn't feel any connection, like he was my cousin or something. Yes, I knew some cousins got it on in some parts of the world, but I wasn't going to go there. "No," I repeated, shaking my head. "I'm not going to go on another date—"

Marcus leaned forward, and before I could react, a hard hand grasped my waist and pulled me close as if to tango. Then he planted his lips over mine.

My brain exploded.

I'm not going to lie and say I hadn't fantasized a gazillion times about kissing Marcus—especially after he'd carried me home *naked*—because I had. But I will say this; daydreams had nothin' on this, baby.

Heat rushed from my lips to my toes like a giant hot flash. When his tongue brushed my lips, I nearly moaned. Okay, maybe I did just a little. Warmth pounded through me as his hand cupped my ass. I opened my mouth and our tongues touched.

Oh. My. God. I think I just spontaneously combusted.

He tasted like a fine wine, and I found myself wanting more. There was nothing gentle about his kiss. It was feral, almost with a desperate need, filled with a fiery passion. I fell against him, intoxicated by his scent, his taste, all of it. Desire pounded in my veins at the feel of his hard body pressed against mine. A sliver of thrill hit when he let out a tiny growl. Damn. I couldn't remember the last time I'd been kissed like that. Oh, yes, I could—never.

My head swam. I was kissing Marcus. I was kissing the chief and I liiiiked it.

I pulled back before things got messy, which was me ripping off my clothes and jumping the chief right there on the platform. Hell, I nearly saw stars. It was *that* good.

"What the hell was that?" I growled, trying to get my composure back. But I knew exactly what that was. That was a rip-your-panties-off kind of kiss. The pulse-pounding hell-of-a-kiss left me breathless and wanting more. Oh, dear.

Marcus stood there, still wearing just a towel and a smug smile. "What do you think it was?"

My jaw fell. "If you did that just to prove something to Adan, I'm going to kick your ass—which is a very fine ass—but I'm still going to kick it."

Marcus laughed. "You're a Merlin. You figure it out." And with that, the half-naked chief closed the door, leaving me standing on the landing all hot and bothered and a little breathless.

Chapter 20

Marcus had kissed me. And I'd kissed him back.

It was a good thing I walked back to Davenport House alone, trying to sort out what the hell had just happened. High on emotions, I waddled like a drunk, never really focused on where I was going. I was drunk on a kiss. A freaking kiss.

You'd think I was a teenager, reacting to her first kiss. But Marcus's kiss had sparked something in me that I hadn't thought I'd ever feel again, not after what I'd experienced with my ex. A thrill of emotions sifted through me.

The possibilities, the connection between us, and the heat—oh, yeah, there was that.

Guess Iris had been right. There *had* been something between us. Either I'd refused to see it, or I just didn't want to because I was afraid. I'd had my share of bad experiences, so the possibility of starting a relationship with Marcus terrified me. Was I even ready for it? Did I want this?

There was no denying the sexual chemistry between us. Hell, you could build a bomb with it. But there was attraction and then there was… everything else. Sexual attraction could only go so far. You needed to be compatible. You needed to be friends. Relationships took hard work. Was Marcus a relationship guy? Or did he want to have hot, out-of-your-mind sex and just leave it at that?

And that look he gave me? He looked… smug. Like he knew the effect his kiss had on me. *Arrogant monkey.*

I couldn't and wouldn't let my emotions make my decisions. Because those types of decisions ended up being stupid. I had to be smart. Kiss or not, I wasn't sixteen, and though the chief was sexy as sin, I had more pressing matters to deal with. Like a ring of power and a crazy witch who wanted to do me in, that's what.

The Night Festival's music and the sound of voices faded behind me until I could only hear my shoes hitting the sidewalk as I walked further and further away. There were two more nights left of the Night Festival. Now that Winnie knew I was onto her, I hoped Marcus moved quickly because I doubted she was going to stick around much longer.

The silver rays of the moon vanished as a dark cloud snuffed out its brilliance, bringing forth the scent of rain. I hit Charms Avenue and made a left, pushing my thighs a little faster. I did not want to be caught in the rain, though the idea of some cool rain might be just the thing to extinguish my hot, hormonal flashes.

There I went again, thinking of Marcus. Damn him and his hot bod.

Just don't do it, Tessa.

I walked faster. Sparks of light pulled my attention to the sky again.

"Green lightning? That's weird?" But this was Hollow Cove, where weird was a necessity, a way of life. Besides, the green lightning was probably just part of some gimmick from the Night Festival.

When the air dropped by twenty degrees a moment later, I knew something was definitely wrong.

I halted, listening. A darkness crept all around, like a smoky, slithery mass that whirled itself like an ethereal black mist.

"Okay, definitely *not* normal."

Immediately a cold sensation crawled over my skin like I'd just stepped into a human-sized refrigerator. A second later, a surge of heat moved along the surface of my skin, from the tips of my fingers and toes to my head. A hum of energy filled the air as a familiar pulsing flowed in and around me.

Magic. Raw and powerful magic. The Elder ring.

Someone was pulling on its power. I was certain of it.

"Winnie? Is that you?" I mocked and cast a glance around but saw only the thick darkness. "Come out, come out, wherever you are."

I waited, not sure what to expect. I tapped into my will, pulling on the energy of the elements around me as I focused on the power words I'd memorized. I'd love to use one on that witch.

"How about you come out and we do this face to face? What do you say?" I called out, holding on to my magic and letting it tingle in and around me as it begged for me to release it. Okay, maybe not smart since she had a power ring. But I wouldn't show her fear. If I did, I was dead. This bitch had already tried to kill me once. And once was once too many.

With a sudden crack, the darkness shifted, thinning and pulling away until I could see the shadows of the street again. Only, it wasn't.

The street had changed from a road of quaint homes to a dark, faerie-tale wilderness with a thick forest and glowering trees. I was both seriously impressed and a little scared. I knew the ring amplified the wearer's power, but this was some serious glamour.

"Nice trick," I laughed, though it sounded forced and a little high. It dawned on me that I couldn't hear the Night Festival's festivities, or the crickets, or any of the night critters.

I weaved a power word on my lips, my heart pounding hard in my chest as I glanced around. This was hard-core magic, not some quick and dirty trick. It took concentration, and I knew Winnie was here somewhere near.

"Impressive," I called out, thinking I should be feeding her ego. "Spooky, but still impressive. So, why are you hiding? You're the one with the ring? How about you come out and show me your big, badass self, huh?" I had no clue what I was going to do once I saw her. I thought I'd just wing it and see what happened. Yeah, good plan.

I felt a sudden, slithering pressure on the back of my neck, my instincts' way of telling me someone or something was watching me.

A sudden buzzing reached me followed by a loud grinding and the snap of branches breaking as a sudden powerful gust of wind hit me. I took a step back as the air grew thick with electricity. I knew what that meant.

Lightning flashed above me, lit with a sudden angry green fire that slowly faded away. Sounds rang through the air, the crackling of lightning and the roar of thunder following. The angry clouds pressed in all around me, gracing the tops of the trees and way too low to be natural. That was no ordinary storm.

"Oh, shit."

A bolt of lightning slammed into the ground, two inches from my foot. Heat blared at my face like an instant sunburn. The bitch was trying to zap me like a fried chicken.

I had a split moment's thought of going after her, but this was *her* forest. She'd created it, and she could be anywhere. I might never find her.

"Time to go."

I spun and ran into the forest, which was technically, I hoped, down Stardust Drive. I ran hard toward the direction I believed was Davenport House, though all I saw was more and more trees.

The air crackled again. The buzz of electricity was so close it hummed over my scalp.

Instincts flared and I pulled on my will and shouted, "Protego!"

A white, semi-transparent half-sphere burst into existence, lifting over my head and back down into the ground.

A bolt of green lightning hit the half-sphere just above my head and bounced back.

"See? You're not the only one with a bag of tricks," I shouted, raising my fist for added effect.

I wavered as a slip of dizziness hit, the payment for using magic. Magic always took what was owed—a piece of the witch's life force—and made it its own, serving the spell.

Another bolt of lightning hit the top of my half-sphere and then another. My half-sphere shook, leaving the acrid scent of burnt hair.

I knew if I stayed here, right under this damn lightning cloud, I'd end up bald.

The air above me sizzled and popped. I crouched low, let go of my will, and when my half-sphere fell—I ran.

The lightning slammed into the ground where my foot had been a second ago.

"Ha! You missed!" I shouted. Very immature I know, but the fear in my gut was making me crazy. I put on a burst of speed and ran between trees and shrubs that shouldn't have been there.

The forest was dense and dark, and if it weren't for the magical lightning that lit everything in an eerie green glow, I'd be running blind. The air smelled of wet leaves and pine needles, which would have been normal, except for the acrid scent of sulfur that had a way of burning my nostrils.

Through a break in the trees, a light shone. It was faint, but I saw it. Light meant the end of this forest glamour, or so I hoped. There had to be an end to Winnie's magical reach.

I made for the light at a jog, just as a loud humming rose around me like I'd just stumbled upon a giant beehive. I slowed to a walk, not liking this one bit. The throbbing of my heart crammed my ears with a rapid beat.

Clicking, chirping, and buzzing came at me from everywhere at once. "This is going to suck," I mumbled and planted myself.

A dark mist came forward through the trees.

Scratch that.

Not a mist, but a cloud of thousands of bugs.

CHAPTER 21

The critters hovered for a moment and then they joined together, whipping around as they began to add themselves to a single mass. I nearly threw up in my mouth as it took shape and stood up, an enormous creature of vaguely human shape made of thousands of different insects. Green light shone from twin holes in its insect-writhing head. It stood about nine feet tall and twice as thick as me. Its legs were as wide as tree trunks, with its arms nearly just as large.

"Bugs? Seriously?" As a witch, bugs didn't bother me. They were a crucial part of our ecosystem. I was always the first one to save house spiders, catching them and letting go outside. But thousands, perhaps, millions of creepy crawlers coming together to make a giant humanoid creepy crawler? That was a whole different, skin-crawling-creepy story.

The bug-creature lifted its head and opened its mouth. "You are hard to kill," it said. Its voice was a sound like that of a harmonica, and not at all like Winnie. But I knew she was in there somewhere, controlling this beast with the ring's magic. "But I will kill you."

I gave it a finger wave. "Winnie? Is that you? Glad you dropped the suit. I'm digging the bug-lady outfit, though. Or is it lady-bug?"

"You should have left things be," said the bug-creature, swinging its head from side to side. The slipping and crawling of thousands of bugs skittled and hummed, adding to the overall eerie effect. Damn, it made my skin want to crawl off my own body and run away.

"Oscar-worthy visual effects," I told it. "But I'm not about to let you kill me. I do have some self-respect."

Critters moved along the thing's face, pulling and spreading until it looked as though it was smiling. Yikes. "I'm going to do much worse to you... than what I did to her."

I flashed a smile. "Thanks for the heads up."

The bug-creature raised its arms, gesturing and making my skin tingle. "You're nothing. Just a washed-up wannabe witch who happened to be born into the right family. You're no Davenport witch."

I pursed my lips in thought. "Tomayto… tomahto…"

Bugs slipped over its features into a deep frown. "You should have stayed away. Should have stayed in New York."

I cocked my head. "What's the matter, Winnie? Were you not hugged enough as a child? Is that it?"

The bug-creature lifted an arm and pointed at me. "You're finished."

"Me finished? Nah. I'm just getting warmed up."

The bug-creature thrashed its arms and wailed, a sound of thousands of angry wasps and howling wind.

My jaw gritted as I gathered my will and focused, tapping into the elements as energy coursed through me. "Come on, ladybug."

Then, it opened its maw, or the part of crawling bugs that looked like part of the jaw, and I could see the darkness inside, moving in a slippery blackness.

Shoots of wasps and locusts spilled out of the bug-creature like a fireman's hose. (Yes, I know how that sounds.)

I lifted my arms and cried, "Ventum!" Pouring out my energy as I reached for the wind.

A powerful gust blasted from my outstretched hands and hit the shoot of bugs like a giant swatter. The force sent half of them blasting in the opposite direction while the other half smashed against the surrounding trees.

I felt a slip of energy as the power word took payment. But I was high on adrenaline, and I had a hell of a lot more fight in me.

By the time I heard the howl, it was too late.

A bug-made fist smashed into the side of my head. I fell to the ground on my knees, blinking the pretty white and black stars from my vision as I tasted blood.

"Ouch," I spat on the ground. "Not bad."

The bug-creature laughed, a horrid, buzzing, wet cackle that sent a jolt of fear through me, and it nearly made me throw up.

"You definitely don't hit like a girl." I staggered to my feet, tired but mostly pissed. "But neither do I."

I'd learned a new power word a few weeks ago. Probably the most dangerous. They'd said never to use it. Witches probably died using it... and I was just crazy enough to try it.

The bug-creature rushed me.

The power of the elements stirred in me.

"Evorto!" I shouted as power and magic coursed through my outstretched arms and lashed out at the bug-creature.

The creature staggered as the power hit, and its makeshift eyes glowed green, full of hatred. Its body grew and grew as a foul greenish smoke rose from its body. It opened its mouth to scream but exploded into a mass of insect bits and guts as though it had swallowed a grenade.

I ducked, but of course, not fast enough, and was hit by slippery goops and tiny hard things I did not want to think about. Thank the cauldron I closed my mouth in time.

Exhaustion swept over me with the effort of the power word, and I scowled down at the slop of insect blood and guts.

"You're a nasty piece of work. You know that?"

I knew Winnie wasn't done with me yet, and I wasn't about to sit around and wait for her next trick.

Feeling like I was in serious need of a shower, I started running again.

Something hard caught me in the chest and sent me sailing backward like I was hit with a two-by-four plank.

I hit the ground hard, my breath escaping my lungs. Rolling over, I tried to get some air into my lungs, but every breath sent jarring pain through my ribs. Well, damn. I thought I might have broken a rib or two.

Weaving a power word in my head, I got to my feet, letting my magic spindle around me.

Wood snapped, and a twenty-foot oak tree bent forward and swiped a branch as thick as my waist towards my head.

Well, shit.

I dropped to the ground and rolled again, my power word evaporating from my brain as fear replaced it. Leaves grazed the top of my head, telling me I'd just missed it.

"Great. Now the trees are attacking me." Backpedaling, I shot to my feet, adrenaline masking some of the pain in my chest, and sprinted forward, not knowing where I was going and not caring. I just wanted out of this forest.

At that moment I knew two things. One, I had to get that ring from Winnie, and two, if I didn't get out of this godforsaken forest, the trees were going to crush me like a bug.

The loud grinding of wood split the air behind me—

Something grabbed my ankle and yanked me back. I screamed as searing pain flared up around my ankle and something cold cut through my skin.

I whirled around and saw a dark green vine with black thorns wrapped around my ankle. Well, at least I knew where the pain came from.

"I really hate your forest!" I shouted.

I kicked at the vine with my other leg, and the damn thing tightened around my ankle, making me hiss. Gritting my teeth, I reached out with my fingers searing in pain, slipping and sliding around my blood as I desperately tried to tear the vine from my ankle. But the more I pulled, the tighter the vine squeezed.

"I hate these vines more!" If I wasn't in such pain and scared out of my mind, I might have admired the magic, the control of the elements like this. But right now, it felt like someone was taking a razor blade to my ankle and sawing.

A few seconds of trying to pull the vine free and failing, my hands were shredded, oozing blood and looking like the time I'd been attacked by a horde of feral cats because I tried to pet one of them—okay, grab one of them.

A snap pulled my attention to the left. And then I watched, horrified, as another vine from hell lifted from the ground and wrapped around my other ankle.

Oh. Shit.

Then a third. A fourth. A fifth and sixth.

"Why do I get the feeling something bad's about to happen?"

The vines around my ankles heaved and I suddenly found myself hauled up into the air, swinging upside down from my ankles and staring at the ground.

Okay, that's when I *really* started to panic.

Blood rushed to my head, making it hard to focus. My ribs burned with the effort to breathe. I blinked at the upside-down world and watched as the vines joined the trees, whipping through the air apparently of their own volition. They writhed together into what I suspected was a make-shift baseball-tree-bat.

The trees were going to use me as a witch piñata.

Oh, hell, no.

That jumpstarted my survival mode. Screw this. I was going to burn them all down.

The vines around my ankles tightened, as though they'd sensed what I was about to do. Shaking with effort, I hauled myself up, clasped my hands around the vines at my ankles, tapped into my will, and cried, "Accendo!"

Fire blasted from my palms as the magic tore from me in a blinding burst of agony as if I'd thrust my hand into my stomach and ripped out a clump of entrails. The fire crawled and spread over the vines, wild and hungry until it climbed up and reached the trees beyond. The scent of burning wood became obvious, mixing with the hard aroma of sulfur.

And just like any fire in the woods, it spread, growing until the world around me was a wash of pretty oranges and yellows and reds. And then, as though the curtains of Winnie's magic fell, the glamour lifted, revealing familiar rows of houses and neatly trimmed hedges.

It worked. Which also meant now I was loose.

I hit the ground hard, back first, followed by my ass. "Ow."

"Tessa? What on earth are you doing on the front lawn?"

I knew that voice. It belonged to a tall, pointed-looking witch who could send you running with just a frown. Dolores.

I rolled over and blinked. Dolores stood on the porch, hands on her hips. "What on earth happened to you? You look terrible."

"Thanks."

Dolores let out a sigh. "Well, you caught us just in time. We were just about to head out to the Night Festival. Stop lazing around and get in here." She stormed back inside the house.

Wincing in pain, I turned over on my back again and stared up at the black sky peppered with brilliant stars. "Why me?"

Chapter 22

I drew up a chair and sat next to Beverly at the kitchen table. Tired and exhausted from my ordeal with Winnie playing the forester, I just wanted to take a hot shower and crawl into bed.

But I couldn't rest, nor could I feel the soothing comforts of a feathered pillow. My mind was too busy imagining Ronin's head exploding.

"I can't believe he didn't come back here," I growled, my head pounding. "When I *explicitly* told him to bring her here. We don't know who cursed Iris. They could be at the festival." I shook my head. "I can't believe he would do this."

Beverly smiled at me. "He's a vampire, darling," she said, as though that was answer enough.

"Well, I'm going to strangle him when he gets here." If he took Iris back to his place and pulled his vampire mojo on her, I was going to castrate him. Iris was still only just recovering from her curse. I had no idea if her magic could handle a vampire's gift of persuasion.

"He's so dead." I grabbed my phone. He hadn't answered any of my texts, twenty of *"You bring back Iris now, or I'm going to cut off Little Ronin!"*

My mood had worsened when I saw the texts from Adan and the five missed calls. "Tessa. I'm worried about you. Call me," the message had said.

Great. I'd missed the chance to apologize to Adan while I'd been too busy getting my ass kicked by bees and trees to answer the phone. Now he must have thought I was a giant asshole. Adan was a classy, nice guy. He deserved an explanation.

I made the mental note to call him as soon as I woke from a small nap, which my body desperately needed. It was half-past one in the morning. I didn't function well that early, and I needed some sleep.

Right after I kicked Ronin's ass.

"Here. Drink this." Ruth placed a cup of something hot in my hands. "It'll heal your ribs and take care of the bruising and the scratches." Her blue eyes rolled over my face, and she forced a smile.

"I look that good, huh?"

"You've had better days, darling," said Beverly, a faint smile crossing her face.

I sighed, braced myself for the awful tasting drink, and took a sip. Yeah. Worse than I thought. "Tastes like toads," I ground out, making Ruth break out into a fit of giggles. Not that I would know what toads tasted like. It just fit. Grimacing I took another sip because I knew I needed it, and I'd be a fool not to trust in Ruth's healing drinks.

"What *I* want to know," said Dolores as she took the chair directly in front of me and sat with a large book in her hands. "Is if Winnie killed Myrtle and took the Elder ring... why does she want to kill you?"

I gagged as I took another gulp. "She knows I'm onto her, that's why. She told me as much with her giant ladybug puppet." The thought of that eerie bug puppet had my skin riddling in goosebumps.

I'd told my aunts everything as soon as I had dragged my butt into the kitchen: Gilbert's keeping the Elder ring a secret, Winnie's involvement, and her trying to kill me (skipping the part where Marcus had planted that rip-my-clothes-off kiss on me).

I tipped the cup and drank the rest of the foul-smelling healing liquid. "So, anything you know about this ring would be really helpful."

Dolores dropped the heavy book on the table, making everyone jump. "I'm way ahead of you." Her long fingers flipped through the pages and then pointed to a particular page. "It says, and I quote, *'the Elder ring is a powerful magical object that dates back to the fifth century created by the witch Samuel Wordsworth by use of a celestial metal.'*"

I leaned forward in my seat. "Celestial metal? You mean… metal from Heaven?"

Dolores stared at me through her eyelashes, frowning. "That's exactly right. Now, don't interrupt."

"Sorry," I smiled at her and her cute frown.

Dolores cleared her throat and began to read again. "*The ring helps the magical practitioner channel their magic. As a magical instrument, the ring centralizes all magical properties—elements, ley lines, and celestial—and thus acts as an amplifier, which gives more complex and powerful results. Though the ring is magical, it is, however, very difficult to master and requires much concentration and incredible skill to wield its power. Only advanced and skilled witches are known to have wielded its magic.*"

I let the words sink in for a moment, which was basically what Gilbert had said, except the part where it was made with celestial metal. That part was really interesting. Still, something didn't fit. "I never took Winnie as someone who possessed *incredible* magical skill."

Beverly gave a harsh laugh. "With a name like Winnie, the only skill she should have is with a dancing pole."

I let out a laugh and immediately regretted it, as my ribs were on fire. "But maybe that's exactly what she wants others to think," I said. The thought flitted through my head as the words spilled out.

"That she spins around a pole naked?" asked Ruth, her back against the kitchen sink as she towel-dried a pot.

"No." I shook my head, trying not to think about Winnie spinning around a pole, which was really hard, now that it was in my head. "That she's ordinary," I told them. "Invisible. Not capable of skill or great magic. But when in fact, she's a total badass."

Dolores leaned back in her chair, her brows pinched in the middle. "It wouldn't be the first time a witch purposely goes under the magical radar. Janet Moony always downplayed her abilities. Though in secret, or with her close friends—me—she'd let her true skill show." A shadow crossed her face. "She passed away a few years ago. Some witches don't like the attention."

"It's perfect. Smart," I said, feeling a warmth settle inside me. The constant pain in my ribs eased, making it more comfortable to breathe again, thanks to Ruth's magical healing drink. "That way, no one would suspect poor, ordinary little Winnie."

Ruth laughed. "Sounds like a wiener."

I laughed. God, I was tired. "Tonight, I saw a glimpse of what she's capable of, and it's not good. If this ring is as powerful as you say, we can't let her keep it." The cold that licked up my spine told me this was just the beginning. Winnie had plans for this ring. Otherwise, why steal it? She'd killed for it. She was dangerous. Guess what? I was dangerous too.

She'd tried to kill me, and now it was payback.

"You're absolutely right," agreed Dolores, and I lifted my gaze to her. "There's a reason why the Elder ring is kept locked away. In the wrong hands, it could have devastating results."

Beverly shifted in her seat and picked at her red, perfectly manicured nails. "If she's still in Hollow Cove, we'll find her. No one tries to kill my only niece and thinks she can get away with it. Not in my town."

"How are we going to find her?" I asked. "I don't think she'll be in her trailer. She's not that stupid."

Dolores's expression went pensive, as if making a decision. "We can track the Elder ring," she said. "Its power is a unique source with its unique imprint and magical energies. All we have to do is a quick location spell and follow the residual magic traces. Shouldn't take very long."

"You think she acted alone?" asked Beverly after a moment.

"She could have friends with her," agreed Ruth.

"No. She acted alone," I answered. "I don't think you can share the ring's power. Plus, she killed Myrtle. That tells me that she doesn't want anyone to know. She comes off as a greedy bitch."

"And ugly," added Beverly. "Don't forget ugly."

"We don't have the element of surprise anymore," I continued. "She knows I know. Which means she probably knows I've already told you and Marcus. If we don't stop her soon… it'll be too late."

"If you told Marcus," said Dolores. "Why hasn't he made an arrest?"

I let out a sigh. "He needs more to go on. Proof that I don't have at the moment." Like the ring, preferably with Winnie's finger still attached to it. "He said he'd look into it."

"Oh, he did. Did he?" Dolores's face took on a dark cast.

Restless, I glanced at each of my aunts. "Can the Merlin Group arrest her?"

The three sisters were quiet for a moment. "If you mean... do we have a jail or prison to put murderous and dangerous half-breeds?" asked Dolores. "Then your answer is no. The nearest witch prison is the Grimway Citadel in New York. We protect the town with spells, wards, and all the magic in our possession. We don't have dungeons or barred cells. We're not jailors."

Beverly laughed softly. "I was a jailor once," she said, a wicked smile on her face. "Handcuffs were involved... a whip... and a helluva lot of whipped cream."

Not going there. "I know it's her. But I can't prove it. I don't have witnesses, no magical fingerprints, nothing. But if we could get her to confess... then Marcus can arrest her." And let him deal with all the rest, right after I kicked her sorry ass for cursing me and trying to kill me.

"Don't worry, Tessa," said Dolores, a strange look in her eye that I wasn't used to. "We've got ways to make people talk."

Beverly gave me a sly smile. "Yes. And I'm really good with a whip."

"Or we could just toss her in one of my cauldrons in the garage," added Ruth. "It's worked before."

I flicked my gaze over to Ruth, wondering where my cute, innocent aunt had gone. "Do you have something that can give me a boost of energy? Like a witch's version of a Red Bull?" I knew the idea of sleep was useless. I was tired, but if we didn't stop Winnie now, we'd lose her and maybe never find her again.

I couldn't let that happen. We had to do something... now.

"I know what you're thinking, Tessa." Ruth walked over to me. "But you're in no shape to go anywhere."

"I am," I told her, my eyes moving to each aunt. "We need to do this tonight. It can't wait." The fact that no one interrupted me was enough to know they agreed, though they didn't like it. I looked at Ruth again. "Do you have something?"

Ruth smiled at me. "Yes. Goblin bones and poop of gnomes. Let me fetch some."

"Sounds... delicious." Yikes. "I'm going to need all the energy and strength I can muster to find Winnie."

"You're looking for Winnie?" said a male voice from the hallway.

I turned to see Ronin and Iris walk into the kitchen. Both fine. Both alive. For now.

My anger button exploded, and I shot to my feet, my chair falling with a crash behind me. "Ronin! I'm going to *kill* you!"

The half-vampire raised his hands in surrender. "Whatever I did, I can assure you it was with consent."

"I'm so mad at you right now," I growled. "Told—you—Iris—house." Damn. I couldn't even speak. "I ought to flog you."

"Can't wait," said the half-vampire, smiling.

"Sorry, Tessa," said Iris, her voice filled with guilt that matched her face. "We… lost track of time."

I glowered at him. "You're so dead."

"Before you ladies bring out the whips," said Ronin quickly, his hands still in the air. "The only place you're going to find Winnie is at the beach." He hesitated. "Winnie's dead."

Chapter 23

What's that expression again? No rest for the wicked? It really should say, no rest for the *witches*.

We were running.

My thighs pumped as I ran along the sand. Every step felt like my feet weighed an extra fifty pounds. The grunts and curses behind me told me Iris wasn't far behind. Ronin was sprinting ahead of me. If it weren't for Ruth's homemade energizer drink that hit me like twenty expressos, I'd be cursing right along with Iris. But now… I just flew over that sand like it was a walk in a park. I was Wonder Woman. No, Wonder Witch. Look at me go!

I ran like a gazelle, the golden dunes of Sandy Beach spread out before me. Moonlight glinted off the waters of the Atlantic Ocean, the waves rocking a few sailboats in the distance. The sounds of the waves crashing upon the shore brought a lot of memories of me playing on the beach and searching for seashells and neat looking rocks to add to my collections.

Large shingle-style homes, spread out with several hundred yards between them, stood above the rolling hills down to the shore. It was a dark night, but with the moonlight, it was manageable. I managed to start making out shapes in the darkness. It wasn't hard to pinpoint where I was going. The bobbing flashlights a few yards away on the shore were a dead giveaway.

During the day, Sandy Beach was crawling with local half-breeds, bathing in the sun, or out with their kids. At nearly two in the morning, it was deserted except for the owners of those flashlights and us.

The flashlights were all clustered together, supposedly standing around Winnie's dead body. It wasn't that I didn't believe Ronin that Winnie was dead. I just had to see it with my own eyes. Who knew? It could be a trick. The Elder ring was powerful, maybe even powerful enough to glamour a dead body into looking like her. At this point, anything was possible.

With my heart in my throat, I reached the body. Marcus looked up at me and for a moment while those pretty gray eyes locked onto mine. I forgot where I was and why I had run across the beach like a manic she-devil was after my soul. My pulse increased just a tad. That kiss had done a real number on me.

Control yourself, Tessa. It's not like I haven't been kissed before—just not like that.

Next to him stood Cameron and Jeff. Their big silhouettes seemed more imposing in the dark, and the fact that they wore black clothes didn't help. Their faces were barely visible cast in shadow.

The air moved next to me. Ronin promptly stepped in front of me, somewhat obstructing the view. "Told you. Damn. She looks like a Russian doll, all bloated like that," said Ronin, bumping into my shoulder. "Not that I'm into dolls or anything."

Marcus angled his flashlight to give me a better view of the body, and I strained not to flinch.

I looked down at what I was told was Winnie's body, but it was barely recognizable.

The body lay on its side. A large branch as thick as my arm pierced through her chest and came out through her back. Long strands of seaweed were wrapped around her arms and legs. The front of her red, pinstripe jacket was stretched tightly against its buttons like it was three sizes too small. Deep lacerations and abrasions marred her face and hands. Her eyes bulged out of their sockets, and I couldn't tell what color they were. Her lips were bulbous like she'd done way too many lip injections and looked like a duckbill. A thick tongue hid any signs of her teeth. Small chunks of flesh were missing, probably from tiny fish while she was in the water.

I didn't know much about rigor mortis, but I knew bodies bloated a day or two *after* they were dead. Either this wasn't Winnie, or the water had accelerated the stages of decomposition. Or perhaps, this was magic.

Because I felt it. Magic. Just below the surface, faint, but it was there. A light pulse of energy hummed like the beating of wings.

I reached into my bag and yanked out a small globe the size of an apple—Dolores's witch light. She'd given it to me before I left along with the spell that would light it up.

Holding out my hand I said, "Da mihi lux." *Give me light*.

The globe vibrated against the palm of my hand, and then a light shone through it warmly, as though I was holding a light bulb. It illuminated my hand and arm in soft yellow light. The globe shot into the air above me, and I nearly cried out in excitement that it actually worked.

The globe zoomed past me and hovered in the air just above the body, illuminating the scene in a soft yellow glow.

I was both glad and horrified to have the scene lit properly. Now you could see *every* gruesome detail.

Movement caught my eye and Iris unscrewed the lid of the vial Ruth had given her before we left, tipped her head back, and chucked it like you would a shot. Then, she knelt next to the body toward the head—and plucked a couple of hairs from the scalp.

Strange witch, that one. That's why I liked her.

"Hey! Don't touch that." Jeff marched over to her. "You can't do that. You can't remove evidence. What kind of idiot are you?"

Iris blinked up and him. "Why not? She's dead. It's not like she's going to miss them."

"You can't disturb a crime scene," growled Jeff. Though I couldn't see the expression on his face, I was betting it was a deep scowl. "There's still lots to examine. Evidence to bag. Details. We need those to determine the cause of death."

"You mean that giant toothpick in her abdomen isn't a clue?" I asked him and immediately regretted it at the look of pure fury on his face. "Well, I'm almost positive she wasn't killed here." Whoever she was.

"I agree," said Marcus, pulling my attention to him. "They probably tossed her into the ocean, hoping the current would take her away. But those of us who live here know the current in Hollow Cove always tends to bring us back to the shore. That's what this looks like to me."

I looked at Marcus. "So, you think the killer isn't from Hollow Cove?"

"I don't," answered the chief. "They wouldn't have done it this way if they were from here. They would have buried the body."

"Well." I straightened and let out a long breath. "I can tell you that magic was involved with her death."

"They thought sticking her in water would wash away the magic," said Iris, arching her brows knowingly.

"Exactly. But it didn't. We can feel it," I said, knowing that Iris could feel it too. I stared at the bloated face and chest of the witch, knowing the answer to the question I was about to ask. "How long has she been dead?"

Marcus stared at the body. "Without a proper autopsy, it's impossible to tell. Judging by the state of the body, looks like two or three days. But if magic was involved… maybe a few hours. I won't know for sure until I get the results from the pathologist."

Dread was heavy in my gut. "Are we sure this is Winnie?" I asked, my eyes on the swollen face, knowing I'd seen Winnie at the festival earlier tonight. "Look at her. It's really hard to tell. She could be anyone." She was wearing the same clothes I'd seen her in the last time I saw her, but then again, this could be someone else in her clothes. "Winnie could have pulled this off. She could have killed someone else and faked her own death." If anyone could pull this off, she could. And with the ring's power, anything was possible. I wouldn't rule anything out.

"Who else would it be?" said Marcus. "After we spoke I went to look for Gilbert, who wasn't in any shape to talk. I went looking for her instead. She wasn't in her trailer. No one had seen her for hours."

So, he had believed me. "You found her? You found the body?"

His gray eyes wrinkled at the corners. "No. A couple who thought they'd enjoy a bit of naked on the beach did. I happened upon them on my way here."

I whipped my head and glared at Ronin.

He raised his hands. "It wasn't me. Though I do enjoy a bit of naked on the beach."

The fact that Iris hadn't looked up at us and was now picking off a button off the dead woman's jacket and stuffing it inside her pocket told me that Ronin was saying the truth. Or maybe she was just into dead bodies and not Ronin so much.

"Okay," I breathed, still not convinced this was Winnie.

"We can smell her," offered Cameron, who immediately clamped his mouth shut. "I mean… what I mean to say is," he stammered, rubbing the back of his neck. "She has a witch scent. She's a witch."

"Okay… so she's a witch," I agreed, trying hard not to smile at his awkwardness. I knew shifters (though I still didn't know which kind they were since I'd never seen them in their beast shape) had a keen sense of smell. I wouldn't doubt for a second that she was a witch. But it didn't prove this was indeed Winnie.

Cameron nodded. "Most of the water washed that away and it's hard to smell beyond the stink of the sea, but yeah. It's there. She's definitely a witch. Ah… excuse me."

I watched as the husky shifter intercepted a curious Martha and an older man I didn't recognize from coming too close to the scene. Martha caught me staring at her and waved her hands enthusiastically, like we were old pals from way back when, hoping I'd let her get a closer look.

"Tessa! I want to know all the gruesome details!" she cried. Cameron dragged her back along with the rest of them.

I turned my gaze back to the body to see Iris poking at the dead witch's face with her fingers, which drew a scowl from Jeff. He looked like he was about to strangle her. Ronin, bless his vampire heart, was edging closer between Jeff and Iris, his taloned fingers out with a strange smile on his face as he stared at Jeff, not that anyone took notice.

"We won't know if this is Winnie Wilde until we do a DNA test," Marcus said, drawing my attention back to him. "Once we match the DNA from her trailer to this body, we'll know for sure."

"How long is that going to take?"

Marcus pulled out his phone from his jacket pocket. "Not long." He texted something. "Maybe two, three hours tops," he answered, not looking away as he typed.

I knelt next to the head as Iris pulled away strands of seaweed from the body, took a sniff, rolled it up, and dropped it in her pocket, making a large vein throb on Jeff's forehead.

Still wondering if this was truly Winnie, I leaned over the body to get a better look at the face, careful not to breathe in the scent of rotten flesh.

But when Iris pulled another thick clump of seaweed from the body's neck, my heart rate went from sixty to a thousand. Fear sent icy pricks racing down my limbs.

"Oh, no," I mumbled. The tension in my voice made Iris drop the seaweed in her hand.

Her wide eyes looked like a witch with her fingers in the spell jar.

"What? What is it?" Marcus knelt next to me, his handsome features creased in worry. "You found something?"

My eyes fell back on the body, to the vines with sharp thorns wrapped around her neck like barbwire. I recognized those vines.

The same vines had tried to kill me.

Chapter 24

Reason tried to force its way through my brain, but it seemed it was having a hard time catching up and processing what I was staring at. Whoever tried to kill me had killed this witch with the same MO.

I still was not certain if this was indeed Winnie, but whoever it was, she died a horrible and very painful death. We were dealing with a true psychopath, someone who enjoyed killing and torturing.

A stirring of unease slid through me. My gaze rolled over the vines, seeing the deep gashes around her neck. I swallowed hard. This could have been me.

"Whoever did this is the same person who tried to kill me tonight," I said, standing up and feeling a small ache around my ribs. Ruth's tonic was wearing off.

"Wait—what?" Marcus jumped to his feet. Panic and then anger flashed in his eyes. "Someone tried to kill you? When? Why didn't you call me?"

I waved a hand, thinking it weird that he thought he was my number one emergency contact because of what? The kiss? "Long story, but yeah. And they did it by using those vines," I said, pointing at the body. "Before that, though, there was this bug-creature—"

"The bug-creature?" Marcus crossed his arms over his chest, his phone still hanging in his hand. "You were attacked by killer vines and a bug-creature. Are you serious?"

I shrugged. "Usually not so much. But now, yes."

Ronin and Iris both laughed. Loved these guys.

I looked over at Marcus. "I hope now you realize I had nothing to do with this."

Marcus kept his gaze on me. "I never said you did. I was following protocol."

"Right. Protocol." I tried to glare at him, but my stupid face was trying to smile instead and probably making me look constipated. "You'll take care of the body. Right?" I knew my aunts had mentioned once or twice that Marcus was in charge of "cleaning up" crime scenes, and I was glad of it.

Marcus watched me, his gaze going sharp on mine. "That's right."

"Okay. Well, I'm done here." I reached out, grabbed the witch light that was still hovering above the body, and muttered, "Averte lumina." The light went out and I dropped the globe inside my bag. "Text me when you get your DNA results," I told Marcus as he gave me a nod, still looking pissed as hell at me. Strange, but I kind of liked it.

I looked at Ronin and Iris. "Come on, guys. Let's go."

Together, the three of us started making our way back through the sand dunes.

"What are you doing?" asked Marcus.

I looked over my shoulder at the chief, who was striding behind us. "There's a killer on the loose and a magical ring to find. I still have work to do."

"I'm coming with you," said Marcus, his voice firm.

I shook my head but didn't stop walking. "Why? You just said you were going to take care of the body. I'm *a* body, but not *the* body."

The chief was suddenly next to me. "Someone or something tried to kill you tonight... twice if you count the earlier curse."

"Okay. It wasn't the first and won't be the last." As a Merlin, I knew I was a target now. It was part of the job. It was something I'd have to live with from now on.

"You need protection," added the chief.

Ronin snorted and I glared at him. "I can protect myself, thank you very much. I'm not totally helpless."

Marcus walked along next to me, his shoulders bumping into mine as he walked. "With two tries on your life... I'm not so sure—hey!"

Iris moved her hand from Marcus's head. I hadn't even seen her move. The little witch was fast. She looked at me and winked. "I've got some hairs if you ever want to curse him."

I laughed. "Iris... you and I are going to get along just fine."

We reached the grassy knoll where the beach ended and the boardwalk started. A mob of half-breeds with wide eyes and wider expressions rushed past us and headed down toward the scene on the beach. The Martha-gossip network at its best, no doubt.

I felt sorry for Cameron but not so much for Jeff.

It was a perfect night for a stroll. Ronin and Iris mumbled to themselves as they walked ahead of us. With a warm breeze, the tall lampposts that connected to the boardwalk gave a more romantic and even mystical feel. Yet, even with all this pristine beauty, I couldn't shake off the dread that was slowly becoming a giant boulder inside my gut.

If Winnie was dead, if that was truly *her* dead body on the beach, who killed her? And who had tried to kill me?

Iris turned around, gave Marcus the once-over, and then winked at me. Yeah, not so subtle, especially when Marcus stuck out his chest a little more with a confident smile on his lips.

I felt like I'd dunked my head in lava.

I could have told the chief to buzz off. Could've. Would've. Didn't.

Looked like I couldn't stay mad at the chief for very long. Yup. I was in *serious* trouble.

Iris halted, dropped to her knees, and began to scrape up what looked like gum from the floorboard. I hoped that *was* gum and not something more sinister and smellier.

And just when things couldn't have gone weirder, they did.

A tall handsome witch strolled our way with the confident grace of someone who knew they looked good. The light of the lampposts hit his hair in a way that it almost looked like it was glowing. His smile would have women throwing themselves at him—possibly naked.

Crap. That handsome devil was Adan. Guilt was a hard ball that sprouted from my gut and fell to the ground between my feet somewhere. I forgot to call him. *Whoops.*

"Adan, hi... uh—I'm so sorry I didn't call you back," I stammered, as the tall witch came over. I didn't like the fact that I had to do this now with an audience. He wore a white T-shirt that snugged his fit chest under a black leather jacket and jeans. He looked fantastic with his blond hair arranged in just the right kind of messy. He was a terrific guy. Just... not the guy for me. "I shouldn't have left like that without an explanation. I'm a giant asshole. And I understand if you hate me." The guy did not deserve that.

"You left?" a smile appeared on Marcus's face that I wanted to slap off. "Must have been a bad date." A new grin hovered above him as he looked at Adan. "What did you do to make her leave?"

Ronin rubbed his hands. "I knew tonight was going to be exciting."

I glared at Marcus, wanting to jab him in the ribs. "It wasn't like that," I said, as Iris appeared in my line of sight off to the left. "Adan was a perfect gentleman. The date was perfect. I'm the asshat." I looked at Adan. "I am *truly* sorry. My life is a mess right now, with all the murders and being *blamed* for murder. I know it's no excuse. I just... wanted to give you a call and explain—which I'm doing a lousy job of—when things settled down a bit." At this rate, that was a giant never.

Adan lost some of his smile as his gaze lingered on Iris for a moment. I didn't blame him. She was a very pretty witch, though a little eccentric at times. Perhaps she should have gone on a date with him.

His eyes met mine and he flashed a casual smile. "No worries. I understand. Just glad to see you're okay."

Cue in more guilt. "Still friends?" I knew that was probably not what he wanted to hear, but I wasn't going to drag this witch into my hectic life when I didn't even know what I wanted. Well, I knew I didn't want to date Adan.

Adan's eyes flicked to Iris again. Maybe I shouldn't feel that guilty. I then realized I'd forgotten to introduce Iris to him. "Adan, this is my co—"

"I heard they found a body." A muscle twitched on Adan's face as he scanned the area behind me toward the beach.

"We did," answered Marcus, his tone all business.

"Whose?" Adan's gaze was still focused on the beach behind me somewhere.

"We don't know yet," responded the chief, his low voice penetrating. "But I'm sure we'll find out soon enough."

"How did they die?" asked the tall witch, his eyes everywhere but on us. "Do you know? Or do you have to guess that too?" His tone was polite, but there was also a sharp edge to it.

Marcus straightened, hints of steel tightening his face. He watched Adan with interest but didn't answer as his face twisted in annoyance. I was too tired to watch this testosterone fight.

"Carry on with the pissing contest, boys," I said quickly. "But we're leaving."

"My money's on King Kong," said Ronin as excitement flashed on his face at the prospect of a fight.

I rolled my eyes, my previous discomfort slowly turning into annoyance. "It was great seeing you again, Adan. But we need to head back. Right, Iris? Iris? I-i-iris?" I turned around, wondering why she didn't have my back. Her face was pale. And with her already pallid complexion, she looked like a human popsicle. "Iris. What's wrong? Tell me you didn't put that gum in your mouth." I cringed. "Iris? Are you okay?" I squeezed her arm gently. The witch looked like she was about to spew chunks.

Iris stared straight ahead without blinking, her eyes round and filled with fear. "It's him."

"Yeah, it's him," I said, my voice low. "It's *Adan*. I told you about him, remember?"

Sudden panic flashed on her face. "No. It's *him*. I remember now. He's the one who cursed me."

CHAPTER 25

You know the feeling when someone tells you something you can't quite get your mind around, and you've got that deer in the headlights look? You feel the wheel of your brain turning as it tries to catch up to the words. Well, I was having one of those moments.

"What?" I whipped my head around, my brain finally having caught up. I looked at Adan, seeing the all-around good-looking, charming, and polite witch, and not seeing how he could have cursed Iris. But then again. I didn't really know him.

I blinked and said, "Adan?"

"Involuta!" shouted Iris as she flung her hands forward with a vicious, murderous expression on her face.

I'd never heard that spell before. The magic between us White and Dark witches was a tad different. But there was no mistaking the tone of voice and the lethal look on her face.

Adan was going to get it.

With a pop of displaced air, Iris's body shuddered, her skin pulled and stretched, and then her frame shrunk, until a black and white goat stood in her place a moment later, her clothes a crumpled pile next to her hooves.

"Baaaa!" cried Iris the goat. "Baaaa!"

"Oh, shit." Ronin was next to the goat in a second. "What the hell is this?" He jumped back and forth around the goat, his hands splayed like he wasn't sure whether to touch it or not. "Iris? Baby? You okay in there? Okay, let's everyone calm down. I can work with this. Okay, now you've got hair—or is it fur? I don't mind women that go a little native. Turns me on. Gives me jungle vibes."

Well, at least now he could see her. Either the curse had evolved, or this was something else.

I stared at Adan and gave him my best hard stare. "Did you do this to her?" Though I didn't detect any sudden influx of magic, nor did I hear him utter a spell. His calm demeanor made all my warning flags go up, screaming to me that Iris was right.

The bastard had cursed her.

Adan lifted his hand. A plain gold ring that looked like a simple wedding band looped his index finger. I hadn't noticed it before but now it winked in the light of the streetlamp. The Elder ring.

I couldn't feel any magical pulses coming from it, nothing that would indicate a ring of power. But then again, Adan probably knew how to conceal the ring's power from being discovered.

He caught me staring. A smug satisfaction tugged the corners of his mouth up into a wicked smile. "She got in the way of my plans," he said.

Dark anger slid to the forefront of my mind. "You mean she discovered you were a lying murderous giant sack of crap? Smart girl."

"Weak witch," mocked Adan.

My jaw clenched. "The more your lips move, the more I want to drop kick you in the throat." Now I hated this guy, really hated him. He had me fooled, had us all fooled. I couldn't believe I felt guilty about standing him up. I needed to up my asshole radar.

Winnie had never stolen the ring. It had always been Adan.

From the corner of my eye, I saw Ronin take a step forward toward the tall witch. Canines bared, the half-vampire looked like he was about to take a chunk out of Adan's jugular. If I were a vamp, I would too.

"You cursed me too. Didn't you? When I tripped outside of Myrtle's tent. You put your hands on me," I said, realizing that was precisely when the headaches had started. And I never even noticed. "You killed Myrtle and Winnie, and all for what? The ring? For a little more power?"

Adan made a sound in his throat like I was a simpleton. "You know nothing."

"Enlighten me, dumbass."

Adan looked at me with an infuriating, satisfied-male look on his face. "You Merlin witches are all the same, insufferable know-it-alls."

I beamed. "You're welcome."

"That's it." Marcus pulled a pair of iron cuffs from inside his jacket. I knew exactly what those were. Iron was a natural magic repellent, so those cuffs would keep Adan or any magic practitioner from doing magic. "You got any spells to knock out this bastard? I'm tired of his mouth." He looked at me with a sly smile.

I grinned back. "You bet." Gritting my teeth as I pulled on all the elements around me. The air, the earth, the water, all shook with deliberate power. I felt it resonating through the elements around me as much as heard it, all echoing as they answered my call. Adan might have been able to curse me once, but he was going down.

Marcus shifted his weight next to me and crouched low, like he was about to hit Adan like a linebacker. Either that, or he was about to beast-out into his King Kong alter ego.

And Adan... just stood there, hands loose at his sides, with a self-confident smile on that damn handsome face that I wanted to jump-kick.

That's it. Now I was pissed.

With a power word on the tip of my tongue, I tapped into my will, pulled on the energy of the elements, and cried, "Inflitus!"

Only the kinetic force I'd called upon didn't hit Adan.

It hit me.

A sonic boom exploded all around us. I let out a howl as the explosion of magic slammed into me and blasted me off my feet. The air whooshed in my eyes, my clothes, and flapping hair as I soared in the air and flew fifty feet back.

That is, until I hit the tree.

Have you ever hit a tree at thirty miles per hour? Me neither until then.

I smashed into the tree trunk, feeling like a car had hit me in the back, and slid to the ground. If I hadn't begun to decrease in speed when I hit it, the crash would have killed me or left me paralyzed.

But I was alive. Wiggling my feet and my fingers, I wasn't paralyzed. Just in loads of fiery pain. My breath was slow and ragged, and everything hurt. Pain reverberated through my head and down my back. It was a miracle my spine wasn't shattered. I was going to need a bucket full of Ruth's healing tonic to heal this.

"Tessa!"

I managed to turn my head and blink, seeing a blurred version of Marcus. I groaned in pain, feeling like my limbs were useless, overcooked spaghetti noodles.

My mind was jumbled, and my thoughts were skimming through the hazy dull state I was slowly pulling out of. I must have hit my head pretty hard. An internal yelp of pain resounded in me, and with a push, I felt my magic leave me.

"Are you okay? How do you feel?" he asked. Panic slid behind the chief's gray eyes as he crouched beside the tree. "You hit that tree hard." He shook his head. "But you're alive."

I swallowed, my vision clearing. "I think… I think my spell backfired… it hit me… instead of him." I took a labored breath and laughed. "Damn. I almost killed myself with my own magic." But it had been Adan. Somehow, the Elder ring had propelled my magic onto me.

"Can you stand?"

Before I could answer, Marcus scooped me up in his arms. I was too tired and in too much pain to protest, though I didn't want to. There was something comforting and soothing about being in his big, strong, manly arms again.

I looked around. Fear hit when I remembered where I was and why I was here. "Where's Adan?"

The first thing I saw was Ronin petting Iris the goat's head while she glowered at him, and yes, she could do that.

But there was no sign of Adan. The witch was gone.

Chapter 26

"I can't believe I got beaten by a hit of my own magic," I drawled. "I feel like such an idiot. That's got to be some record in the book of the biggest failures of witch history." My arms ached from having them up over my head for more than two minutes.

Ruth's arms worked around me as she wrapped a magical healing dressing around my stomach and back. As soon as her magical bandage touched my skin, the pain in my back eased, and the burning on my skin dropped to a manageable throb. I had to hand it to Ruth, the witch knew what she was doing.

I wrinkled my nose. "Why does it smell like cabbage?"

Ruth gave me a pointed look. "It doesn't matter what it smells like as long as it works."

Dolores stood with her hands over her chest, her back leaning on the counter. "You're not the first witch to have had their magic hit them in the ass. But I'm sure the ring had something to do with it."

I nodded in agreement. I'd seen firsthand what the Elder ring was capable of. Now it was lost in the hands of a madman.

"Done." Ruth stepped back as I pulled down my shirt over her bandages. "You can turn around now."

She moved to the kitchen sink, turned the tap, and began to wash her hands. I guessed she didn't want them to smell like cabbage.

Ronin and Marcus, who had been instructed to step into the hallway and turn around while Ruth worked on my dressing, came back into the kitchen.

Ronin gave me a tight smile. "You all wrapped up like a mummy, Tess?" He took the seat next to Iris, who hadn't spoken a word since I'd performed the spell to transform her back into her witch self.

"I am." My heart squeezed at the pain on Iris's face. Everything had gone terribly wrong tonight.

"How you feeling, Tessa?" Marcus came to me, his beautiful face stretched with worry. I wasn't used to this gentle side of the chief. He was all muscle and power and dominance. This softer side... well... I liked it.

I smiled at him. "Like a wrapped gift." Our eyes met, and a surge of warmth went through me, disquieting and thought-provoking. My skin tingled at his nearness. I looked away before any of the others noticed the heat that was happening between us.

From the corner of my eye, I saw him hesitate, like he wanted to sit next to me but then thought better of it. He moved to lean against the wall opposite the kitchen table.

With my pulse throbbing a little quicker, I pulled my attention to Iris. "What can you tell us about Adan, Iris?" If I could get her to talk, maybe she'd pull herself out of her downward spiral for a little moment.

The Dark witch blinked and looked up me. "He and I..." her lips trembled, and I saw her take control of herself with great effort. "He was my boyfriend."

Ronin made an angry sound in his throat. "He's dead. I'm gonna rip his jugular."

"Take a number." I leaned forward, surprised that Ruth's magic dressing kept me from moaning in pain. "You're remembering."

Panic and then anger flashed on her pretty face. "He wasn't always such an asshole—

wait—no, maybe he was always an asshole. I was just too stupid to see it."

"Don't," growled Ronin. "Don't put yourself down. People can be great actors. Especially when they're after something."

Iris laughed without mirth. "Well, he sure as hell fooled me. He fooled me real good." Her face was strained with emotions. "A year I wasted my life with him. One year of him playing me." She shook herself and rubbed her face. "I found out what he was planning to do."

"About the ring?"

"Yes," answered Iris, her cheeks darkening. "He had all these papers and pictures lying around his office. It didn't take a genius to figure out what he was doing. And then he cursed me to shut me up."

"Insufferable witch," cursed Dolores, looking as mad as I'd ever seen her.

Ronin moved his chair back, balancing it on two legs. "He's dead. He's *so* dead."

My thoughts went to earlier tonight when we'd first encountered Adan. He hadn't been enthralled with her beauty, after all. He was just surprised to see her as a witch again and not as a ghost goat.

"I would have spent the rest of my life as some goat specter if you hadn't helped me," said Iris.

My heart clenched at the pain on her face. "Hey. You saved my life. Guess that makes us even." Not even close. I owed her, and I wasn't giving up. "Do you know why this ring was so important to him? Apart from the uber power it bestows?"

"He was broke," Iris continued. "The entire Williams family lost their fortune by bad investments and gambling a few months ago. He told me this was his way to get the family name back. The glory." She laughed low. "He wants to be a king or something."

I raised a brow. "A king?"

Iris nodded. "King of the witches. Or something equally stupid."

"He's lost his mind," ground Dolores. "There is no such thing. There are covens, groups, councils. There has never been a witch king, and there never will be."

"Tell that to Adan," said Iris. "I told him he was being an idiot… and then… well…"

"You joined the animal kingdom," I said, seeing a tiny smile on her face, but then it disappeared in the folds of her scowl.

Iris sniffed. "The thing is… Adan was never really good at magic. He never excelled like his father or even his mother. It was always a struggle to do magic, or so his mother said. I've seen him pay for spells that a five-year-old witch could do. It was a touchy subject, and he never let me do magic in front of him... he got... really mad."

I really hated that guy.

"He's a bigger loser than I thought," grumbled Ronin. "I love killing losers. Oh, I'm gonna hunt that bitch down."

"The thing is... without the ring," said Iris. "He's as magically potent as a rock."

"He's got small penis syndrome," I said, all eyes on me. "The ring is his Viagra."

Ronin snorted and high-fived me. Loved him.

"So the curse he put on you..." I said, wondering how Adan could pull something off like that if he wasn't magically inclined.

Iris met my eyes. "He bought it on the Shadow Market. A Dark curse from one of the worst Dark witches. All he had to do was say the invocation phrase and the curse would work itself. He gloated about it just before he did it."

The Shadow Market was the half-breed and paranormal community's version of the human Black Market. I'd never been, but I heard it assembled the worst of our people.

Silence covered the kitchen for a long time.

"He wants to rule over all of you," said Marcus, his eyebrows high. "All the witch covens and clans." He pursed his lips and said. "If he thinks he can rule the Merlin Group, he's a bigger fool than his ego." He smiled. "Love to see him try."

"Well, you just might." Adan wanted to make himself king? Over my dead body.

Iris shifted in her seat. "What happened to me tonight... does that mean I can never do magic again?"

My throat throbbed at the anguish in her voice. I opened my mouth and then closed it when I realized I had no idea. Unlike me, whereas my magic had simply bounced off Adan and hit me instead, Iris's spell hadn't worked at all. It had just turned her back into a goat.

Dolores and Ruth exchanged a look. Dolores let out a sigh. "We don't know. Until we figure out the exact spell he cursed you with, I'm afraid we can't reverse it."

"And if he dies?" I said, remembering the curse Samara had put on Dolores. The curse had left her because its caster was dead. "It should lift the curse, right?"

"It should," said Dolores. "Yes, that would most definitely lift the curse."

"Let's do it." A chair slammed as Ronin leaned forward. "You know where he lives. Right?" he asked Iris.

"West 57th Street in Manhattan. It's a high-rise apartment in New York City near Central Park."

Ronin spread his hands. "What are we waiting for? I say we go and take care of this sonofabitch right now."

"New York is hours away," said Marcus. "Even with the fastest plane, it'll take you about two hours. Driving from here to the airport—that's another two hours. By then, Adan will be long gone. Now that he knows we're onto him. I don't think he'll just wait around in his apartment to see who shows up."

"You never know," I said. "The guy is a total douche. He might be doing exactly that. Having a drink. Thinking he's won." Though I had to admit, it was a long shot.

Ruth shuffled forward and put a hand on Iris's shoulder. "Don't worry, dear. I have a few concoctions that will keep the curse dormant. Unless you want to be a goat again?" She smiled, her eyes wide and hopeful. "Goats are so cute. I've always wanted a goat. We have the perfect garden out back for a goat—"

"Yes, thank you, Doctor Doolittle." Dolores pulled her sister away from Iris. "I know this is hard to accept, Iris. But for now, there is nothing we can do. It's up to the Merlin Group in New York now and the Dark witch council," commented Dolores. "It's out of our hands. Adan is gone. We have to accept it. That reminds me, I need to call Greta and tell her. Knowing that miserable witch, she'll probably tell me this whole thing is our fault." She mumbled darkly to herself as she walked out of the kitchen to the hallway where the landline phone was.

My gaze moved to Iris again. Emotions cascaded over her, frightening in their rapidity: dismay, fear, anger, betrayal.

I knew what it was like to be betrayed by the man you loved. It hurt like a sonofabitch. And with time you learned to live with it, you learned to accept it, and then you moved on.

Ronin was watching her with a frightened look on his face, his jaw clenching, and his body shaking like he didn't know whether to hug her or leave her be. He looked like he was in hell.

I couldn't let Iris live the rest of her life like this. A witch who couldn't do magic... well... was practically *human*. Nobody wanted that. Seeing how she was dealing with it now, I could only see a dark depression on its way. I didn't think she'd recover from it. Adan, yes, she'd recover from him. But not being able to do magic ever again? No, I didn't think so.

I had to do something...

The back door to the kitchen opened and Beverly walked in, her face flushed. "Girls. We have a problem."

I stilled. "Adan's back?" Good, I was going to find that witch and pop his head off like a dandelion. I was almost giddy with excitement.

"No," said Beverly, tucking a strand of blonde hair behind her ear. "Though I wouldn't mind showing him to the basement if he was."

"What is it, Beverly? You're all out of condoms?" sneered Dolores.

Beverly shook her head. "It's the paranormals at the Night Festival. They've gone completely mad. Rumors of Adan have them all up in a frenzy. Well," she put a hand on her hip. "They almost tipped poor Ben's tank over. Can you imagine? Well, maybe I should invite Ben to stay with me in a hot tub for a while. Until things settle down."

Ruth giggled. "We don't have a hot tub."

"Honey," said Beverly. "I can find a hot tub."

"Okay, okay," Dolores waved her hands impatiently. "So what you're saying is… the festival's gone mental? Is that it?"

Beverly shrugged. "Yes. We need to get down there and talk some sense into these people before they ruin everything and there won't be a Night Festival tomorrow."

"Let me get my shawl," said Dolores. Her gaze snapped to me. "You stay here, Tessa. You're not fully healed. This is an easy fix. Beverly and I can handle it. And I'm very good at making people listen to me." Dolores moved out of the kitchen and disappeared down the hallway. Beverly moved quickly behind her, her heels clicking on the hardwood.

"I better go too," said Marcus, looking at me. "People paid good money to see five nights at the Night Festival. I have to make sure we get them. Are you going to be okay?"

I smiled. "I am. Ruth's magicked me back to health," I said, and Ruth beamed before she moved back to the stove.

"Come on, Iris." Ronin gestured with his hand. "The distraction will be good for you. Plus, you don't want to miss Dolores's showdown. Best show of the year, trust me."

At that Iris gave a little smile and followed Ronin out the back door. Marcus watched me a beat longer than necessary before he too got up and left through the back door.

"You're not going, Ruth?" I asked, watching her stir her simmering pot of what I suspected was something to help Iris.

Ruth turned around. "No. I feel so terrible about what's happened to Iris. She's so unhappy. I just can't stand it. I need to make sure my potion is the best it can be. No witch should not be able to do magic. It's unnatural. Oooh. I just hate that Adan."

"That makes two of us." I sighed, wishing I could find a way to get to New York. "I could summon that cute demon dragon Obiross again." I shook my head. "He won't be fast enough, though. It's just too far."

That's it. I'd failed. The murderous witch had gotten away, and there was no way I could stop him.

Anger rising anew, I thought of how that bastard Adan had vanished like he'd been beamed up by Scotty on the USS Enterprise. It had been the trick of all tricks. Just wish I knew how he'd done it.

"If only I knew how he vanished like that," I said. "It was so weird. Just vanished, like he'd stepped into another dimension." A thought occurred to me. "Maybe he stepped through a Rift into the Netherworld?" Rifts were gateways to the demon realm. They were gaps in the Veil—that invisible layer that protected us and kept the Netherworld's creatures from crossing over into our world. "Maybe he's hiding there?" That was a longshot. I'd never heard of witches, Dark or White, crossing over. But I was running out of ideas.

"He probably just rode a ley line," said my aunt, stirring her pot.

All the hairs on my body, yes, *all* of them, rose. "What did you say?" My heart pounded in my throat as I stared at my aunt.

"Adan," said Ruth as she turned around, looking like a slimmed-down Mrs. Clause with her rosy complexion and fluffy white hair. "He probably just jumped a ley line. That's how he did it. That's how he *vanished*."

Chapter 27

It took a few moments to register what Ruth had just said.

I mean... I knew ley lines were powerful, and witches and other magic practitioners drew from them... but riding?

"Why don't *you* jump the ley lines," said Ruth, as she put the spoon of red glob in her mouth and tasted it. "You'd be there in an instant. Hmm. Needs more mandrake." She pinched some green powder from a container between her fingers and sprinkled it over her steaming pot.

I leaped to my feet, my heart thrashing in my chest like I had a jackhammer in there.

"Ruth? What do you mean *jump* the ley lines?" I didn't remember reading anything about jumping ley lines in any of the books Dolores gave me to read. Why the hell not?

"Ride them." Her happy face met mine. "Didn't you ever ride the ley lines when you were little?"

I blinked at her. "No. I think I would have remembered something like that."

"Well, some witches use brooms. But those of us fortunate enough to live near a ley line and know how to use it ride them."

"Ride them?" I questioned.

"That's right. It's really quite simple. Yes, it might hurt a little, and maybe you'll end up losing an arm or a leg—but it's a lot of fun." Her blue eyes were wide and filled with excitement. "And don't worry. If you lose an arm or a leg, we can always track them down using a tracker spell…" She cocked her head to the side, thinking. "Attachment is a little more complex…" She patted my shoulder. "But you never know till you try."

"Great pep talk." I stared at my aunt. I would have to be mad to try and ride a ley line. But what other choice did I have?

"Why didn't Dolores or Beverly tell me about riding the ley lines?"

Ruth shrugged. "Probably didn't occur to them. Did you tell them how he disappeared?"

Come to think of it, I didn't. "No. I was too busy yapping about how I kicked my own ass."

Ruth let out a howl of laughter. "I hope you stay with us forever." She turned around and started humming, stirring her pot.

She had no idea how those words affected me. My eyes burned at the thought. I'd never had family who'd wanted me before, and even at almost thirty years of age, it felt amazing.

I blinked the burn from my eyes. Adrenaline surged, making my legs shake. I was pumped. I was going to do this.

"Ruth," I said, my pulse rising. "If he did ride a ley line, that means he knows where to find them, right? It means… there's one near where he lives."

"Yes," answered my aunt without turning around. "That sounds about right."

A mix of adrenaline and excitement coursed through me and was intoxicating. I grabbed my phone and Googled Mapped the address Iris had said. And in less than thirty seconds, I had his address in New York. Not so smart after all, you giant asshat.

"Adan must have a map of the ley lines then. He knew which one to ride that would take him home." Some of my initial adrenaline was fading. "But riding them is dangerous, right?" Because losing a limb sounded dangerous to me.

Ruth laughed as she spun around. "Well, if you mean... can you die from riding a ley line? Then yes. But then you shouldn't worry about that because you'd be dead." Her eyes were round as she laughed again, though this time it was creepy.

O-o-o-kay. "So... how do you do it? How do you know where you're going and when to stop? I don't want to end up in Antarctica, though a trip somewhere warm would be nice."

Ruth tasted the potion again and set her spoon down. "Well, each ley line has its stops, like a train has multiple stops—unless you take an express train. Then you go straight to your destination," she added with a grin.

"Okay, okay," I said, urging her on. "And then?"

"So, you jump the nearest ley line to you that goes through to New York where you want to go and just count the stops. Thousands of ley lines are placed at strategic points around Maine. You just have to pick the nearest one to you that will take you where you want to go."

That didn't sound half as bad. "How do I know how many stops I need?"

Ruth raised her finger and then rushed out of the kitchen and disappeared down the hallway. She reappeared with a small black pocketbook. "Here. There's a map of the ley line network. You can count how many stops before you land in New York City."

I grabbed the small book called *The Ley Lines of North America* and stared at the page where Ruth had left it open for me. It was a detailed map of the ley lines of the East Coast. There were hundreds of them, thousands, going north and south, east and west. I spotted a few that went from Maine to New York, and I even spotted the ones right here in Hollow Cove. "Where's the ley line that goes through Davenport House?" I pinpointed the one Adan used near Sandy Beach. Though it wasn't far, it would still take me ten to fifteen minutes to get there. I didn't have any more time to waste.

"Right at the front door," answered Ruth. "Didn't you ever feel the magic when you first walked in? You get used to it after a while. But that's where the ley line crosses through the house."

Of course. I'd always felt that prickling against my skin, the hum of magic that buzzed through me and settled inside. The door was the entrance to the ley line.

I stared down at the page. It was also the same ley line Adan had used. I noticed little stars along the ley lines at equal intervals. "Those are the stops," I said, my finger shaking with excitement. "Twelve stops till I hit the stop near 8th Street near the corner of West 59th

Street." Near Central Park and steps away from Adan's expensive apartment.

Your ass is mine, buddy.

A mixture of anticipation and fear bubbled up, fear that riding the ley line might cost me a few limbs, but I couldn't deny the excitement.

I leaned forward and kissed the top of my aunt's head. "Ruth, you're a genius."

She blinked up at me and shrugged. "I know. But don't tell anyone." She winked.

Without another second to waste, I grabbed my jacket, bag, and phone and dropped the tiny black book into my bag. Then I rushed to the front door.

I blinked staring at it like it was the first time I'd laid eyes on the front door. Now that I knew it was the entrance point of the ley line, I was nervous.

"Here." Ruth handed me an umbrella.

I stared at it in my hand. "Why do I need an umbrella? Am I going to pull a Mary Poppins?" Maybe I wasn't going to ride the ley line but *fly* the ley line. Say what you will about Mary Poppins, but Julie Andrews was a badass.

My aunt smiled and said, "You never know. It might rain in New York."

I grabbed the umbrella. My nerves fluttered inside my gut, tightening until I felt like I might puke. "Uh… how do I do this?" I'd been through this door a hundred times and I'd always landed where I was supposed to.

"You need to reach out with your will and tap into the ley line," said Ruth. "Once you are connected, you just have to open the door and step through."

Sounded easy enough. Until you did it wrong and half your body ended up in Madagascar.

I had a moment's hesitation. Going at this alone was not smart, but we all knew crazy was in my DNA. Besides, by the time I found the others, it might be too late.

I took a deep breath and let it go. "Here goes nothing."

I drew in my will and reached out to tap the ley line. A burst of sudden energy hit me, and I staggered, feeling a vibration in the ground. I leaned my energy and focus on the ley line. I could feel its trembling energy beneath my feet, beneath Davenport House, rushing by like an enormous river ready to sweep me away.

I knew if I didn't step into it properly, it would kill me. But I was running out of time and options.

"It's just like a train," I muttered. "Just like riding a train."

And so I gathered my courage, reached out, turned the doorknob, and stepped through.

Chapter 28

Well, screw down my nipples and call me Frank.

This was *not* at all what I thought it would feel like. But I'd never been inside a ley line, so how could I possibly know the insanity I'd gotten myself into.

I felt like I'd been tethered by a rope around my middle and suddenly jerked forward. I let it all out and screamed like a banshee, wondering if Ruth could hear me or if I was already out of earshot.

I screamed as my feet left the ground, and I was speeding forward in a howl of wind and swirling colors. It was a miracle I was upright, well, at least I *thought* I was upright. But it was really hard to tell when everything around me was a blur. My body was moving, pulling forward on a ley line like an invisible train on jet fuel.

And I kept on screaming.

A mix of fear and exhilaration hit me like ten shots of whiskey, just as a surge of adrenaline shook my body. I laughed. I screamed. I think I might have peed.

It was amazing.

Energy rushed through my head, my body, everywhere. Then, I felt a sudden release as the images around me slowed until they weren't blurred anymore. I could finally make out a road with streetlights, cars, and a string of houses. It was like staring out from dirty glass. I could see the town, but it wasn't clear.

My body was propelled forward again, and we were off.

Okay, so that was a stop. Good to know.

It hit me then that I'd forgotten to ask Ruth how to jump off. How did I make a stop? If I tried to read that ley line manual book, I'd throw up all over myself. I was prone to motion sickness, so I couldn't read or text in a moving vehicle. A little voice inside me told me reading while in a ley line would be worse.

After only about fifteen minutes, or what I believed was fifteen minutes, I hit the eleventh stop. Nerves hit, and I wasn't sure if I was shaking because of my anxiety or if this was just the normal effect of riding a ley line.

If I missed my stop, I was screwed. If I didn't jump out properly, I was screwed.

And just like that, the propulsion around me slowed.

This is it.

The images around me focused, and I could see tall skyrises and billboards flashing in the night. I heard the loud honking of cars along with all the sounds of traffic. There was no mistaking where I was, the familiarity of it—this was New York City.

Damn. Was I about to appear in the middle of the street, surrounded by thousands of people? Yeah, that's exactly what was about to happen. At least it was still dark, which would hopefully work in my favor to help disguise my sudden apparition. Everyone knew New York City housed tons of crazies, so no one would notice or care about one more crazy witch. I hoped.

The ley line, the images, slowed to a stop.

I pepped myself up.

One... two... THREE!

I pitched myself to the side. My feet slammed into the ground, and I staggered and then fell. Everything spun like I'd just fallen off the merry-go-round after using it for an hour.

"It worked," I said, stunned, and slowly pushed to my feet. I looked around quickly, at the throng of humanity that was still mingling around at nearly three in the morning, but no one paid any attention to me. Not even a glance.

Holy crap. I'd arrived in New York City and in once piece. Yay me!

Nausea hit, and I stumbled forward and puked next to a parked car. Fantastic.

I didn't have time to worry about who saw me puke my guts out. I needed to get to Adan's apartment.

Having lived in Manhattan for five years, I knew it well. I wheezed in a breath, stunned and shaking. That's when I realized I'd lost Ruth's umbrella. Must have dropped it in the ley line when I jumped off.

With the nausea gone, I took off at a jog up on 8th Avenue, my legs still shaky, but I pressed on until I hit West 57th Street and turned left.

I hadn't given much thought about what I was going to do to Adan when I saw him. A karate chop in the throat came to mind.

But when my thoughts turned to Iris—the endless look of absolute desperation and sadness that she could no longer do magic without shifting into a goat—a well of fury rose in me. Yeah, that bastard was going down.

Then 4779 West 57th Street came into view. My jog slowed to a jerky halt. I glanced at Adan's building, wondering how anyone could afford such luxury—not anymore apparently. It stood ridiculously high, so I had to lean back and put my head back if I wanted to see to the top. A limestone beauty, it was accentuated by light fixtures shining on every floor, making it look like the building was made of gold. It looked massive and permanent like it wanted you to stop and take a look. The building was cocky if such a thing was possible.

Shifting gears, I walked up to the glass front door, stepped inside, and moved past the doorman. The elderly man's face was lost in wrinkles and folds of skin, and at the moment his eyes were closed, and a deep snore came from him. The dude was snoozing standing up. Now, that was a first.

Trying to look inconspicuous while moving my legs faster than necessary took some skill. But I made it to the elevators without being stopped. With my heart pounding in my ears, I hit one of the elevator panels' up button and stood back.

I didn't have to wait long for a ding as the doors swooshed open. I stepped inside and pressed the level ten button with a shaking finger. The elevator jerked as we ascended, my heart racing as we climbed higher until the elevator chimed again, and I rushed out.

There was a fifty-fifty chance Adan was still in his apartment. If he was organized and smart, he would have taken a ley line away from the city. Possibly to another country.

I was hoping he was a big ol' dummy.

When I reached the door with the number 1006, I was drenched in sweat. Nice. I was sweating in places I didn't even know I had pores.

I had no idea what to expect once inside. Was Adan a lone ranger? Or did he have a posse of witches with him? Maybe I should've asked Marcus and Ronin to join me. It would have been a lot easier to take him down with three of us.

Maybe this wasn't such a good idea.

But there was only me. And no time for second-guessing. I had to be enough.

Adrenaline whipping through me and feeling like the female version of James Bond, I reached out and turned the doorknob. It turned easily and wasn't locked. If it wasn't locked, that meant that Adan was probably long gone.

Still, I had to be sure. I pushed in and closed the door gently behind me. Letting out a shaking breath, I waited, expecting the pulsing of a protection ward to hit me as I stood in the entrance. But there was nothing.

Was it normal that I was both excited and scared at the same time? Probably not.

The apartment was dimly lit, but I could still see that it was enormous, like twice the size of Davenport House's first floor.

"Okay, so, it's nice. But he's still an asshole," I whispered to myself. My shoes padded along the rich hardwood as I crept forward, feeling like I was in the grand hotel foyer.

A definite bachelor pad, it contained lots of black and mahogany with the largest flat-screen TV I'd ever seen. It was practically a movie screen and took up an entire wall facing a few couches and loveseats. A coffee table was topped with glasses and bottles of rum and whiskey.

A large fireplace sat on the opposite wall with a couch and two chairs facing it. It was empty. Past the fireplace was a large open-concept kitchen with a massive island that could seat eight people and still have room. Hallways branched out on either side of me with doorways and other rooms disappearing into shadows. I walked to the middle of the apartment and stood there for a moment, listening for any sudden sounds, like someone in a hurry and packing, but all I heard was the beating of my own heart and the muffled traffic from outside.

At first glance, I would have thought a normal human male lived here. But when I looked closely at the sigils and runes embroidered into the pillows on the couches along with the drapes and carved into the wood of the dining room chairs, I knew a witch lived here. Only now, I was fairly sure no one lived here.

Damn. The apartment was deserted. Adan wasn't here, and I'd missed my chance.

Anger followed by despair came for me, cold and hard. I'd failed at getting the Elder ring back and helping Iris.

The floorboards creaked behind me.

I spun around.

In the shadowed hallway stood Adan.

CHAPTER 29

I'd done some really smart things in my life. *This* wasn't one of them.

I'd jumped the ley line to defeat Adan, but now as I stood staring at him, I had no idea how to do that.

"Well, well, well. If it isn't the Merlin Police," laughed Adan, a surprised look on that stupid face of his. He dropped the suitcase he'd been holding and gave me a hard stare.

"Going somewhere?" I asked, my mind whirling with ideas and trying to form cohesive plans but failing. I looked at his right hand and saw the Elder ring still looped around his finger.

Adan's face hardened until all his smooth handsome features wrinkled and twisted into something truly vicious and ugly. It was as though he let go of the disguise, like he was tired of pretending to be the good guy. The monster was out.

"How'd you find me?" he spat. Gone was that beautiful, gentle voice, replaced by a harsh, flat tone.

I beamed. "Google is my friend. So is Iris." Okay, time to formulate a plan of attack. He was going to use the ring's magic on me. That was a no-brainer. I didn't have the power to match, so I needed to use my brain. I had to outsmart this bastard. I just didn't know how I was going to do that.

The smile materializing over Adan's face gave me the creeps. "You're alone. Aren't you?" He took a firmer stance, his head tilted in enjoyment and his hands clasped before him. "A pretty face without the brains to match. You're a stupid witch if you think you can take the ring from me."

"Bring on the stupid," I said, knowing the shitshow that was about to happen. "'Cause that ring is coming with me." Wow. I was full of myself tonight. Blame it on the ley lines.

Adan shook his head. "At least Iris knew when she was beaten. And yes, I beat her. I beat her *real* good." The pleasure in his voice had bile rising in the back of my throat.

Bastard. "The only one who's getting beaten tonight is you, my friend." I pointed to my shoes. "With my shoe up your creepy ass."

I laughed at the constipated look on his face. He had murdered two people and cursed two people. The bastard deserved worse—much, much worse.

"Tell me." I smiled. "How do you fit all that stupid into that small head?"

Emotions cascaded over him in a fluid torrent. The witch had a very sensitive ego. Poor baby. "I think I'll *beat* you too," he said, that creepy smile returning. "I'm going to *beat* you till you cough up blood. Then I'm going to choke you to death while on top of you, still *beating* you, so I can see the light go from your eyes."

Nice. I gritted my teeth. "You are a seriously demented sonofabitch. I might be new to all this. I'll admit... I don't know much. But one thing I *do* know is you're *never* going to beat me, creep. I'll kill you first."

Adan laughed low, the sound empty and hard and chilling me to my very soul. How the hell did I ever consider him sweet and kind and a gentleman? I must have been out of my mind.

The witch came forward until only a couch sat between us. I saw frustration and rage flicker over his features. He splayed his hands, and the Elder ring on his finger glowed a brilliant yellow light.

My pulse thrummed at the rising of power that oozed from him, a power that resonated in the earth, in the air, the ley lines, in everything around me—the power of a god. It iced through me, and for an instant, I couldn't breathe. The sheer force of his power seized me and had me taking a step back. Pinpricks of power crawled over my skin, and I stared at the ring. This was unimaginable power fueled by a murderous creep.

Yup. That was some serious magic mojo.

A wild impulse to flee filled me, born of the ring's magic. Gritting my teeth, I forced myself to stay still, channeling my magic with my will.

The only way I was going to win this was to get the ring *off* his finger. Once it was off, I was golden. I just needed to take it from him.

But first, I needed answers.

"There's something I just don't get," I began. "Why kill Myrtle? What does she have to do with all of this?"

"She doesn't," he answered, surprising me. "Contrary to what people think, Marvelous Myrtle wasn't a fake. In fact... she was the real deal. She took one look at me that night... and she knew. I saw it in her mind. She knew what I was about to do."

"So, you killed her," I said, remembering how she'd freaked at what she saw about me.

And then it hit me—through me, Myrtle had seen her own death somehow. She knew our lives were interconnected, but she just didn't know how exactly. It was why she threw me out. All that screaming wasn't about me. It had been about her.

"And then you killed Winnie because... she saw it too. Didn't she? Or she found out you killed her friend." I stared at him hard. "The only fake one is you, Adan. You can't even do magic. Can you? You have to buy your spells because you can't perform any. You're magically impotent." Oopsy.

Adan snarled and flicked his wrist.

My lips parted and a shot of his magic hit me.

I let out a howl as I flew back and hit the back wall hard, slipping over the fireplace mantel and smashing onto the floor.

Ouch. Now, *that* hurt.

My body rose, like I was lifted by an invisible giant's hand, and I hit the wall again. My head smashed hard against the drywall, and for a moment I saw multicolored stars.

Laughter reached me, and I blinked to see Adan walking toward me with a cruel smile on his face, but what I saw in his eyes sent primal fear rolling through me.

Pulse thrashing, I tried to free myself from these invisible restraints, but I couldn't even move. My arms and legs splayed out, pinned to the wall by his magic. By the ring's magic.

I might not have the use of my limbs, but nothing was wrong with my mouth.

Focusing, I pulled together energy from the elements around me. The power poured into me, spinning and simmering with a quivering life of its own.

I shaped it and shouted, "Accendo!"

A ball of fire shot from my palm and smashed against Adan's chest.

The witch stumbled, great yellow and orange flames rising high above him. The fire's heat warmed my face as it grew and wrapped around him until he disappeared under sheets of flames.

I stared surprised. I never thought it would work, but it looked like it did.

"Gotcha, you bastard."

I waited for the wailing and the smoldering reek that followed burning a creature.

But it never came.

Adan just... shook himself, like a wet dog would after a bath, and the fire went out. He looked at me and gave me a smug smile. "That's the best you can do?" he laughed.

Okay, he might have won that battle. But the cocky witch had made a mistake.

While he concentrated on removing the fire that surrounded him, he'd let go of the magic that held me.

"Son of a bitch," I swore, lunging.

I slammed into him, knocking him flat on the hardwood, but he didn't stay down long. He jumped to his feet, his face creased in what I suspected was another volley of the ring's magic.

Forget using my magic. I used the three sessions of self-defense classes I took in Manhattan and kicked the bastard in his balls.

When in doubt, go for the balls. It always worked. And no matter how big and strong they were... they *always* fell.

"You bitch," wheezed Adan as he fell to his knees, his hands covering his groin.

"Aww, does that hurt?" I smiled my best selfie smile at the groaning witch.

I saw my window of opportunity and went for it.

Adrenaline spiked as I lunged for the ring.

Something hard smashed the side of my head and I staggered and fell to my knees. He brought his hand up and punched me on the cheek, hard. My breath hissed out in a pained gasp.

Focusing, I tapped into my will of power, calling on the elements, and shouted, "Infli—"

Adan flung up his hand, and my power word died in my throat. A strange sensation hit me with a wave of cold fever, causing my skin to break into a sweat as I started to shake.

Clenching my jaw, I tried again. I called to the elements, pulling at the energies—

And nothing.

No answering hum or prickling along my skin. No electric current spindled inside my core. There was just a void. My magic was gone. My well of power empty. It was as though Adan—the ring—had taken my magic from me.

Adan laughed at the fear he saw on my face. "Who's magically impotent now, bitch?"

I narrowed my eyes. "Still you. And I bet you have a small penis too."

Adan raised a brow. "You've got quite a mouth."

"I know."

A smile of satisfaction blossomed on his face. "That's both your lure and your downfall."

"I beg to differ."

"I'm going to kill you, Tessa Davenport."

"No, you're not, Adan... uh... whatsyourname again? I forgot. Guess you're not that important to me."

His eyes narrowed. "But first, I'm going to torture you... Nice and slow. It's my gift to you, Tessa. You'll feel everything. I promise."

A smart witch knew when she'd been defeated. And a smart witch knew when to split.

Time to go.

Terror overcame all my training, fear turning into survival mode. He was too strong. The ring was too strong. Without my magic, I was as good as dead.

I spun around and bolted for the door.

Adan slammed into me and we both crashed onto the coffee table. My bag flew over my head as I toppled over. Bottles and glasses smashed against the hardwood floor as I tried to scramble away. Strong hands grabbed me, yanked me off the table, and shoved me on the floor as he pinned me with his weight.

"Ready for a little beating, witch?" Adan said, his eyes dark with hate and desire.

My pulse pounded as I felt him pull more from the ring's magic.

"Get off me! You bastard!" I shouted as I thrashed and kicked under him. "Get off—"

Cold, rough hands wrapped around my throat, cutting off my air. My heart beat wildly and I couldn't breathe as I realized what was happening.

Adan's magic raced through me as his hold around my neck intensified. A blackness flooded my mind, and I panicked as I felt myself extinguish.

I teetered on madness, unable to breathe and unable to think. I tried to scream, but it was useless.

Fear iced through me when he didn't let go. He kept squeezing and pushing me with his body on the floor. "You stupid witch," he said in disdain, spit flying in my face.

Adan made a sound of pleasure when he licked the side of my face. "I think I'll kill you first. Then I'll beat you."

Stars marred my vision. I had no more air in my lungs, just the constant pressure of Adan's hands around my throat as he kept squeezing, harder and harder. The pleasure in his face at watching me die, getting aroused by it, was the most horrible thing I'd ever seen.

He was going to kill me, and I hadn't the strength to stop him.

My hands fell uselessly to my sides, and something sharp sliced my finger.

A tiny flare of hope kindled in my chest followed by that primal fury of wanting to live and to kill this bastard before he ended me.

With the last of my strength, aided by that will inside my soul, I wrapped my hands around a sharp, glass shard, cutting into the soft flesh of my palm and fingers. And slammed it into his jugular. It hit his flesh with a meaty thump.

Two things happened at once. First, Adan let go of his hold around my neck. And second, he jerked back off of me, reached for the glass poking in his neck, and pulled it out.

Everyone knew *never* to do that. Guess he really was the moron I thought he was.

I sucked in the air, gasping and gagging as I dragged myself back from Adan and the fountain of blood that spilled from his neck.

Yikes. My stomach churned. I didn't realize how gory and gruesome it would be. If he hadn't tried to kill me, I might have felt sorry for him. But the only emotion I had left was anger with maybe a little satisfaction thrown in.

A wet gurgling sounded from Adan's mouth as he tried to speak, his eyes wide in sudden terror and panic. The bloodied shard of glass rang as he dropped it and it hit the floor. He pressed his hands to his throat, just as he fell over to his side unmoving until I saw the life drain from his eyes. Thick torrents of red blood pooled from the hole of his neck, finally slowing to nothing.

I swallowed and winced. My throat felt like I'd drunk some razor blades. After staring at Adan's body for a full minute, making sure he didn't blink or twitch—I wanted to make sure the bastard was indeed dead—I stepped around the pool of blood and stood next to his right hand, shaking from spent adrenaline. A golden ring winked up at me just waiting for me to grab it.

Breathing hard, I gazed at it. If you were like me and had not only read *The Hobbit* and *The Lord of the Rings* multiple times but had seen the movies at least fifty times—each—you did not want to touch that pretty little gold ring. You know what I'm saying?

I moved to Adan's kitchen, grabbed a dishtowel off the counter, and rushed back. Using the towel like a glove, I carefully grabbed hold of the ring and pulled, surprised at how easily it came off. Almost like it wanted to come off.

I folded the towel around the ring and dropped it into my bag, letting out a shaky breath. "Okay. It's time to ride the ley lines."

And this time, I was truly excited.

CHAPTER 30

One week had passed since my little altercation with Adan the douche. The Night Festival was long gone. They packed up and left the following morning after their last show, and not a moment too soon in my opinion.

The Night Festival, though I had been so excited at the thought of seeing and discovering new things in my paranormal community, had turned out to be a bust. If I never had to suffer through one again, I couldn't be happier.

A cool morning breeze wafted through the open kitchen window, bringing forth the scent of fall and the promise of cooler weather and spectacularly colored leaves. Fall was my favorite time of the year. I loved the cooler weather, fewer bugs, and fresh air. And having Samhain coming up made my mood skyrocket, bouncing in the clouds.

"Coffee?" asked Iris, a steaming cup in her hand.

"Love some."

Iris smiled warmly and placed the coffee in front of me on the kitchen table. Then she went to pour herself a cup. Her hair was up in pigtails with matching pink scrunchies, and she looked like a doll.

Iris, the aunts had decided, was to stay with us at Davenport House. That is to say, until *she* wanted to leave. She had an open invitation. Her guest bedroom had become her own room. We'd all bonded with the Dark witch. There weren't that many witches in the world, and we witches, White or Dark, had to stick together.

Besides, I loved having the eccentric witch with us. She made Ruth look more normal.

"How are you feeling?" I asked the Dark witch, seeing that her color had returned to her pretty pixie-like face.

Iris turned and smiled. "Like I could curse someone, you know."

I matched her smile. "I know the feeling."

When I'd arrived back at Davenport House with the Elder ring that morning, courtesy of a ley line, Iris had jumped into my arms and hugged me until I couldn't breathe.

"It's back! My magic! All of it!" she'd hollered to my ear, my face wet with her tears.

Yes, I'd jumped a ley line back home—just not the same one.

Turns out, you don't *use* the same ley line when you want to go back in the opposite direction to where you'd originally *jumped*. You ride a *different* one.

I'd learned the hard way after going back and stepping into the ley line on the corner of 8th Street and West 59th Street, and then jumping out after I counted the twelve stops, only to find myself surrounded in palm trees and smothering heat.

Thankfully, my little black book explained clearly that you needed to find the ley line going *north*, back to Maine, and not south. Ley lines were constantly moving in one direction. After about an hour of wandering around the hot climate, I'd located the right ley line north and made it back home in one piece. I was a pro.

Ruth walked into the kitchen, a vial with a blue substance in her hand. She carefully placed it next to a pile of spellbooks on the counter.

"Is that for Marcus?" I asked. I'd admit, the fact that I didn't know what my aunt was supplying the chief had me going a little crazy.

The last I heard from Marcus was the text he'd sent a week ago, telling me that the body that had been washed up on Sandy Beach was indeed Winnie. With two dead bodies in his town, the chief had been super busy with the aftermath of the cases. Their families came down on him hard, blaming him for the murders, for not keeping them safe, and I was glad Merlins didn't have to deal with that kind of crap. Though I did feel bad for Marcus.

Ruth spun around. "I was thinking of Belgian waffles for breakfast this morning. What do you say, girls?"

"Sounds great. I love Belgian waffles." Iris pulled the chair opposite me and sat down.

I wasn't giving up. "Why can't I know what's in that vial?"

Ruth put her hands on her hips. "Ask Marcus. Now. You want waffles or do you want me to make my special tomato omelet?"

I sipped my coffee. "Fine. Waffles sound great," I said, and Iris snorted. "What? I'm going to know what that blue stuff is. And I'm going to make Marcus tell me."

"I bet you will," smirked Iris, and she winked. "And all kinds of other things, you dirty witch."

I laughed hard. It felt great. "He does drive me crazy sometimes." More like, all the time.

Iris leaned her elbows on the table. "Has he asked you out yet?"

"Who asked who out?" Beverly sauntered into the kitchen smelling like fresh soap and roses and dressed like she was going out. She went straight to the coffee pot and poured herself a cup.

"If Marcus has asked Tessa out yet," answered Ruth as she pulled out a bowl and dumped some flour into it. She cracked open six eggs and mixed them in with a whisk.

Beverly took a sip of her coffee and leaned against the counter. "If he doesn't, he's a fool," she said and smiled at me.

"Who's a fool?" Dolores walked into the kitchen and dropped a stack of papers on the table. At the look of surprise on my face, she said. "I'm having a meeting with Gilbert about his wanting to limit five pounds of butter per customer. Anyone going to tell me which fool we're talking about?"

"Marcus," said Iris, a smile on her face. "We all want to know why he hasn't asked Tessa out. Because we all know he has the hots for her."

"He does not," I said as my face flamed. That kiss was still fresh in my mind. I had expected him to call or even text, but he didn't. Maybe he had his reasons. He did have his hands full with the two murders. Maybe I was reading too much into this kiss. But what a kiss it had been...

And there was still that lingering question I wanted to ask him... why he'd put a question mark next to my father's name in my file. I hadn't asked him yet, partly because he'd know I had broken into his office but mostly because I wasn't ready yet to know if there was any truth to the question mark.

But I *was* ready to know who that pretty brunette on his arm was. I hadn't forgotten.

Iris's phone buzzed and she picked it up. A smile spread along her face as she read the text that had just come in. Probably from Ronin. The half-vampire had fallen hard for the Dark witch, and it seemed like it was reciprocated.

"I almost forgot. Here, Tessa. This came in the mail for you today." Dolores handed me a white envelope.

"Thanks." Curious, I took it and read the return address: The Institute of Paranormal & Magical Objects, New York, New York, HB10028

"Who's it from?" asked Iris, leaning forward seemingly trying to see through the envelope.

"The Institute of Paranormal & Magical Objects in New York," I answered, wondering why they would want to write to me.

"Didn't you return the Elder ring to them?" asked Beverly. "Please tell me you did."

"I did." Weird. "I wonder what they want?" I tore open the envelop and pulled out a thin piece of paper and a check. "Holy shit."

"Language," scolded Dolores.

"Holy shit," I said again, looking at all the zeros on the check. "It's a check." I looked up at them. "It's a check for *fifty thousand dollars*."

"No way!" Iris slid over the table and landed next to me, snatching the check into her fingers. "Oh my god. It is. I've never held so much money before."

"Me neither." I stared at my aunts. "Why would they give me so much money?"

"Did you read the note?" said Dolores, in her matter-of-fact tone.

I picked up the letter and read it quickly. "They say it's a thank you for returning the Elder ring." My heart was thrashing in my chest. "You know what this means?" I set the paper down. "It means I can finally get rid of that giant debt." I sat there in my chair, a sudden weight lifted off my shoulders, like that huge load of carrying so much debt and worrying about when and if I could pay it back was gone. "Can this be for real?"

Iris licked the check and nibbled a corner. "It's real."

I let the paper fall on the table, feeling surreal and happy. I could finally start saving for a car and not have to borrow my aunts' ancient Volvo.

"Ooh! A job's coming in." Ruth dropped the flour bag she was holding, and it exploded into a cloud of white dust on the floor and all over her toes.

An electrical buzzing came from the toaster. There was a sudden pop, and a card came flying out. Ruth snatched it up easily.

"Is it a new job?" I asked, feeling lighter with my mood lifting. I felt invincible. Today was going to be a great day. I just knew it. I felt it in my bones. Maybe I'd even give Marcus a call. *I felt crazy.*

Ruth handed it to me, her face screwed up in worry. "It's for you."

"What's the matter? What does it say?" I took the card, Iris's chin grazing my shoulder, and saw Dolores and Beverly inch closer to me.

I swallowed and read.

Dear Ms. Tessa Davenport,

Your presence is required at High Peak Wilderness, New York, on October 31st, 9 a.m. to begin your Witch Trials or your Merlin license will be revoked.

Sincerely yours,
Greta Trickle, Witch Trials Training Division, Director.
Merlin Group, NY

Oh, crap. I was being summoned to the witch trials.

Don't miss the next book in The Witches of Hollow Cove series!

ABOUT THE AUTHOR

Kim Richardson is a USA Today bestselling and award-winning author of urban fantasy, fantasy, and young adult books. She lives in the eastern part of Canada with her husband, two dogs and a very old cat. Kim's books are available in print editions, and translations are available in over 7 languages.

To learn more about the author, please visit:

www.kimrichardsonbooks.com

Printed in Great Britain
by Amazon